Rage

"God did not create evil. Just as darkness is the absence of light, evil is the absence of God."

"Only one who devotes himself to a cause with his whole strength and soul can be a true master. For this reason mastery demands all of a person."

— Albert Einstein

Contents

Preface

I'm not sure if I heard the deafening sound first, or felt the heat of the stressed metal wrapping around my body. It was something like how the super hero character Iron Man must have felt. His suit of armor would automatically fly toward him, in bits and pieces, and reassemble around his body to a perfect form. Only, this was not in perfect form, it was perfect chaos. The disorganized movement of metal, plastic, and other matter came at me with the speed of a bullet. Like storm clouds engulfing a city, darkness dominated as the metals formed a cocoon around me. I closed my eyes just at that moment, not wanting to see any more of what was to come. I turned off all my senses, going deaf as well. In the darkness and the creepy silence, I sensed nothing. Time seemed to stand still. Yet, within the seconds of calm, ironically, the rage overwhelmed me.

I don't know where all my anger came from. It must have been like a project over time, a work in progress. I have been through so much in my life. My career with the CIA was stressful, to say the least. I made it my first priority and at times, shamefully, put my family second.

I was always expected to keep my cool. To analyze each situation, and respond responsibly and effectively. Throughout the whole Yemen camp situation, losing my best friend, dealing with death and the threat of death, I remained strong. I maintained the ability to keep calm and reason clearly. We contained that situation, probably saving our powerful nation from a debilitating demise of the government.

Why I let this routine criminal investigation get to me has no explanation so far. I ponder about it every day with no answers. All I can say is, if you think I'm in bad shape; you should see the other guy.

My name is Jack Owens, forensic accountant for the CIA. I was recruited in college with the promise of an exciting career working for the United States government. I was young and it sounded really cool, "Hi, I'm Jack, CIA." An excellent pick up line for the ladies and, a once in a life-time opportunity. Only thing was, I never got to use that line on anyone since my job was of a covert nature. Since graduating from Emory, my life has been a series of ups and downs and tragedies. At least until I found my true love. She was the one that changed my world.

I am trapped in a never-ending dream state. Instant replays of reality versus fantasy; at times I cannot tell the difference. There is so much I want to say. My mind speaks but no sounds come from my mouth.

Day after day, week after week, I lay here. My mind frustrated with never-ending replays of the past; and the music. The sounds of the Smashing Pumpkins "Bullets with Butterfly Wings" over and over again. Sometimes I visualize Billy Corgan standing in front of the microphone singing "*Despite all my rage I am still just a rat in a cage,*" the bright and colorful lights glaring. These moments take me away from the past events; a short reprieve. I suppose I am in a hospital, maybe I am dead and this is purgatory or some test before moving on to heaven.

I hear sounds; real sounds, and sometimes my brain lets me interpret what is happening around me. Today my beautiful wife must have been close to me. I know this because I sensed her touch radiating throughout my body. I cannot tell you where she touched me, my arm or a kiss on my cheek. My mind makes up things, but something had to spark my senses. I could smell her perfume, imagine her holding my hand, a tear running down her cheek. I miss her and I want to tell her how much I long to feel her soft touch; to kiss her lips, to hold her hand. I want to tell her she is my world and I love her. I want to hold my adorable baby boys. They need their dad and I need my family. I want to tell them I'm sorry for all that they had to endure because of me. I need to return to them, none of us can be whole without the other.

North Carolina – Senate Committee meeting

"Good morning, thank you Mr. Chairman, Mr. Lieutenant Governor. I have asked to speak today in order to present new information affecting our state, and the country as a whole. Four years ago you all witnessed the unthinkable. Impostors infiltrating our government with the sole purpose to destroy the very backbone that has created and kept our glorious country a free nation. A nation unified, where the expression of hopes and dreams are an individual right of each and every person.

Jihad according to Wikipedia means "*to struggle in the way of Allah.*" In the Muslim world it can be interpreted as *a war or struggle against unbelievers*. This is generally viewed as a peaceful means to promote the Islamic way of Allah as the only acceptable way of life.

Terrorist extremists twist this otherwise peaceful religious command to have a more military purpose. They rant of the war against *infidels*, those who do not believe. This war allows followers to break the true meaning Muslims have followed for thousands of years. This includes violence against all non-believers. The

4

brainwashing of young and old alike and the promotion of hate in the name of Allah is becoming more and more acceptable worldwide. As the non-Muslim world becomes accusatory to the general Muslim communities due to the actions of these extremists, the bad guys score another round by building animosity between these otherwise peaceful social groups.

America's youth, some who are lost and in need of guidance, find themselves indoctrinated into this fantasy war. They can be our greatest danger. They are the least expected part of the threat to our great country."

The closed session audience of senators and other government officials sat quietly as Senator John White continued. They have heard all this before, but afforded him the respect he deserved. After all, he and his covert operation of four years ago probably saved America from a great disaster.

"You all have heard this before, and this is only the tip of the cataclysm approaching. I still believe the threat of four years ago remains. There are people in top positions of our government, as well as teachers, doctors and the like, who are not what they appear to be. Look to your right and left. Anyone in this room can fit that scenario. You all know from the past, this is not paranoia that I preach." The Senator knew this first hand. His son

Carlton was a T2. His second born by minutes, William, was a T1. The Yemen Jihadists used these acronyms when referring to kidnapped western infants. A T1 was the second born twin (raised by his American family) and T2 stood for the first born who was taken and raised in Yemen. *There's a joke in there somewhere but my mind isn't playing along.* Anyway, Carlton was taken at birth under the guise of being stillborn. They brainwashed these children in a simulated American town in Yemen and raised them as Jihadist western impersonators. When one of the twins gained an influential status, or joined a government position, the trained T2 replaced and disposed of their T1 twin brother or sister. The imposters would then proceed to influence situations that benefitted the Jihad.

The crowd seemed a little annoyed at the recall of the past situation; and insinuations. The chatter grew louder. The senator continued before he lost control of the group.

"Ok, today I have something new, but not so new. The threat of Al Qaeda is growing; not just covert operations like the Yemen Camp situation. Funding out of the United States and Mexico is probably the biggest source of money for them. Al Qaeda is becoming the new drug cartel threat. Through human trafficking and drugs, money is being moved in and out of this country. Funding for cells here and abroad is growing at a frightening rate. We need to invest in a tactical war against these new sources of revenue that our enemies have taken over. With your support I will take this to the Hill."

The senator said his piece, the response turned out to be less than what he expected with many shaking their heads. In his mind John White and his covert group had already started the process of breaking up the funding sources.

Secret Agent Oliver Jones

He waited patiently in the shadowy corner. This is not the first time he covertly spied on his prey. His keen sense of sight and smell allowed him to prepare for taking down the long awaited perpetrator. Like others before him, he trained from birth to achieve these great skills. There was a slight scratching sound, then he saw the evil creature as he unknowingly made his way past the agent who would take him down showing no mercy.

Secret Agent Oliver Jones first met Jack Owens during a midnight surveillance Op. At first he wasn't sure if he could trust this smug looking example of a human being. Yet, he sensed something that gave him confidence. He was certain this was a person who could be an asset; one he could eventually trust.

Oliver had no safe place to sleep and the nights were getting cold. After the second time they ran into each other, Jack offered Oliver a place to stay. Immediately a friendship ensued. At first his wife Katie was hesitant but the little people in the home convinced her to let him stay. After all, he was a stranger; although, he was young and good looking with an innocent face. At times he could be playful and the children really took to him. Other times he seemed so serious, they understood that he had a job to do. It did not take long before the Mrs. of the house took to the feisty new addition as well.

It has been several months now and the two Agents work together often to protect evil from ascending upon their family.

Chapter 1 - Control

Carmine Caputo walked down his long driveway. The sun came up an hour ago and the dew still glistened in the bright light. The tree lined private road, saturated with carefully placed floral arrangements and natural wild flowers, attracted a variety of colorful little birds. Their chirping music echoing throughout the forest-like path. "Where the fruck is the damn paper?" mumbled the tall man, with a girth equal to about half his height. He had a hardened face and almost never smiled. Drinking the night before at one of his clubs left him with a hangover. The pattern of his brick driveway made his head hurt even more. People in the neighborhood knew who he was and what he did for a living. The paperboy was afraid to drive onto the property. He often got out of his car at the entrance and threw the paper as far up the private road as possible.

"There you are, you mutter frucker." Slurring his words to himself, he bent down to pick up his daily paper and saw her shadow. The young lady was like a dark angel glowing in the bright sunshine. His headache seemed to ease as his attention was diverted. She startled him though, and he almost lost his balance. "Who the fruck are you? Ah, who cares, you are easy on the eyes."

"So handsome, you are the big man? Where are your bodyguards? Aren't you afraid someone like me might molest you?" The attractive, very sexy lady winked, and he immediately realized his robe might not be covering his manhood well enough to hide his peaked interest in her. "I am Carmine Caputo; who would mess with me? Except perhaps you; you could mess with me, it would be fun." She smiled, "No time for fun today, boss." Carmine disregarded her remark, "How about some breakfast?" He waved for her to follow and walked on ahead. He mumbled, "The wife and kids are visiting her dumb sister for the weekend." His head began to ache again, *damn that hangover*. She left him lying face down on his fancy brick driveway. One bullet to the back of the head. A typical mob type hit.

Carmine Caputo's death would create havoc amongst his associates and rival business partners. A war over territory will allow outsiders to move in on his operation.

The simple theory of supply and demand began as product on the street became scarce. Prices went up and the immediate demand had to be filled. Since the terror cell that planned Caputo's hit knew of this need, they stepped in and provided their own product to a well groomed market.

The guy on the street corner has a supplier, who has a supplier, who gets bulk from a distributor, who has a larger distributor, who buys from an importer. All this adds to the end user's cost and the degradation of product quality.

A new importer planning to sell directly to the last distributor could make twice as much money with less risk. The profits would be directed back home and to local cells to fund terrorist actions in the United States.

Eventually the drug operations would expand across borders up north and operation would culminate in Mexico right at the source.

The revenues grew quickly, and a way to move the money without traceability, became a new goal for the terrorist factions controlling the operations. The increase in human trafficking and money laundering inundated the justice system.

Chapter 2 – June 2012

We had been in our new home in Dix Hills, New York just over a month now. While still living and working in North Carolina, my wife received an offer to work with the Manhattan District Attorney's office. This surprise offer came immediately after she passed the Bar. An offer like that does not get turned down unless one is out of their mind. Katie Claire, my beautiful fantastic wife of four years, mother of my precious twin boys, now three years old, deserved this. She had been through some tough times and yet she persevered. She took charge of her life, my life, and that of our family. Although she has said this of me many times, the truth is, she is the strength in all of us.

I asked her what she wanted, her reply was the same each time asked; "We have been through a lot and we are settled here. I love my home and the boys have their cute little friends. We are at peace and happy. Maybe we shouldn't uproot and risk all the good we finally have." We discussed her future in North Carolina and I knew she needed more. Katie is brilliant, and although she comes off as this sweet and caring young woman, which she indeed is, she can be ruthless and determined for a cause. And God help anyone in her way.

So after some intimate pillow talk, the decision was made in the middle of the night, to move to New York and re-build our lives there. For me it was easy. My team has had a successful couple of years tracking bad money and averting the formation of terrorist cells by bankrupting their operations. That, plus my part in preventing one of the most covert terrorist plots in American history four years ago, I could ask for most anything and get it. The latter is a whole story in itself. The next morning I met with my boss, who also had become one of my best friends.

Chapter 3 – Transition

"Good morning, Sally, is he in?" Sally May smiled. She was a good secretary. Not all that bright as one would expect for a government intelligence employee. I guess she was efficient and made sure Kevin Sorenson, AKA the boss, always kept to his schedule. At thirty something this cute girl from somewhere in the Deep South was still single. I think it was her smile, which she did a lot and probably should refrain from doing so, keeping her mouth mostly closed for that expression. Evidently her family lacked dental coverage when she was younger. "Good morning, Agent Owens, he sure is, give me a moment." There goes that wicked smile again.

Kevin Sorenson was all business and projected a hard-ass image in public. I closed the door behind me; "Don't you give that girl dental coverage?" Kevin gave a good hearty laugh, "I do but I think she likes her mouth the way it is, she must think it gives her blond bombshell character. Besides, she may still be single but she always seems to have a guy in her life." I shrugged my shoulders, "Maybe it makes for a good..." I made a perverse gesture. "Ok Jack, so what's up?" And so our discussion began, all joking aside.

"Dinner last weekend was nice; Katie and I needed to get out. Between her studying, my traveling and the boys, social time has been pretty much limited to, zilch." Kevin leaned back, "Well, it was nice, and imagine that, we didn't talk shop at all. We will have to plan another night in a few weeks. Perhaps you two and the boys can come out to the lake house for a long weekend." Kevin and his wife Margaret had purchased the lake house about five years ago during a down market and got a really good deal. The place was awesome. It was a four bedroom "A" frame type home, common for a lake house. The previous owners really did it up with a new kitchen and renovated bathrooms. All granite with marble floors in the entryway and terracotta in the bathrooms. The three guest bedrooms were on the top level of this three story home. Each had its own little terrace overlooking the lake or the woods. The master bedroom, Kevin and Margaret's private domain, was located on the main level of the house. It was offset by a long corridor, affording privacy, and had its own bathroom with a Jacuzzi. While taking a nice soak you look out from the huge bay window at the gardens and forest behind them. True tranquility. The wall opposite the four post bed had a gas fireplace and to the left, French Doors overlook the lake. Truly magnificent.

We had spent a few weekends with them, and on occasion, my co-worker Donald Graham and his wife Nancy joined us as well. Nothing is cozier than sitting by the fireplace in the winter sipping cognac or in warmer weather, outside around the huge fire pit with a cold beer and a good cigar. Mind settling, relaxation; just what the doctor ordered. Kevin interrupted my momentary daydream, "Margaret and I will probably retire up there; I am for sure, ready."

I tried getting my nerve up to break the news. Kevin gave me a lead-in, "So, my friend, what's on your mind that you invade my space first thing this fine morning?" I figured I should get it over with, quick and easy. "So Kev, we have had one hell of a run since the big take-down." Jack paused and unwittingly switched gears; "Hey by the way, I got tickets to the Yankees; sky box seats. I think the four of us should plan to go to the game. It's the first Saturday afternoon in September." Kevin was a bit perplexed at where his friend and subordinate was going with his conversation. "Jack, what is it, can you get to the point? I have a meeting in ten." I took a big breath and exhaled slowly, "Katie got a job offer in New York, Manhattan ADA. She gets to be a trial lawyer." "That is wonderful news Jack, is she going to take it?" I'm not sure why, but I had the feeling I seemed awkward, and it was embarrassing. "I think so. It will mean us moving there."

17

Kevin leaned forward in his chair, "You know what this means my friend; you will need to apply for a transfer." Shrugging shoulders and grinning, "Looks like that is the only option. I'm sorry boss, you and this office have been fantastic to me. You have helped me so much in my career and have been a good friend." Kevin stood up and put his suit jacket on; "And I will continue to be a good friend, just not your boss. As you know, I have top connections in New York. I will make the calls and set it all up. This is great news and the change will be good for all of you." I was at ease now, relieved that my boss was not upset. "She has to start in three weeks, things will move quickly. I will stay with you for a few months, or as long as you need me to. I will need time to get my family settled in the new home; wherever that will be." Kevin reassured me that he would coordinate the transition and make sure there would be communication between his office and the New York office.

"Make sure to let Sally know the dates for the Yankee game. Margaret and I will plan a long weekend, and get to see your new home, if you have one by then."

After dinner that evening Katie tucked the boys in, and I read them a story from their favorite DR. Seuss book, "Green Eggs and Ham." We retired to bed early. "So, Kevin is onboard, he actually offered to coordinate my transfer. We are all set. Tomorrow I will call a broker and get that part started." Katie was in the master bathroom as Jack was talking to her from behind a partially closed door, she had just come out of the shower. "That is great Jack, I'm excited."

My very beautiful and sexy wife entered the bedroom part of the master suite. Her hair still wet and wearing the black negligée, my favorite; low cut, sheer, short enough to show just the right amount of what was needed to show. I sat up against the headboard on the bed, "Now, I am excited."

Katie climbed on top, facing me, neither of us saying anything. She was resting on her knees, kissing my lips ever so gently. I put my hands around her waist, caressing her as she started moving up and down on me. "You are so beautiful." "Shhh, don't wake the boys." I kissed her again and then let my tongue continue the caressing allowing my hands to control the motion. Katie whispered in my ear just before she took a little nibble, "You are my life and my love." I felt my breathing begin to quicken. Time would run out soon for me so I lifted my wife off and down to her back and took control of the situation. I needed to slow things down. Starting at her toes, her cute little toes, moving up her body using my tongue and hands to pleasure her. "Stop! I can't take it." It was like using the TV remote, I pressed pause, "No, don't stop, take me, NOW!" I did as asked, no complaint from my team. We came together. If one could produce a graphic video of the moment, it would be Fourth of July, fireworks and all. The musical group 'The Doors' blasting "Come on baby light my fire."

I held Katie close, "We are destined for good things to come. Life will be grand." Katie took hold of my hand while pressing her backside tight into the natural curvature of my body, "It will be interesting for sure. Change is good, isn't it?" "Very good."

In stereo: "Mommy, Daddy."

Chapter 4 – Abducted

Her high school classmates voted Karen Masters "most likely to succeed." Tall, ironed straight dark hair, black eyes. Every guy in her school fantasized she was his. Her mom taught high school French and never had any problem keeping her students' interest. Especially the male students. Some swore they were twins and when made-up and in heels, it was sometimes hard to tell which female was the elder of the two.

Karen started her freshman year at Syracuse University with high hopes of earning a degree in Biology. She had not decided if medicine or research was a direction she wanted. She was young, and had time to decide. Karen's roommate, Andrea, was from small town in Indiana. At first, the girls struggled to find common ground. One night Andrea convinced her roommate to go to a frat party. "Come on, we can meet some cute guys." "Miss serious," Andrea's nick name for her; "Let's have some fun." Karen turned down most offers to "grab a drink", "hang out" and various other attempts by her roommate to break the ice. For some reason, this night she was amicable to trying to have some fun.

The frat house of Phi Delta Sigma was hopping. The music was loud, but not as loud as the crass young men were as they slurped beer from various weird contraptions... "Here, take a hit." Karen liked pot, but only smoked occasionally. She found it hard to study after getting wasted, even a day later. For some reason her tolerance was low and the effects lasted longer than it did for her friends. "Ok, just one hit." Andrea gave a disappointed look and both girls laughed. Karen coughed hard. "Damn, whoo." She took a few more and really felt the effects. "Hey Karen, look at those two guys, they are cute. Let's go over there." She grabbed her roomy's hand and pulled her along. "Hi!" "Hi yourself." Introductions out of the way, they smoked another joint that the boys offered up. They were all wasted. One of the guys suggested, "Let's go upstairs, I have something really awesome to smoke." They found an empty bedroom. The blonde haired boy, Tom, short for Tomas pulled out a case containing a device that looked like a fancy e-cigarette. "We are not into cigarettes guys, yuck." Andrea made a face. Tomas told his friend to close the door, "Not enough to share with anyone else." He pushed the little button and inhaled, then exhaled a thick white vapor. They passed it around, each taking a few puffs before it ran out. "Wow this is some good shit, my head is floating." Andrea laid her head in Karen's lap. Karen asked, "What is this stuff?" Her head was spinning and her body felt as if it were floating around the room. She never felt so good. All the pressures of school and life in general no longer existed, at least not for now. "Electronic freebasing. Expensive but worth every penny. You girls are really hot. Sex is awesomely intense on this stuff." Tomas offered his hand, gesturing they move onto the king sized bed. Andrea raised her hand to the sky, "Count me in." Karen was in dreamland, "Some other-time. Come on Andrea we should go." "Are you kidding, go where? We are here baby; we are here." Andrea started laughing uncontrollably. Karen found herself laughing as well.

Like switching channels, Karen was unaware of how she ended up tangled in a web of sexual frenzy. The four were naked and having sex. She did not know whose hands were caressing her, whose mouth she kissed or which guy brought her to orgasm. "Holy mother of…"

There were more parties like this and Karen did not recognize her addiction to the drug or the sex-drug combination. By her third month at school, she looked anorexic. She made excuses to not go home for Thanksgiving, telling her parents that she had to study.

"Tomas, I need a refill, hook me up." "You have some cash babe? I can't front it anymore." Karen had no cash, her cards were maxed out. Soon her parents would be notified that her tuition had not been paid. "Please…" She gestured to the bedroom but Tomas said, "No cash, no vapor. Besides, I got a date and it's not you tonight."

Karen started to shake. Her world was imploding. "Here Karen, take this number, call it. This guy will hook you up. He will expect some serious appreciation. Dress nice and be really cool."

Karen knew it was wrong, and dangerous. She saw what happened in the movies to girls who made these calls. Desperation drives all fear away. Karen made the call and took a taxi to a motel outside of town. The ride took over an hour and the fare read seventy two dollars. She began to panic. A tall, long haired guy walked toward the cab. "Karen?" She nodded. He handed cash to the driver and opened her door. "Hmm, muy bonito. Come with me, I will take care of all your needs tonight." Karen started to recognize fear at its worst, but there was no turning back now. Somehow she understood she was about to trade sex for drugs. She needed to get through tonight. Tomorrow she would work on getting straight and turning her life around.

At first he was gentle and spoke nice to her. "Would you like a drink? Here, take a hit on this." One hit and she was off, floating around the room. The world once again animated, she felt good. His hands were all over her. Her clothes were off, she had no recollection of that action. She closed her eyes for one second and they were in the shower. Her host took her from behind then aggressively forced her to go down on him. The channel switched and she was on the bed, wet and slippery. He had rubbed oil on her and now assaulted her with his tongue. She felt as if she could take no more when he finally came. At last, he was done and she could mellow out. "Here take another hit." Karen pushed it away. She needed a break. Her head was so high she thought it might detach from her body. The shock of his back hand on her face made her jump. "When I request something of you, it is a demand. Do not question – do it!" He again offered the pipe to Karen. This time she inhaled a dose. The pain in her face immediately went numb to gone. The man left the room and she heard talking. She now realized how heavy his accent was. Then she heard conversation in Spanish. He came back in, accompanied by another man. "This is my brother, he would like to smoke with you." The other man took a hit on the vapor pipe and handed it to Karen. Fear started to overtake her. Her host put his hand on her shoulder gently, "Take a hit." She did as told. Both men then had sex with her. Things got rough at one point, she understood she was being raped and could do nothing about it. She brought this on herself. It was the drugs. Before sunrise, three more men were introduced into the room of horrors.

"Get up and shower, then we will take you home." She washed the blood off herself, a result of the severe abuse from the night before. She knew what had happened to her but only remembered small bits of the details. Her head was still mixed up. Her body hurt really badly. The hot steamy water ran over her aching body. Karen did not recognize that she was in a state of shock. All of a sudden her breathing became rapid and her heart pounded. She cried hysterically, unaware she was being watched. One of the men involved in the assault handed her a grimy towel and abrasively said, "Get Out! You're done."

The van had no windows in the back where she was seated, and it was bumpy. They drove for at least a few hours. This was much longer than the cab ride she took from the university to the den of horrors. Karen started banging on the partition. Ten minutes later, the van stopped. The doors opened and the sunlight blinded her. "Why is it taking so long to get me home?" The man's voice, not familiar to her, and much older than her abuser of the previous night said, "We had to make a stop. Stay in the van!" Karen ignored the instruction and tried to get out. His fist met her face and she was thrust backward into the vehicle. A minute later a young girl's body was tossed into the van. The heavy thump of her body hitting the floor made Karen jump, hitting her head on the vehicles roof. The door slammed shut and the van started moving, tires screeching. "Oh my god, what did they do to you?" The girl looked to be around fifteen or sixteen. She was beaten and unconscious. Her clothes were filthy and disheveled. They drove all day, Karen cried and pleaded to her abductors, but was ignored. The van made two more stops, and two more girls were put in the van.

The next morning, the van stopped for gas. A voice told them to be still or they would be beaten severely. Karen's body still ached from a combination of drug withdrawal and her physical abuse. It appeared that the other girls suffered from the same painful combination as Karen. The need for a *fix* and the lack of food and sleep kept them weak, limiting their ability to put up any resistance. The other young girls were hysterical. Karen understood what was going to happen to them, and to her. Several more hours passed before the van pulled off the road. She could tell by the smooth to very bumpy change in the road. The doors opened again, and this time two men with guns entered the van. The girls were blindfolded, gagged and tied up. "We are close to the border ladies. Your new life awaits you. Sweet young American girls fetch very good money." The doors slammed shut. Darkness prevailed, only death, it seemed, could set them free.

Chapter 5 - Katie Claire Owens (July)

Some would think starting a new job, in a new town, in a new home at the same time, is taking on way more than any one person should attempt. For Katie Claire Evans Owens, it was what she termed as "The Project." The short amount of time that she called North Carolina home, she married (me, of course), dealt with a psycho terrorist bitch, and gave birth to the two most beautiful baby boys. Such little time, and so much history. The move to New York seemed intimidating at first, but as she thought about it, she understood it was the right way for her and her family to move forward. Leaving the bad memories behind and expanding on the good had to be the right plan of action.

"What a gorgeous morning;" Katie sung to herself as she got out of bed. Her handsome and courageous husband still sleeping; my snoring probably sounded like a twister moving across the Kansas plains. She looked at the clock, six-fifteen on the button. She never had to set an alarm; somehow her internal alarm clock never failed her. She needed to get dressed and out of the house in thirty minutes, or she would be late for the start of her second week on the job at the Manhattan District Attorney's office. First order of business; look out the bedroom balcony window at her new lush garden-lined backyard.

Squirrels played near the side fence, one chased the other and then they did somersaults. She noticed a blue jay watching them play from a branch on one of the many pine trees that lined the property. The in-ground pool was recently redone with new stone around the perimeter and a new sky blue liner. The trees and flower beds made excellent use of the early morning sunrise to reflect their images in the glistening water. It felt like a daydream every time she looked out at her property. She loved her new home.

I found this *perfect* house while on an assignment in New York. It was before Katie got the job offer. It had been on the market for a few weeks during a bad time for home sales. The owner's husband recently passed away, tragically, at the age of fifty-three. The home was too much for the widow to manage and she wanted a quick sale. As soon as we decided to make the move, I called the listing broker to find that it was still available, and at a more reasonable price.

I had no trouble convincing Katie that this was the home we should raise our family in. "Jack, I love the fact that it has five bedrooms; room to grow our family. I love the fact that the kitchen is brand new and so modern. But;

you had me at the gardens." Of course I knew how much my wife admired the White's North Carolina property with the magnificent gardens and pool and fountains. Our home would be a bit more on the modest side, but still lush with beautiful foliage; and a nice pool as well.

"Jack, I'm going." As I opened my eyes, squinting from the bright sunshine flowing into the room, I had to smile, "You look beautiful and very professional." Katie walked around our king sized bed and leaned over me for a sweet goodbye kiss. I smoothly slipped my hand under her skirt, moving upward to dangerous territory when she pulled away. "No time, save it for later, stud. Oh, and make sure you get the boys to daycare on time." Before any chance of comment from me, she was gone. I am so proud of my wife. She worked really hard to pass the Bar and deserved this opportunity.

About a week after the interview, Katie had not heard anything from New York. She started getting upset at the thought of an offer being made to another candidate. The good husband that I am, I offered to ask Senator White to make a call; he knew just about every DA in the country and most owed him in some way. Katie was adamant that no outside influence be used. "I have to do this on my own. I am a perfect candidate for this position and if they don't realize that, then it will be their loss as much as mine."

Katie was right, they told her she was their top choice from the beginning. The interviews after hers just proved them all the more correct in their choice.

Today she would be given her first case. They were short-staffed and the caseload was off the charts. In addition, the mayor's office consistently put pressure on them to close more cases with "wins." The pressure was on, and as promised during her job offer meeting, she would be thrown in "feet-first."

Chapter 6 - Getting Started

Her new office on the seventh floor of 1 Hogan Place was not what she expected. She did not expect to be back in a cubicle, albeit much larger and equipped with cool shelving and a locking cabinet system. Katie's new space had a new computer with two monitors and a web cam. Pretty cool for a government office. These tools would make for easier research work and allow for online meetings.

"Good morning, ADA Owens, How are you today?" Robin is the sweetest young lady and very efficient. As a shared assistant for the six ADA's in this section of the department, Robin had her work cut out for her. The group consisted of four male and two female prosecutors. "I am just perfect, Robin; thank you." Robin looked so tiny sitting at her reception desk, which turned out to be deceiving. She stood much taller than expected, and once out from behind her desk, her very long and perfect legs offered all the explanation for the visual misrepresentation.

"DA Johnson has called a meeting at ten sharp; I already put it on your digital calendar."

Katie settled in at her desk in her sort of cool cubicle, and started reviewing the huge stack of open case files. The new ADA's routinely received the crappy unsolved cases to review. They dissected the archived cases trying to find mistakes. Then, a decision could be made as to whether a case should be reopened. If she found a re-workable one, she would need to contact the detectives or officers who had ownership, at one of the precincts, then start a new profile for the case. Then, if it looked like new evidence could be obtained, she would present it to the DA for his review and approval; or denial. Often, it turned out to be a dead end; a time filler between current, active cases.

It was nine forty-five, and almost time for the meeting. Anything would be better than what she was doing. Katie knew that finding the needle in the haystack could mean fast-tracking up the ladder of success so she did her best; as she always did.

"Good morning, Katie. We are heading into conference room 'A'; are you ready?" Jason Albright a third year team member and one of the more senior ADA's in this office, waited for her to gather her notepad and allowed her to walk ahead; such a gentleman. He was an excellent mentor. Pretty good looking too, not that that mattered, but no reason not to appreciate pleasantries on the eyes. She smiled and thought to herself, "What, Katie? Jack would think these thoughts about an attractive woman in his office." The old "look but don't touch" rule. Katie grabbed her notepad and pen, "With you; thanks."

The conference room, one of three in the suite of offices, seemed larger than the other two. It was a decent size, capable of seating twelve comfortably, and plenty of standing room as well. There was a large screen LCD on the wall and a small buffet area with coffee, as well as a refrigerator for cream and snacks. All the conference rooms were set up the same. ADA's spent many late nights in these rooms during trials. Meals were often brought in, and sweet snacks kept available to boost energy levels.

Chapter 7 – The Case

Katie and Jason were the last of the six ADA's to join the meeting. "Good morning everyone, I hope you all had an excellent weekend and are well rested." Erik Johnson aka "The DA," stood at the front of the room. His appearance was a little intimidating; tall, average looking with a prominent jaw bone. He stood at the head of the conference table, sharp looking in his pinstriped gray suit, displaying no smile as he greeted everyone. Robin was also present to take notes and assist with whatever was needed. "First, I've asked Robin to clear your schedules through lunch time; I hope we can finish up by then." The DA looked uptight, it was obvious he was under a lot of stress over whatever we were about to discuss.

"You all know Jason Levine, Senior ADA. I assume you all know each other but I am following a protocol here, dotting the "I's" and crossing the "T's". Michelle Adams has been with us three years, and she is also a Senior ADA." He was speaking slow and clear and gestured to each attendee using his whole hand as a pointer. He announced each of our names; "Rob Moss, Alex Ritter and Dan Rodriguez. And our newest team member, Katie Evans Owens, who, as agreed, will be known as Katie Owens; even though her business cards reflect the former. Katie, please be at ease with my sarcasm, it is how we all cope with the stress in this office." Katie was tougher than most by this time, her history would tell it all. "Ms. Owens comes to us with very high recommendations, and has resources we hope to be able to make use of for the case I am about to reveal." Katie and the DA had a discussion after she was hired; she agreed along with Jack that her resources would be available as long as there was no conflict of interest between authoritative agencies. And of course, requests remained within the legal side of the law.

Robin was fiddling with the remote, starting a PowerPoint presentation on the wall mounted monitor. "We have been trying to take-down Raul Espinosa for three years. Each time we discover a witness or evidence, one or the other or both disappear. His huge legal defense team slithers their way out and he gets off with a mistrial or some other trick. Robin, are we ready?" Robin, a little flustered, pushed the button and the eighty inch monitor came to life. The iron faced DA sort of smiled, "And here we go."

"Some history; Jason, please." He again used hand signals to indicate his directives. DA Johnson sat down as Jason Levine stood and signaled Robin to start the presentation. The slides displayed facts as well as pictures of Espinosa and known associates. "Our original case was brought against Espinosa for drug trafficking, with his area spread across all five boroughs. The organization is based up in Harlem, but has moved locations locally several times a year. Supplies are imported from Mexico, where a major manufacturing and distribution plant has been set up. Every time we *turn* one of his henchmen, they end up dead or missing, presumed dead. His estimated annual take has been upwards of fifty million per year." Jason had the group's attention. Katie had goose bumps. She was involved in a real case. A case that would be on the books to be studied, if they ever got it closed. "Recently, we discovered through contacts at the FBI, that this mini cartel may be funded by an Al Qaeda cell which recently formed in the area. We do not have all the intel as of yet. At this time, the FBI has detained one known associate of Espinosa's crime family and will update us as they extract information from him. Obviously, he is a prime asset for us and under a serious threat. His associates will do everything possible to silence him. This cell, working with Espinosa, has added human trafficking to the table." Alex motioned for attention, "Where are the girls taken from, and do we know where they are transported to?" Katie's excitement turned sour as she learned more about Espinosa's updated business venture. "Ok, so we are pretty sure, according to FBI info, drug abusers and prostitutes are the main inventory. They present less problems for their captors and in most cases, no one misses them. There have been other missing persons, teenaged girls from good homes whose cases are being looked at as possible ties to this organization as well." Jason went through his slides, updating the team with all kinds of facts and figures. The last slide stilled the room.

"Thank you, Jason. The six of you will be paired, as you can see from the monitor. Jason is the lead on this, all information flows through his team, who will update me daily; any questions?" Michelle Adams had one, "Shouldn't Jason and I work together as Senior ADA's? I mean, Katie is fresh out of law school, and this case is too important to be a learning event at that level." Katie felt just a bit uncomfortable, for sure the boss should have talked to Michelle first. She herself was confused on this unexpected but thrilling challenge. DA Johnson, stone-faced and intimidating, put up his hand, "Each and every one of you will play a very important role here. Building and winning this case will be a tough and possibly dangerous challenge for all of us." Michelle squawked, "But!" The DA would have none of it, "I expect all of you to work in harmony. There is always a reason for how I lay out my plans of action. There is a stack for each of you; take it and read all of it by tomorrow. Make sure to take notes and be ready to start working the case. Eight AM back in here." The DA gestured to the conference room by pressing his finger down on the shiny table surface.

The group disbanded but not before Katie caught the sneer Michelle directed at her. "Katie, please stay for one minute." Jason finished a two minute conversation, off to the side, with the DA, and then it was just the two of them. "I hope you are ok with us being teamed up together. There may be some animosity from the rest of the group." Katie reminded herself to keep a serious face, no smiles, "I am pretty thick-skinned. But I am curious; Why me?" Jason leaned back in his chair, Katie noted, again, how good looking he was; he must have girlfriends lined up. She envisioned slapping herself back to reality. "You are by far the greenest of the group but, you also hold the best credentials for organizing data and research. I believe you did quite a bit for your previous position. I also see from your file that you worked full time while going through law school. To me and to Erik, this means you have stamina and a work ethic that will prove invaluable to us succeeding." Katie had to smile, "Wow, thank you, and yes, I will work really hard. But my husband's career and contacts in high places played a part in your selection as well; Truth?" Jason put up his hand in the "Got me" pose; "Part truth but the other reasons are equally important to us. This is a great career move for you so early in your tenure here." "I am aware of that and

I won't let you down." Jason stood; "Also, I noticed there was some classified information on you, need I be concerned?" Before Katie could respond, "I just wanted to be upfront with you that I have seen all the files on you except that information. I don't require any explanations unless you deem it necessary at some point." Katie acknowledged with a nod. Jason, with a serious expression, said "Enjoy the read, it is massive and just the tip of the iceberg."

Katie returned to her cubicle. Dan Rodriguez was filling a cup of water at the cooler and made a clawing motion as she passed. Katie just ignored his immature gesture.

The pile of documents was huge, she got started with no expectation as to how long the read would take; she had a good eighteen hours to complete it. She hoped she could live up to the stamina part of their expectations.

Chapter 8 – Mexico

He stood proud before his constituents. After all, they are a good people in need of direction. The whole area of this small town twenty miles east of Nogales International Airport, is stricken by poverty and despair.

Juan Carlos Martinez studied political science and public service at the State University at Berkeley. He went on to obtain his MBA at the Haas School of Business. Growing up poor, and a firsthand witness to the devastating effect gangs and drugs have on society, he made it his quest to change the local environment. He vowed to help make his hometown a better place for its people.

After graduate school, Juan Carlos interned for various law firms thinking along those lines. He also interned for the currently seated governor, during his run for a second term. He found his mentor to be incredibly interesting. He thought the governor was a great man who worked *for* the people.

One night, while working late, the proud intern discovered some documents that conflicted with a recent speech made to the people regarding taxes and property allocation for a new business district. Juan Carlos realized the man that had inspired him, was indeed a corrupt politician. At that moment, he decided that he would work his way up the political ladder to fight for the people and his hometown.

After his disappointing discovery, Juan Carlos left the Governor's mentoring program; wisely not revealing the information he uncovered. Through various social circles and networking, he got speaking time and started voicing his political agenda for a drug-free, corruption-free society. He presented a larger picture for all of Mexico, starting with his local jurisdiction. He promised an open office, with an advisory council staffed with half "his" team and the other half civilians, as a watchdog policy.

In a small, poverty stricken area of the town, a young girl looked at herself in the mirror. She and her mother were going to listen to the good man make a speech. She searched her reflection head to toe, making sure her favorite pink party dress was just right. "Momita, why does this feel so bumpy, I no like it." Her mother smiled at her child with tears in her eyes. "You are so beautiful my little angel. I had the dress cleaned and it is just a little stiff. It will soften as you wear it. Besides, we will not be there long, and you can take it off when we get home. Do you want to play with your friends later?" The little eight year old girl smiled at her mommy, "OK,

Momita, but why are you crying?" Her mother wiped the tears from her eyes and cheeks and then smiled again. "Because I love you so much. You are God's little angel and he will always look after you." Mother and child held hands as they walked the short distance to the town square.

On this beautiful warm afternoon, in front of the largest crowd he had ever addressed, Juan Carlos stood before the assemblage, speaking the words of a true hero for the people. He had the estimated two hundred potential constituent's rapt attention. His two biggest fans made sure to get a front row position. His wife Maria, and son Carlo, listened with love and admiration. Maria fell madly in love with Juan Carlos the first time she met him during their third year at Berkeley. They married right after his graduation from Haas. As he spoke, Juan occasionally looked to his wife for her approval. She obliged with a smile, driving his momentum forward.

The crowd applauded and whistled. He had their admiration. His words drove them to desire something more than what they currently had. They wanted to better their lives and believed he would truly stand beside them.

As every good politician knows, physical contact with potential voters is the best format for building confidence and allegiance of the people. Juan Carlos Martinez proudly shook hands with the men and woman who stood before him. He made his way off the podium, patting little children and kissing babies. It all seemed stereotypical to him but his actions were sincere. "My, you look so pretty in your pink dress. Do you have a party after you leave here?" The little girl smiled and gave a little curtsy, "I wore the dress for you; it's my favorite one." She started to pull on the side of her waist. "It isn't always so uncomfortable; Momita said I can take it off when I get home. Good bye Señor." Moments such as this, the smile on a little girl's face is what validates all the efforts made in a political quest.

The police, no one, ever expected what happened next. The blast was loud. The crowd found themselves bloodied by a forceful discharge of nails. Chaos ensued making matters even worse. The police only heard of children being used as suicide bombers in other countries by terrorists. After interviewing eyewitnesses who survived the bombing, the police recognized a new horrifying threat to their locality. In all, sixteen people were wounded and five were killed. Juan Carlos Martinez, the little girl and her mother were the first casualties. Martinez's family were among the wounded.

The war on drugs took on a new face on this day. Those who planned this horrific event thought that they had succeeded. The news media interviews showed how angry the people were. Their outrage, directed at the drug lords and corrupt politicians. In memory of Juan Carlos Martinez, and with his wife's continued support for reform; government and police presence continued to see improvements through better training, hiring of better qualified law enforcement personnel and campaigns directed at informing the people of their rights and responsibilities to their community.

Chapter 9 – Assassin

Every day was the same. CNN morning update, one hour of grueling exercise and body strengthening. And then, morning prayers. Afterwards, a lean high protein breakfast. Like others dedicated to this Jihad, it was all about conditioning. Unlike most, she was a home grown and a one of a kind, not a T-2. The government infidels, hiding under the cloak of their god who was not Allah, and therefore not the true god, would not see this coming. The fools thought that investigating missing twins would produce results in their search and destroy mission. They will learn; to deny Allah is to deny God.

The clock indicated almost 10AM. She had twenty minutes to get to her first class for this dismal Tuesday. Graduating law school with the highest honors opened many doors. She received several offers from various Law Firms. Ever since early childhood, teaching was a dream of hers. She decided to combine both into one career. Her students, only a few years her junior were a concern with the university board during the hiring process. It did not take long for them to realize that they made a wise choice to bring her on as a full professor at their Law School annex. Her ability to control her students and foster strong leaning achievements amongst them surprised none of the elite members. Some have referred to her as having a killer instinct. They had no idea...

She had been called many things. The few words some of her victims managed to say before she took their lives would cripple a meeker person's hearing. Somehow "Professor Palovich" sounded OK to her. Petrović was the original surname of her father, now deceased. She altered it to be a little more Americanized.

Growing up, her father drank a lot. He was an angry drunk and was abusive to her and her mother. Ironically he professed to be a devout Muslim forcing his wife and child to follow the daily rituals of cleansing and prayers. According to him, they existed to please him as the man and head of the household. Like so many, he abused a sacred religion for his own comforts and desires.

Although Ann never witnessed his cheating, her mother always cried at night, alone in her bedroom. One night the wretched man came home drunk and reeking of another. His wife finally confronted him, accusing him of cheating on her and betraying Allah. Petrović lost his temper and beat his wife then threw her down the basement stairs. Ann hid in her bedroom feeling rage at being helpless and afraid.

In the morning Ann quietly approached her father who was drinking coffee and reading the weekly Muslim Observer newspaper. "Where is momma?" Her father did not look up from his paper, "We had a fight last night and she left; she will be back." "But papa, I heard you yelling at her." The red faced man looked up at his fourteen year old daughter and said, "Your mother accused me of being unfaithful. She is the one who is unfaithful, she is a whore! It is not for you to worry, it is of no concern to you. She will be back. And if not, good riddance." Ann cried night after night and prayed to Allah for her mother's safe return. In her heart she knew that would not happen.

A year passed and Ann's mother did not return. She hardly saw her father and when she did she avoided him. He was always drunk and smelly. The doorbell rang, Ann ignored it. Her father usually went to the local mosque with a friend for the late afternoon prayers. Three times the bell rang. Ann ran downstairs to the front door. As she reached the landing she noticed her father slumped on the couch, his body half on, half off.

"Hello Ann, where is your father?" Ann did not look up, she just pointed. "Ah, I understand. It looks like he will be out for some time. He is not a very good father to you, is he?" Ann did not respond and fought hard to hold back tears. "Why don't you come with me to the mosque? Our Imam would like to meet you. I think he can offer some words of comfort to help you." "Can he bring my momma back?"

Ann went with her father's friend to see the Imam. She did not trust this man, but compared to her father, what could be worse? She had never been allowed to enter the mosque. Her father always made her and her mother wait outside while he went in to pray and meet with the other men.

Ann had seen pictures of mosques in her father's newspaper and on television. They were often huge and somewhat ostentatious in design. Her fascination with the structures made her forget her fears for the moment. This local mosque's exterior was simple, more like that of an office building. The interior, however was plush and larger than she expected. She thought it was beautiful, and she felt comfortable and safe within its walls.

The Imam spoke slowly with comforting words of advice and praise. He explained that her father had demons. He offered to teach her the way of Allah and to make her a soldier of Islam. She was intrigued and agreed to his offer. He quickly became a surrogate father.

"Where have you been, are you defiling yourself! Come here!" Ann's father was drunk and out of control and hit Ann hard in the back of her head. She fell to the floor frantically trying to escape further injury. "You are a slut just like your mother, perhaps you should join her in the infidel's hell." He threw himself on top of her, pressing his firm male parts against her. With one hand he covered her mouth and pushed down so hard she felt the back of her head start to bleed. With his other hand he touched her. First on top then lower. She remembered nothing after that except that she passed out. When she regained consciousness her father was lying next to her, bloody and dead.

I always knew my mother did not leave me. We were victims of father's cruel and warped view of what family is. I now understand what love and loyalty should be like. I now know the respect of a true believer. I have a new family; and Father, you will not be joining mother in Paradise.

"Ann, you have an instinct to protect yourself. The ability to do what it takes to remove evil from Allah's chosen world. *He* has a plan for you that I am to help you with. Allah has spoken to me and you are the chosen one. You will take part in the greatest Jihad. You will succeed where others have failed." Ann did not speak, she bowed her head in acknowledgment. She would do anything asked of her to please her Imam, her father. She would follow the word of Allah.

It was a beautiful day, even with the early morning breeze. She waited in stealth mode for the fat man to make his way down the long driveway following his daily morning routine. "So, handsome, you are the big man?"

There would be many more assignments; bloody assassinations, and seductions to make way for the ultimate plan. As Ann neared adulthood, the frequency of assassinations and violent seductions decreased. Unlike her predecessors, she took no pleasure in the brutal acts she committed. She saw it more as an obligation, with a justified end. Now, as she readied to receive her Law degree, she received several offers from prestigious law firms. To her leader's dismay, she turned them down to pursue her chosen profession in education. Her Imam asked to see her. "Ann is a child's name, you are grown up and need a more sophisticated name. One that represents your excellent self-esteem and brilliant mind. You will use Anastasia from now on and use Ann only as a sobriquet for those close to you. You may go on to teach as you desire for now." She did this for several years, educating young law students. She managed several relationships during her tenure, each discouraged by her Imam before it could mature into a longer lasting situation.

Anastasia; college girl, seductress, assassin. She had a higher purpose than random killings and sexual enticements. A more important job than teaching infidels how to be sinners. "It is time my dear for you to make a change; time to approach law firms. You were seen once as valuable to them, now you are even more so. This will escalate your status in society giving you better exposure to those we need to conquer and destroy." Her leaders, after years of preparation for an unknown part of the jihad, finally informed her of her most important role.

She will be the wife of the Vice President of the United States. This they was certain of.

Chapter 10 - Home

Katie arrived home exhausted. The house was wonderfully quiet. As usual, I had to work late. The nanny had the boys asleep already, and offered to make something for Katie to eat, before she left. Katie gave Rosa a hug, and sent her home to her family. Keeping things simple, Katie pulled some chicken and rice from the refrigerator; leftovers from last night's dinner. Our cat, Oliver, sat at her feet and meowed indicating his desire to share in the pre-prepared meal. It tasted delicious, if I don't say so myself. I had cooked dinner a few times this week. As a long-time bachelor, I had to become a pretty good cook; not by choice but for survival. When Katie worked full time and attended law school, there was no other option except "take-out"; and that grew old, fast. I hope she realizes what a good man she has. When she met me in college, she never imagined any sort of relationship between us, aside from the casual friendship through William. William and I were friends since early childhood, inseparable yet independent, and completely different personalities. Damn; thinking about William; what a tragedy. He was her first love and she hated him for the way he ended it with her and for how he let Jane into their relationship. To make things worse, after the whole Yemen camp situation she found out that her

William had been replaced with a *clone*; actually, his "presumed dead" twin brother. At that point, the guilt kicked in, followed by sorrow. By that time she and I had formed a relationship. To Katie, it made sense now. William and I were best friends. We both had different, but redeeming qualities that made us good men, and wonderful partners for a relationship. William will always be missed and his memory has a special place in Katie's heart and mine too. There was a period of time, early on, where I had my own feelings of guilt. I allowed myself to question whether I would give up Katie to have William back. I wondered if, Katie were asked the same question, what her answer would be. For a while, the dilemma aggravated me. The answer, at least for me, is not an easy one; but I am certain of my answer. I finally put it out of my mind. The situation will never, could never occur. Katie and I are happy and have made peace with that situation.

Katie looked at the stack of paperwork as she ate, she was ready to get started, ready for a very long night.

At about 2 AM, Katie caught herself dozing off. She had to review one more file. Her interest was piqued by the overwhelming abundance of data on this creep, yet no hard evidence existed that could put him away. Assumptions and hearsay and missing witnesses, nothing of value. There were pictures of dead, obviously tortured bodies, mostly men, only a few woman and one very young man. She found this disturbing, yet her interest grew with every page and every morbid picture. All this data painted a picture of a psychopath. A cold blooded killer. Yet, nothing tying him to the suggestions of terrorist affiliations. The FBI had one material witness in custody for questioning. She would love to get some time with him. To question him firsthand. Katie could not hold her head up any longer and was ready to call it a night, or morning, when she heard the door open. Her husband was home.

I stood behind my exhausted wife as she sat at the table, head in hands. I kissed the back of her neck and gently massaged her shoulders. "You look exhausted, let's go upstairs and get you into bed."

"I need to put all this away." I took Katie's hand, "Tomorrow is another day; you can do it in the morning." I led my wife up the stairs to our bedroom and directly to the bed. "I'll join you in a minute." I washed up and returned to find Katie fast asleep, her clothes tossed in several directions around the room.

Tip toeing quietly, I looked in on my boys, my little angels, sleeping so peacefully without a care. Oliver, or as we call him, Secret Agent Oliver Jones, protectively slept with one eye open in the corner of their room. I returned to my own bedroom, and climbed into bed next to my wife. I held her close and she responded by moving her body tight into mine. Totally exhausted, we both fell asleep instantly.

The moon was bright, Jack and Katie sat on the cushy porch swing, Hampton Stripes design; the one Katie fell in love with and had to have. They were in their backyard at the house in North Carolina. Katie just found out she was pregnant with twins. Life was good for both of them. Both had made peace with the past and planned a future full of love and happiness. For a moment life seemed simple. They held hands; the night air was cool but Jack did not notice. Katie's touch warmed his whole body. They rocked slowly gazing at the stars. Neither had to speak, yet the communication was so clear. She was the one; Katie was always the one.

Chapter 11 - The Call

The alarm clock blasted at six-fifteen AM, I hit the "snooze button" for the third time, before my cell phone rang; a call this early could not be good. I reached for the phone quickly, trying not to wake my beautiful, sexy wife who looked so peaceful. I am truly the luckiest man in the world. This woman sleeping beside me, never once in all the time we have been together, complained about anything; she is my rock. Who lived through a past of tragedy and terror; lost the love of her life (that is another story, as I said earlier) and yes, there was someone before me (part of the other story) and is raising two incredible boys with a husband who is away on business more often than not? And on top of all that, has a full time career. Oh and she still manages to remain the most beautiful and sexy woman alive, who never leaves her man in need. I live the dream.

The call was from one of the on-call analysts working the night shift. We finally got a break in the case resulting from a routine traffic stop. The car had warrants out for unpaid parking tickets. The driver held the number three spot on the FBI list of suspects from the case I was working on, in conjunction with them. Apprehended in Florida, they wasted no time tossing him on a plane with a Federal Marshal. The scheduled arrival at New York's Kennedy airport posted as 9:15 AM. This guy might be the open book we were looking for, and I wanted to get him before the FBI guys spooked him into lawyering up.

Coffee seemed like a pretty good idea right now. Hopefully, our fancy "Java" machine's "auto on" worked. I am still getting used to our new home. This house is larger than our old one; larger than any house either of us ever had growing up as well. The first few days we considered getting a portable navigation thingy, you know the ones you program and it gives you direction. Then my tech savvy wife discovered Google Maps and tried the "Walk to" function. Ok, it didn't really work and the joke got a bit played out, but it was funny anyway. I made my way down to the kitchen, and with great satisfaction found my fancy machine ready to brew. Two cups were already lined up along with one each of our favorite pods.

I stood looking out through the French doors facing my rather large back yard. The patio and pool seemed so country club like, and the tree-bordered property line thick with colorful flowering plants and bushes, was breathtaking. One would never know that another house existed behind all that. As I looked and daydreamed, I thought how much Rebecca would appreciate our home. Senator John White and his wife

Rebecca are our closest friends. Their son William and I grew up together. He was my best friend and college roommate until a tragic situation took his life. They are older, more like my parents' age, but very young at heart. I also have a working relationship with the senator. My thoughts tend to run wild, thinking back to those days. My boys are at the age when William and I first met at the beach in the Carolinas. I miss those years. Now I get to experience the joys of parenthood. I treasure the moments and the limited time I get with my boys. Which reminds me, Pee Wee soccer starts this weekend.

The smell of the brewed coffee brought me back to the present. Second cup ready, and off I go to awaken my lady, coffee in hand. What else could she possibly want at seven in the morning?

"Hey mister, I need a wake-up booty call." I put down the coffees and sat on the edge of the bed next to my wife. She was laying there in that really hot nighty showing just enough to make me forget my coffee, and my case. Leaning over, I kissed her gently on the lips, a sort of "good morning, I brought you coffee" kind of kiss. I really had to get going; you know, work and other responsibilities. She ran her hand up my thigh and I leaned into her, kissing her passionately. I knew there was no time for this, but the neurons in my brain where in control. Katie paused, her lips a millimeter from mine,

"That coffee smells delish," even her grin is sexy. "Just kidding". So, I might be a little delayed this morning.

"Mom-me."

A good visual would be the stylus on a record player scratching across the vinyl. "Want me to get them?" Katie smiled, "No, I'm guessing that call meant you really need to get going. Besides, Rosa will be here any minute to help with the boys." I guess I won't be late to work; frustrated, for sure. The bad guys better beware.

We really lucked out with Rosa. Our next door neighbor whose children are a few years older than ours used her for years and loved her. Their kids are now in grade school and did not need her any longer. Let me tell you what luck is; this fine woman speaks English almost perfectly and is meticulously clean and always on time or early. She never complains when we ask her to stay late, which with both our jobs, is quite often. She loves our kids and she is now part of our family. Her husband, Armando, is a driller, working the offshore oil rigs for BP near Louisiana. He used to work fourteen days straight then had twenty-one days off. Now he is a supervisor and needs to be on location even if he is not drilling. Armando is only home on holidays, two weeks in the summer, and Christmas week. I don't think Rosa needs the money as much as she craves the family environment. They had no children so I think being a nanny, fills her "family" need.

So, off I go to start my day; so far the possibilities are looking good. The traffic on the westbound 495 was heavy as it usually is during rush hour. I believe the Long Island Expressway's nickname is *"The World's Longest Parking Lot."* Fortunately I get to use the HOV lane as a single driver; a perk of the job. My car has no emergency lights, so I am at the mercy of tired, or just obnoxiously slow drivers. I have exactly one hour to get to Kennedy Airport. Sooner would be even better so I can avoid any confrontations with the other authorities interested in this punk. His name is Manny Menendez and he has a rap sheet a mile long for assorted crimes ranging from petty larceny, to rape, to armed robbery. He was in prison several times and has only been out for eight months after a five year sentence. Now, we believe he is involved in really nasty stuff that could affect the nation's security. That is why the FBI is so hot to nail his ass and try to "turn" him. My interest hits a wider spectrum. There is information that he was working with a group, a cell most likely born from an Al Qaeda faction in Afghanistan.

Whatever genius thought of this HOV lane must have been short-sighted or just plain bored of the project. Why else would they just abruptly end the extra "express" (really a joke) lane at Little Neck Parkway, not continuing all the way to the Midtown Tunnel crossing? One thing I've noticed about the roadways here, there are lots of potholes. In Carolina potholes were just as prevalent as they are here on the secondary roads but the highways rarely had these dangerous holes.

I looked at the car's guileless clock, almost 7:45 AM; I was running late. The Belt Parkway was crawling. The exit for the airport was just up ahead. Once I got into the exit lanes, three merging into two, the airport road was wide open. I pulled up to the arrivals area for Jet Blue, cut off a taxi (*love to do that*) and stole his spot at the curb. Just as I got out of my car, a TSA cop motioned for me to move, so I flashed my credentials and pointed to the ID card on my dash. He just made a face and walked away. I had the feeling he was going to have my car towed, in which case I would have to have him abducted and tortured. I wondered if I could actually make that happen. That could be another story, for another day. I flashed my credentials one more time as I made my way up the stairway to the terminals that were marked "DO NOT ENTER – SECURITY POINT." The text from my associate said gate D6, and there it was. Passengers had just started exiting the gate.

I figured the Marshall would wait for the plane to empty before taking his prisoner off. Looking around, I did not see the other guys yet. I had no doubt they would arrive momentarily. Damn, I was right. I could spot a FED a mile away blindfolded. Two big goons, dark suits, sun glasses, so stereotypical and movie-like.

The passengers were unloaded like cattle being set out to pasture. Most were in shorts and t-shirts. You could tell the northerners from the southerners by the color of their skin. The really tan or sunburned were the New Yorkers. Even though it was summer here, they had to lay out in the tropical sun to out-do their friends back home. Someone should enlighten them that vanity like that causes cancer. I figured the plane was nearly empty, since the families with small children and strollers were starting to deplane now. My potential informant should be escorted off soon.

"Attention, attention, will a Mr. Jack Owens please come to airport security." The announcement was loud and echoed all around. I looked over at my two FBI friends, they were not even looking at me. I checked my cell phone and it seemed to be working fine, showing three bars for the signal strength. I had to ignore two more announcements before it finally stopped. It is amazing how low some will go to win the race. Imagine if we weren't supposed to be working together.

Finally, the last family was leaving the jetway. A little blond haired kid was holding the pant leg of his very attractive blond mother, definitely a native Floridian, as she pushed a stroller with twins. I have to say, that is one brave lady.

There was a moment when the area was clear and no one was getting off the plane; my heart was pounding. I was overly anxious at this point and fighting myself hard not to look over my shoulder at my "competition."

I expected a tall, thin, lanky guy, maybe with a goatee. Instead, Manny was this short, pudgy guy, five-four if he was even that. This guy was wearing baggy pants and a floral shirt. He sort of reminded me of Danny Devito in that movie, "Throw Mama from the Train." He did have a goatee, though. His hands were cuffed in front of him. He had a plastic ankle cuff which allowed him to walk fairly normal but would restrict his ability to run very fast. At this point, he probably knew he was safer in federal custody than free on the streets. For sure, a hit had already been sanctioned. The Marshal escorting him, in contrast, was huge, like a linebacker. No one was getting away from the "Hulk".

I held up my credentials and walked over to them. The Marshal looked at me with suspicion, hand near his concealed sidearm. "Good morning; Jack Owens. I am here to take custody of Mr. Menendez." The Marshal did not speak right away, I noticed his eyes diverting past me.

I didn't need to turn around to know who he was looking at. The two FBI guys had their credentials out and were approaching us. This was going to get ugly. Theoretically, our two branches worked hand in hand in criminal cases originating within the United States. My agency deals with situations out of the US and its territories where the crimes affect or threaten US citizens or our government. Unfortunately, I had a feeling the US Marshal, who is more closely related to the FBI, was going to see it that way and I was going to get screwed.

The big man spoke in a husky voice, "Look guys, I am not going to play referee while you argue this out. I'm tired and this guy is a pain in the ass who doesn't stop jabbering." I had to make my case quickly and quietly. We were in a public place, so I said; "Can we go to the airport security area, so we can hash this out without an audience?" The taller starched shirt said "There isn't anything to talk about, we have jurisdiction." I wanted to say "Not if I make you disappear," but I thought better of it, and the effect it might have on my employment. The big man spoke again, "That sounds like a good idea, let's get this over with." I guess he was willing to play arbitrator. I started to like him; just a little.

The holding area at airport security housed HLS officials as well. I had hoped someone would be there. They would be more inclined to side with me, as our departments worked more closely together. I have a sort of reputation since working with Marcia a few years ago, who is one of theirs. Unfortunately, the sub-Office of Homeland Security was empty of any agents. I figured I had better speak fast and make my case.

"Guys, I realize you have jurisdiction here and I respect that. On the other hand, I am working a case that could affect national security, that I believe has spread past our borders. This guy could be the link to a bigger enterprise. How about giving me one hour with him, right here, and then you can take him into custody." The men in black talked off to the side while the two of us waited. Mr. Menendez was in one of the two holding cells.

I saw them look at me and then they came over to us. "Sorry, Agent Owens, we feel it is inappropriate and in violation of the prisoner's rights since he hasn't been Mirandized." The Marshal stepped forward, "Actually he has, or I wouldn't have been able to transport him; I think thirty minutes is reasonable, I want to get out of here." I was liking him even more now. It was agreed, thirty minutes, the FBI guys had to stay in the room.

"I have nothing to say. What kind of deal are you offering?" "Mr. Menendez, my name is Jack Owens. I am investigating something much bigger than your drug dealing situation. I am only interested in your contacts higher up the chain leading to Raul Espinosa." Menendez leaned back, "Never heard of him." Jack leaned close; "These guys are going to get you for drug smuggling. Your boss, the one you never heard of, will have a hit on you within twenty-four hours of your confinement. They will never let you get to trial. We can hide you, give you a new identity. Have your lawyer contact me. Jack Owens, Central Intelligence, Manhattan office. Do it quick before these guys lock you down and out of my reach. You are much more important to me that you are to them."

"Time's up, you can revisit him after he is arraigned and we are done with our interrogation." I gave one more last look at Menendez then turned back to the FBI agents. "You guys are swell, thanks." I waved to the Federal Marshal and nodded a thank you. Exiting the airport security area, I thought about what a waste of effort that turned out to be.

Chapter 12 – In a Perfect World

So, this is the first, and probably only time, my wife and I would share information about a case we were working on. The DA, in conjunction with the US Attorney, was building a case to bring down the notorious Raul Espinosa for his crimes against humanity. There were many of them that were, and still are, being committed here in the United States. Homeland Security was interested in him as a funding connection for terrorist factions and everybody wanted us, the invisible ones, to find him, and bring him here for trial. Each of them getting credit for their part; that is, all but the CIA. The crazy thing is, officially no one was allowed to share information and everything is top secret clearance. Who needs credit anyway? It's just a job and we do it because we care. *Hmm*.

In a *perfect* world, Manny Menendez would spill his guts divulging the location of his boss. We would find this guy in some secluded mansion filled with beautiful, money seeking whores. Armed henchmen would be ready to wage war for pay in the name of saving their country, or some crap like that. With some luck, he would be located in the US. But more likely, he would be found in some hideaway in Mexico or Venezuela and in the latter two, the need for a difficult and costly extradition. He would, in turn, plea bargain for immunity in exchange for names, places and dates were we could take down the really dangerous threats against our great country.

In the *real* world, Manny will remain silent long enough for the already planned hit to take place. He would be found hanging in his cell, an apparent suicide, for fear of what his people would do to him. Espinosa will continue sleeping with his harem of woman, selling massive quantities of drugs, mostly heroin, and half his profits will go to fund local Al Qaeda cells.

My plan was to be part of making the real world closer to a perfect world.

Chapter 13 – Kate's Case

The train pulled into Pennsylvania Station, otherwise known as Penn Station. Like much of NYC, this multi-purpose structure is split between an underground maze of tunnels and a plaza of stores and food concessions. Above ground, Madison Square Garden and office building. Built in the early nineteen hundreds this century old historical location is the hub of all things NYC. The familiar screech of the subway car as it came to the final westbound stop, alerted riders and woke those rocked to sleep. They had arrived in the dark and famous catacombs under the streets of NYC. Later than usual this morning, the rush hour crowds already easing, Katie traversed Penn Plaza to hop on the downtown line. She, unlike most of the strap-hangers, liked the subway. Today the number 3 train ran express and took her the five stops to her office. She liked to stand or lean against the doors. It had become a sort of game for her. She would test her timing and balance trying not to grab a hanger or pole as the train abruptly started and stopped. She also liked to observe the variety of cultures. She would study facial expressions and imagine what the person was like in a social environment. She did notice that most people seemed unhappy to be riding this mode of transportation. Katie thought, maybe they were just unhappy in general;

How sad. Down south people appeared to be more content, and certainly friendlier. She made her way up the concrete stairs to daylight, pleased to find the morning clouds over Long Island gave way to bright sunshine in the big city.

Katie walked into her office around nine-thirty. As she headed toward her cubical she felt eyes on her. It was kind of creepy. Michelle was talking with Alex Ritter, "We start at eight-thirty or earlier when in a crunch or does teacher's pet think she can do as she pleases?" The bitch turned away and continued her conversation. Katie was taken by surprise, and being new to the team and the company, did not want to continue a losing battle with one of her Senior ADA's. Diplomacy seemed a better option. "Actually I was working all night, till past 3 AM and found some interesting information in the files, if you would like to go over it with me." Without looking at Katie, Michelle snorted, "Sure; let's waste my time because I got plenty of it." Katie had no patience for catty remarks. "No problem, I will explain to Jason why I am late and what I found. Sorry to have wasted even this little precious time of yours. I'll be off and let you continue with your recipe swapping." The nearby listeners may have been disappointed that there was no blood, but they seemed to enjoy seeing someone stand up to their pompous boss. "Jason is in a meeting, you can come to my office." Katie made like she did not hear her and kept walking away. She could feel the tension behind her; it made her smile, just a little.

Her cubicle looked too organized and needed to appear like work was getting done. This part was easy. Katie laid out the files she scrutinized last night and started compiling all the notes she attached to pages. As Katie went through her research, she started pulling her notes and organizing them on her Smart-Board. It took a few hours last week for her to get familiar with this fantastic tool that each team member had access to. After she organized her thoughts the custom program converted them to a PowerPoint or Word document on her computer ready for presentation, or filing for later use.

It was like the data on the board had a life of its own. It was all coming together. Manny was just a pawn, a waste of time and resources. He had no real connection to the higher levels of drug and people trafficking. He was a small time gofer placed in higher profile locations for appearances. The most he would give us is small-time drug deals that probably would lead to another slightly higher level pawn, and never lead to evidence needed against Espinosa. Every lead that seemed to have merit, linked back to Menendez; one big circle of crap. She had to talk to Jack, but first she wanted to update Jason Levine.

Kate walked down the hall toward her boss's office to find Michelle standing a few feet from his door. She appeared to be reading some document. The "she-devil" didn't even try to hide her devious plan to screw with Katie, and grinned as she entered Jason's office. Katie would have none of this, and headed in as well, only to have the office door closed in her face. "Breathe, Katie, breathe." Alex smiled, "She is what she is, and is super territorial." Katie, did as suggested and exhaled slowly and somewhat dramatically, "Why does she hate me?" "She hates everyone and perceives everyone as a threat to her status at the firm." Katie had this pouting look on her face, "But, she does not do this to the rest of you, not like this." "Katie, you are the new kid on the block, you are supposed to file and get coffee; gofer type stuff. We all know it is not your fault and perhaps some of us are a little envious that you started like you were in a senior position. All of a sudden you are teamed with the Senior ADA, and Michelle is bumped aside. You see how that plays out don't you?" Katie leaned against the wall fighting tears. She never really thought about the hierarchy and improper matching that day. She did understand how this looked. "Wow, I'm such an idiot. I have access to resources that can help get this case closed; my connections are why I'm in this position. But, I am good at what I do, and I can work this team equally with the rest of you. I will talk to Jason and have him make this right." Alex put his hand on Katie's shoulder, then thought better of it, and quickly removed it before anyone got the wrong impression and the office rumors started. "Look, Katie, the decision to pair you at the top of the team was not done impetuously; you should not question it, just rise to the challenge. A few empowering words with Michelle might be a good idea. Wait for this afternoon so I can do a little prep work on her. If this team succeeds, we all will have bright futures here, or write our ticket to anywhere we want to go." Katie smiled, "Thank you, Alex, you're a good friend." Alex turned to walk away, after a few steps he stopped without turning, "I'm not sure about the *friends* yet." They each sensed the others smile.

Chapter 14 - Jane

She watched the children as they played jump rope with their friends. The little boy tried to keep up with his sister and the other girls, but he just could not get it right. The little twerps giggled when he tripped on the spinning rope. His frustration was obvious, as his face warped out of shape from his teeth clenching together. Jane almost ran to him as he fell flat on his back. The little girls stopped laughing, one of them offered him her hand, "Are you OK, Mikey?" The little boy rested back on his hands and smiled, "I'm OK, Janie; me tough, I not going to cry." He took his sister's hand and stood up with her help. Once again the girls continued jumping and singing while he remained quietly on the side-lines, out of danger. Jane reminisced of her younger years back in the Yemen camp. William was the smart one, the one to succeed. Yet, somehow he frequently managed to get himself into trouble. His simple yet offensive antics led to severe punishment by the leaders. Jane would sneak to where William was tied up in a standing position for all to see. She would give him water and food and comfort him. Thinking of this made her realize that they had not taken all her humanity from her. It was always there, hidden from those who would take it away.

A little more than four years earlier, Jane gave birth to Janel and Mikael. Throughout her pregnancy she remained conflicted over her decision not to abort them. Jane had never known her parents. She had never been held or comforted. Her abductors, who she saw as mentors, acted more as her keeper. She functioned robotically on command, denied social contact for most of her formative childhood years. This, her leaders, as she knew them, did by design. They groomed Jane into a cold blooded assassin from birth. Every action she took was, by instinct, based on those early formative years. Her mentors psychologically abused her and physically tormented her. Praise for a job well done was what she considered love. Jane existed for one purpose; like others of her kind, kidnapped at birth and raised to fool the Americans, raised to destroy America in the name of Allah.

It wasn't until her jihad in America was foiled that she began to think about her life. She had left a trail of death and destruction for a purpose that failed terribly. Her people abandoned her in a world she was completely ignorant about. She understood what they wanted her to, and believed what they told her. They kept her in a cold, dark, and painful little box.

Chapter 15 - For Love?

At nine months pregnant Jane had gotten used to being confined to her one bedroom cabin a little north of Toronto. She needed to be in a familiar place; so she cut her hair and dyed it darker. When she went outside she covered up as much as possible, and wore "movie star" sun glasses. Even though her enemies would have assumed she would flee back to Canada, they would never think she would return to her last known location. That would certainly be a foolish move, so that is what she did. So far she felt safe, and that is what she needed at that time. Her body tormented her as if the devil was inside, trying to rip her apart. The early stages of her pregnancy were difficult. It was easy for her to hate the two lives seeded inside her. This must be Allah's way of punishing her; a slow death. Things calmed down in her seventh month, and as the living creatures moved inside her, she began to feel things she did not understand at that moment. Or, rather, she could not comprehend why she missed them when they remained still. Her inability to feel remorse or love was a concept she did not know or want to know. But this phenomena that has impacted her life and restricted her in all ways, was growing inside her. Each day her regret for keeping them, diminished a little more. Jane had developed feelings for the little beings growing inside her. Allah's children; Michael's children. She no longer resented Michael for getting her pregnant. After all, she seduced him into staying with her. If she had a tiny bit of the ability to care for someone back then he would still be alive. She should have let him go back to his world and away from hers. He would still be alive, and perhaps she would not have been pregnant.

Sometimes, when Jane would close her eyes, she would dream of him. Michael's touch started her metamorphosis. Her so called friendship with William was fabricated by her leaders. Both of them were together by design to fulfill a jihad that Allah's soldiers on earth programmed into each of them. The sex between them, at least for her, was more of an aggressive, violent nature. She never felt good after, she never thought about it after, and she never really wanted it until they started doing it. Sex was like another program imbedded in her brain – it had to have purpose or there was no need for it.

When Michael touched her, she wanted more. Sex with him created an unrecognized form of love. He had no part in any plan, not hers or her leaders. He stayed there for her, just for her. As Jane began to understand this concept she began to understand love. When her babies were quiet inside her, she missed them; therefore, she could assume she loved them. A work in progress but she wanted to understand more.

Fear of being responsible for anyone or anything besides herself still plagued Jane. If she loved Michael, why did she allow Sarah to finish him off and dispose of him like he was nothing to her? Could she allow something like that to happen to her babies if a more pressing matter came up? This frightened and conflicted her.

Jane made the decision to have her babies and then find someone to care for them. She needed someone who truly understood love and had enough to share with her babies.

Chapter 16 Katie vs. Michelle

Michelle Adams always had a strong personality. Competitive in nature, she would challenge everything and everyone. Early in her childhood, her parents, mostly her mother, instilled a win-win scenario. Starting in pre-school, she had to have a starring role in her class play. The other four year olds had more interest in drawing with crayons or playing with dolls. Michelle would walk around twirling and jumping the ballerina's dance. She was a pretty little girl with dirty blond hair and very distinct features. She did have the look. A few years later, her mom would push her through a series of beauty pageants, many she would win, and some she would not. Those who knew her and her family, especially the other contestants, sat on the fence as to whether mother or daughter were the bigger sore loser. Cheerleading took over in high school and the competition for boys followed. Michelle was not a "mean girl." Her classmates accepted the fact that she came first, and expected to get what she wanted. Fortunately for her, she was equally intelligent as she was beautiful. Without a doubt it had to be Harvard Law. Mother would have nothing less.

Katie respected Michelle's position as a Senior ADA and appreciated her scholastic abilities. She could not stand her personality, and unlike the other co-workers, Katie would not let the Prima Donna push her around. She also had to find a way to work with her if there were to be any chance for a successful career in New York.

While Michelle pushed her way through everything, Katie was so much the opposite, always taking a back seat to the underdog, helping others before herself. For two years while in high school, she volunteered in a homeless shelter. Katie had more free time than many of her friends, as learning was an adventure for her and came so easily. In college she learned to open up more and have some fun. Then she met William, her first real love. A series of unfortunate situations followed, wreaking havoc and betrayal on her love life. Later, she would learn how to fight for real. To survive dangers most only read about in fiction books. Katie remained a decent person despite what she went through, but when she needed to, her claws could be as deadly as a bear's.

The door to Jason's office was open. She was right on time, two fifteen as scheduled. Her boss sat behind his desk and she noticed the two guest chairs opposite him were empty. Perhaps her co-worker decided a late entrance would be more dramatic. As Katie entered, the sun glare from the panoramic window behind Jason hit her eyes, making her squint. The view of downtown Manhattan and the waterfront was awesome. She still felt like a tourist in this fantastic city. Sightseeing time over, blinded vision clear, and a reality check; the bitch was already there leaning against his credenza, damn.

"Hi Katie, on time as usual, come on in and take a seat." Katie smiled without looking at Michelle, "Good morning, thank you." She sat in the seat closest to where her co-worker stood so that she would have to walk behind her to take the other seat. Michelle did not attempt to join them but stayed where she was, facing her boss but behind and to the side of Katie. "Yes Katie, you are always on time, I guess this morning was just one of the known times you got in late." Jason was well aware of the animosity between these two and needed to fix this before his boss got wind of their discord. The DA had no patience for this kind of nonsense in his office. Jason was at the same senior level as Michelle but he was the team leader for this project. "Michelle, please take a seat." Jason motioned with his hand. After a momentary pause, perhaps to indicate she followed the order of her own free will; and as opposed to following her associate's directive, she walked behind Katie and took the seat next to her.

"OK ladies, we all know why we are here. Let's get this over with and move on to important business. Katie, you asked for this meeting, so why don't you get it started."

Katie took a breath, "I am excited to be part of this team. For the most part, everyone has welcomed me cordially, and I have made some nice acquaintances in the short time since I started here." She cleared her throat in an effort to hide her nervousness. "That is most everyone; except for Michelle." Katie turned toward Michelle and looked fiercely at her, and then softened her expression to appear saddened. "I don't know what I could have possibly done to offend you, especially since you hardly speak to me. And when you do, it is nasty and condescending." She turned back to Jason, "This is not a comfortable working environment, and it's not what I am used to." Michelle broke in, "You came in here like you are better than the rest of us, and you, Jason, bought into it. Just because her husband might be a resource for us is not a reason to push me aside. So, yes, I'm offended, in fact I'm pissed!" Jason leaned back, "This is ridiculous, but I see your point Michelle and I am sorry. This was not my decision; it was DA Johnson who put the team roster together." He caught both woman giving him the evil eye as he realized he sounded like he was passing the buck. "Let me explain more clearly and openly. I agree with Eric's structure. The team needs guidance, and Michelle, you are the strongest advocate I have for this project. I know you can keep them focused. It was either you or me in my position, and Eric picked me for no other reason than it seemed right to him at the time. I assure you it has nothing to do with one or the other of us being better at the job. As for Katie, she is the new kid on the block, but not the weakest link. I thought it made sense for me to mentor her while you handle the rest of the team." Michelle looked as if she wanted to blurt something out about a line of crap; her face told the story. Jason put up his hand, "Also, it is true that Katie's husband is a viable resource for us. But, that was not a contingency to Katie's hire. It was, however, part of the reason for her working with me. I can have safe communication, via Katie, without exposure of the resource to the rest of the group. They may assume, but can never be sure. You are part of the inner circle on this. Michelle, this team would be lost without you. You girls need to work this out now, or I will be forced to bring DA Johnson into the discussion. I am going to the kitchen would anyone like something to drink?"

The two woman sat there in silence as Jason Levine left his office. Katie jumped right in. "Look Michelle, we don't have to be friends but we do have to work together. I am sorry if you are uncomfortable with this scenario; think about how I feel being thrown into this. These people are your friends and business associates, and they have nothing but respect for you. My first few days here, your name is all I heard from people in the office. I thought you were like Super ADA. I was so anxious to meet you. What can I do to fix this situation we are in? Please don't say resign." Michelle smiled, the first genuine one Katie ever saw from her. "I guess I have been pretty rough on you. And you quitting did cross my mind, but just for a moment. You are a good kid and seem really smart. I am good with a truce." Katie reached out her hand and they shook; "Friends?" Michelle stood, "Not just yet; business associates for now."

Katie could not help wondering why everyone kept avoiding the "friends" thing. She had this overwhelming feeling that the competitive nature of this niche of the legal world was such that, getting along as business associates was as much as one should expect. Being a friend might indicate the commitment not to stab someone in the back for the purpose of improving one's own status.

Chapter 17 – Taking a Break

Katie's day presented stress she never expected. The pressures of the job, a tough case with huge media exposure; these things are healthy stresses. Office politics and petty nonsense create stress that wears you down and can make your day a real drag.

"What do you say we take a drive out to the Hamptons or Montauk this weekend? The boys can play on the beach and we can have a sort of mini honeymoon." My stress levels needed the break as well. I never would take the time off, but this move we did for Katie, had more of an effect on her than me. In my job, I always had to be adaptable to change. Katie is a homebody. Don't get me wrong, she loves adventure and travel. She just needed to know that her home base, her roots were there for her to return to. This job offer presented a new adventure for her, but it meant moving her safe and comfortable home base to a new and unknown environment. Once the excitement of *new* wore down, reality set in. I am sure she is happy we did this and comfortable enough at her new job. I, on the other hand, miss my old team and boss, who also happened to be my good friend as well. But things for me, as I said, are easier and my situation here is pretty good too.

Katie needed this getaway. "Sounds great honey, you make the arrangements and I will see if Rosa is up for a paid getaway. This way we can spend time on the beach with the boys during the day while Rosa enjoys some R&R." I remember that smile. The one reserved for me that held a whole sensual story in itself. "Nights are for us, we can play honeymoon again." Did I mention how much I love that woman?

I decided on East Hampton for our weekend. The weather remained warm for mid-September and the forecast called for dry and sunny; perfect as perfect could be. The hotel rates drop after Labor Day so good deals were available. Booking took a bit of effort as the beautiful weather gave lots of other families in need of a getaway weekend, the same idea. I thought about taking the Long Island Railroad. The boys love trains and this would add to their adventure. Then I considered all the luggage, toys and other items of necessity and changed my mind. Instead, we would drive out East in Katie's SUV.

I researched East Hampton on the web. There is a lot to see on eastern Long Island. Even though we had limited time to explore, we had to go to Montauk. The boys would love the Lighthouse and there was a great breakfast place according to all the write-ups I read on Yelp. I also reserved some time for Sag Harbor; the travel reviews were on the money; it was awesome. The East

Hampton shopping took care of most of Katie's needs; I took care of the rest.

We both arranged Friday off so we had a three day weekend. Fortunately, Rosa also cleared her busy weekend schedule so she could join us. I packed the car Thursday night so we could get an early start Friday morning.

According to what I read, the town of East Hampton dates back over 350 years. There still remains some of the original puritan values amongst the twelfth generation original families. Nowadays the area is over-run by the rich and famous, who party there day in and day out, all year long. To us commoners, it is the exotic getaway we can occasionally afford to enjoy.

We arrived around 10AM at the B&B. I lucked out getting two rooms of the twelve that were available for guests. The place turned out to be amazing. With easy access just off Montauk Highway, the small fortune it cost to stay there was well worth it. We were close to the beach and not far from all the points of interest we wanted to explore.

Katie decided we all should go into town and walk around for a while, then have lunch. Rosa wanted to see the town as well, so she joined us. Once you see one souvenir shop, you've seen them all. I have little patience for this, but the women enjoyed it and the boys were too naive. I will set them straight when they are a little older. For lunch, we found a pub-like place that had salads for us, and burgers for the boys. With our bellies full, we walked a bit more. At around 2PM Katie declared "beach time," so we split up. Rosa continued on her own. I returned to the B&B with Katie and the boys. "I'll meet you at the beach, I need to make a few phone calls." I knew she would not be happy. "You promised; three days, no business." I did, but she should know me well enough by now to expect some variation of my *good* intentions. I can't help it. "Thirty minutes, Jack, or tonight will be cold and lonely." OK, I set my alarm. Truth is, I hate the beach, actually the sand. I like the amenities like the beer, and the ocean.

Katie set the boys up with pails and shovels and dug her sand-chair in a few feet from the water. The day turned out absolutely gorgeous, and she relaxed the second her feet hit the sand. The boys loved the beach and could spend hours building funky looking sandcastles. "Mommy, when Daddy help us?" "Soon, baby boy, soon."

The chill was unexpected, there was no wind and the air temperature must have been at least seventy degrees. The intense sun kept the sand lovers warm on this early fall day. Something seemed weird. Katie sat up and looked around. She had that sense of someone watching her. She looked around. There were a few kids and a dad flying a kite to her left and some teenagers tossing a Frisbee. To her right, she noticed a young couple romping under a blanket, they were far enough away so the boys would not see or understand at the least. Katie remembered those intimate moments on the beach with me the first year we were together. The prior months had been crazy bad for both of us. Then she thought of William. This made her sad. Yes there was William, he may be gone physically but he had a history with both of us. Neither of us want to forget that, and that is ok with us. It is a shared part of our history that allowed us to evolve to where we are today.

That uncomfortable feeling still plagued Katie. She decided to call it a day. "C'mon boys, grab your pails, time to go." I had just arrived. "Hey, where you going, I just got here?" Katie jumped, "You startled me; hi." I asked, "Is everything alright?" "Yes, I just had this strange vibe, like someone is; oh never mind I am just being silly." Being in vacation mode I let that one slip. Shame on me. "Hey did you notice those two over there, they made their own little tepee." Katie gave one solid knuckle in my arm. "Ouch. I got sand in between my toes so we need to stay a while, relax a bit and make a tepee." This time I was ready and dodged the attempted response. "Go help your boys." And so I did. We had a grand time building a sandcastle with the coolest water moat around it. Katie seemed stressed when I arrived, but as she laid there soaking up the sunshine, she looked relaxed again. She had the comfort of me watching the boys and her. She looked goddess-like; all oiled and glistening in the sun. That night I got to rub another type of oil on her silky smooth skin. Then we played in our own tepee.

Sunday approached all too quickly. We met up with Rosa and the boys and all headed into Sag Harbor to a really cool breakfast place called Estia's. We had the best Mexican style omelets and burritos. The boys shared chocolate chip pancakes and really delicious French toast; ends cut off. I helped in getting rid of them. This place is a little out of the way, but came highly recommended. The wait wasn't too bad for a Sunday morning. We got there around 8:30AM, Katie wanted time to explore town and then get some beach time before heading home.

The sun's rays kept the day warm once again and for mid-afternoon, this felt really nice. I sat on a sand chair reading a DeMille novel. I love the suspense. Who knows, maybe I can learn a thing or two from his suave characters. I can relate to some of them. We dug in close to the water so the boys could build sandcastles and we could keep a close watch on them. The water rushed uphill, just touching my toes. It felt awesome. Katie must have bought a new two-piece in town yesterday because I never saw this one. There must be a Victoria's Secret in town. This was the kind of suit any man would want his dream girl wearing. On the beach, without me around – no way. But, I am here and it works for me. Two kids, and she looks as good as the day I met her. *I am a lucky man.*

OK, I got distracted, I am seriously in vacation mode. Katie all of a sudden seemed restless. "What's wrong?" She sat up not looking relaxed any longer. "I have this feeling, like someone is watching me, us. I had the same strange sense yesterday as well." I looked around, "Why didn't you say something?" "I felt silly and paranoid." My professional instincts kicking in, "With all that is going on, nothing is silly." I started seriously scanning the beach mongers. The tepee couple were back, this time no tepee but they kept it north of "R" rated. Not them. Two guys, sunglasses and speedos, most probably not them. Everyone fit a similar look and all seemed to belong. Then I spotted something. A young guy in a Hawaiian short-sleeve shirt, shorts and sunglasses. He seemed to turn and walk toward the sand dunes just as I spotted him. "I'll be right back, can't hold my bladder any longer." Katie called after me, "What's wrong with the ocean?" Woman do that, not men. Well, at least we will never admit it.

I moved as quickly as possible over the hot sandy beach. My bare feet burned and my legs ached. Did I mention that I hate the sand? "Ouch, damn it!" A broken shell caught the bottom of my foot at the top of the arch. I reached the dunes where they parted to the parking lot and beach house. Scanning the parking area revealed nothing, no one resembling the one I was looking for. I walked around the concession area, no luck. Parents waited on line, some with kids pulling and whining, others loaded down with family food orders to go. Most of the stuff they had looked awful, that is, awfully good. I had to resist sneaking a chili dog.

Katie watched me as I approached, she was smiling so I knew she didn't pick up on my attempted surveillance. Or, perhaps something else. "Who wants ice cream?"

The boys bellies full of dessert and Katie calm, this weekend turned out to be what we needed. "So, success?" My wife leaned in for a nice sexy kiss. "Very successful, thank you." Rosa even looked like a changed person. Too bad we had to return to the real world.

Chapter 18 – Finding a Home

Indecision for Jane was something of an unknown phenomena. All things had to have a purpose and a direction. She did not weigh factors like how this would affect her, or anyone else, for that matter.

Now she was *conflicted*. Is it possible she wanted her children? Did she need them? Could she love them? These crazy thoughts ran around in her head making her dizzy. She started to consider her decision to give them up, as a mistake.

Sunday morning around 4 AM, Jane went into labor. Alone, with no one to help her, she started to panic; an emotion not normal for her. The doctor Jane used early on, started asking too many questions so Jane told her she was moving, and would find another doctor in her new town. Jane had one person she could call. The new bar manager that her old friend Pete had hired. Pete cautiously remained a loyal friend of Jane's and this woman became part of their little facade. The story of Jane's supposed ex- cop husband worked once again. This allowed Jane to have some social contacts that she trusted, sort of her inner circle. Jane would talk woman talk with Marne and found some comfort in their *friendship*. Marne and her husband lived close to Pete's pub and only about an hour from Jane's place. When the time had come for her to expel the two lives out of her body, she called Marne.

It rained hard that morning, and it took her friend over an hour to get to her. When Marne walked into Jane's cabin, she found her doubled over on the floor. "Oh my! Jani girl, Marne is here." Jane tried to smile and reached for her friend. Marne helped her to the bed and proceeded to get Jane ready to deliver. "Ok, sweetie, put this nice big pillow under your butt. I guess tonight I am your midwife. Ed is working. I left him a note to call Pete and let him know." Jane held her breath, sweat pouring out of every pore in her body, her face almost blue. "No, no Jani girl, don't push just yet." Jane started to huff and puff to calm herself and some of her normal color returned. Then the cramping started and she wanted to scream, but her disciplined grooming would not allow for that. Marne examined her and noticed some crowning of the first baby's head. "Now we are ready to push; take a deep breath."

Almost two hours passed until her babies finally joined the world of infidels. It appeared as if a great weight no longer held her down. For nine months she felt as if every breath was shared. Now she could take a deep one and it was all hers. It felt good. "Your babies are beautiful. A brother and a sister to look out for each other." Jane smiled a forced smile. Her mind would speak to her now as it had been doing for the whole pregnancy. *What kind of mother could you be? Oh, one that could kill her own flesh and blood for a cause.* Jane began to experience something new, another misunderstood emotion, tears.

Jane slept for a few hours, awakening to see Marne seated in the chair near the bed, holding one of her twins. The babies made baby noises and she figured the other slept in a small cradle that Pete borrowed from his sister. Jane became anxious, this horrible feeling overcame her and she lost control. "Get those things out of here, I don't want to hear that noise!" Marne jumped almost dropping the male child she held so dearly in her arms. "Jane, calm down honey. You are just overwhelmed from the long morning we had. These are your beautiful baby boy and girl. Here, why don't you hold your son? He needs his mommy." Jane tried to sit up, "Do not bring that near me! Please take them away." Jane realized she could not love these babies; not like a normal person. She never knew of this emotion called love. No one ever showed it to her so why should she, how could they expect her to share anything with these little beings. Besides, they are surely cursed coming from an infidel father and a mother who failed her god.

"You take them, you can care for them and love them as your own." Marne was mortified. She never saw this coming. Jane was a fairly private person and shared little about earlier events in her life. She never mentioned family or even close friends. As far as Marne knew, Jane had no past. Anytime Marne would ask about her childhood or family, Jane quickly changed the subject. After a few times, the subject was dropped and never brought up again. All anyone knew was the bad marriage Jane escaped from and the abuse her husband laid on her. The basic story of Jane's exile to Canada. As for the only other friend in Jane's life, Pete, he followed another story. Jane worked for the United States government, now a rogue American spy who had been betrayed and framed by her country. Pete swore to keep Jane's secret and backed her other fictitious story to protect what he believed to be the real truth. Based on what he had witnessed of Jane's talents during the attack on his bar, her story appeared more than believable.

"My beautiful friend, you are hysterical, I am so sorry. I will help you in any way you need me to. I will help care for your babies until you are ready to care for them yourself." Jane did not smile and tears ran down her cheeks, "Thank you." She passed out from exhaustion.

Marne thanked god for her good cell reception as Jane had no phone in the cabin and she never noticed her on a cell. "Hi Ron, it's me, yes the babies are fine. Jane is not though, I think she has a bad case of postpartum depression. We are going to take these darlings in for just a bit until she feels better. I will ease them back into her life."

Ronald, a good man, rarely said "no" to his strong-willed wife. He met her at a food dispensary for the needy where they both volunteered on weekends. She was a "do-gooder" as he often recited the phrase. Marne knew he would have accommodations prepared for the twins when she returned home with them.

Jane woke up about an hour later to a sweet melody Marne sang to her little babies. For a moment she forgot her anxiety and then remembered her request. "You will make a great mom. I will find a way to help financially when I can." Marne's back was to Jane and she did not turn around. "Now, Jane, we haven't made any decisions yet, you promised to sleep on it. Besides you have me to help you anytime you need me." "I love you Marne, you are their mom now. I cannot possibly care for them. I am not capable of loving them." Marne tried to interject but Jane went on, "So much has happened to me in my life that I can never tell you or anyone. I have done the most horrible things. Terrible things have been done to me as well. Raising them would only infect them with the disease I carry within me." Marne turned toward Jane

98

and raised her voice to take control of the one sided conversation. "But Jane, you never spoke like this during the last few months we have been friends. I had the impression that you loved your babies and wanted them. You seemed happy." Jane now smiled, "I thought I did. I tried so hard to want them, to love them. I hoped they would help me change but in that moment when it was time, just before they entered this cruel world, I realized the truth about me, and about them. Deep down inside they represent evil to me. I cannot overcome this." Marne remained speechless. She was sure her breathing had stopped and she was about to black out. "The babies belong to you and Ron now."

Marne and Ron raised the twins as their own. As the first few months passed, Jane made herself scarce and rarely spoke with her friend except during brief encounters at a local shop or when visiting Pete. Jane occasionally looked in on them out of curiosity. She watched them from covert hiding places by their home and at various parks and playgrounds. When they turned about three years old, she started to get strange feelings as she spied on them. Jane had the urge to touch them to see what they felt like. She would daydream of how they smelled. Something scary started happening to her.

Chapter 19 - Tying Things Up

Jane had been contacted shortly before giving birth to her twins, by an Al Qaeda cell operating out of the States. They put her in touch with a small cell in Canada not far from her. The American contact originally expressed interest in her twins which Jane prevaricated, telling them she aborted. She did not consider whether they believed her story and was sure they had eyes on her. This may have been part of the reason she needed to remove the little beings from her life. Later, her local contact told her they had other expectations for her, and she should be ready when they call. In the meantime, they wanted her to lie low and agreed to provide her with some funds to sustain her.

No longer accustomed to others controlling her, Jane needed another plan. With no allies back home or here she was on her own. Her own people were now the enemy. She once read a proverb that now seemed to make sense. "The enemy of my enemy is my friend." She would use this and perhaps resolve several problems tormenting her life.

Jane needed to take care of some things first. Money was not an issue, as she had saved quite a bit of her secretly funded income. The instructions given to her by her local contact to keep the "burn phone" with her at all times in case they called, made her angry. She did not like another control in her life. Regardless, she would keep it close, and pray to Allah that it stayed silent a little longer.

The fall air was crisp, but still comfortable enough for Jane to wear a mid-season jacket. She had grown used to the changing climates and the extreme cold that saturated her new homeland for more than six months of the year. Her first year after leaving the hot Yemen desert was tough. Each year, she grew more comfortable with the climate, and thought she preferred the changing seasons to the constant heat of the desert.

The children, *her* children, were playing in their front yard. Jane needed to be closer with them. What she was planning could liberate her or be the end of her.

"Excuse me! Why are you watching my children?" Marne spoke in an angry defensive tone. She had just come around from the side yard with a garden hose in her hand. If the year was 1800 and in the "Wild West" she would be Annie Oakley and perhaps Jane would be Belle Starr. Fortunately, the hose had not been turned on yet and Jane was safe. Marne remained guarded all the time; fearful that Jane's crazy ex-husband would come looking for his kids.

Jane turned around and Marne dropped the hose. There would be no shoot-out today. "What are you doing here?" Jane looked around to see if her *friend's* loud outburst drew any attention. Jane started walking toward Marne. "Just stay there – we had an agreement. If you gave them up then you would stay away." "Something has come up, I need to see them... in case; I may never have the opportunity again." Marne did not know what to do but had enough compassion to hear what Jane had to say. "Better come inside."

"Mommy, Mommy who is that lady?" The little girl was so cute with her beautiful blond hair pulled back into a long pony tail. She was Jane, mini style, at least in looks. "This is mommy's friend Jane; Jane this is Jani and this handsome little man is Michael." Jane said "Hello" and reached out in an attempt to hug the little girl. Marne stepped between Jane and her children, picking up Jani and grabbing Michael's hand. "Let's go inside and I'll make some tea." Jane thought to herself how much she wanted to knock Marne out right now and take her kids. She felt rage building and fought hard to stay in control of her temper.

"You kids go and play now and let the grownups talk." In unison both said "OK, Mommy," and left the kitchen. Jane smiled, "You did good Marne; they are incredible and seem so happy." "They are, so why are you here, do you want to ruin that?" Jane reached into her inside coat pocket and removed an envelope. "Here, take this, it is for them, use it however you see fit for them. I am going away for a while, if things don't work out; well… anyway, if they do I'll be back. If I make it back then everything from my past will be cleaned up and I will be safe, my kids will be safe." Marne had that killer look again, "You mean *my* kids – don't you?" "Yes, of course, *your* kids will no longer be in danger and we can all relax."

Jane stood and put her arms out, Marne got up and stepped toward her. They hugged and as Jane let go she put her hands on Marne's shoulders and looked directly into her eyes with a laser-like stare; "If I come back I will want to be a part of their lives, maybe like an aunt. I will want the opportunity to watch them grow." Marne's jaw dropped, her thoughts running wild, but she had no words. Jane seemed so scary, dangerous in her tone. Jane removed her hands and relaxed into a smile, "Now go get those little darlings so I can give each a hug goodbye."

As she held each of her estranged children, she felt their warmth and vulnerability, her heart pounded heavy. She took in their unique smell embedding it in her mind forever.

Chapter 20 – Jack & Jane

My day was mostly uneventful. Most of the morning and a good part of the afternoon was spent pushing paperwork at my desk. The office was quiet, with most of the other agents in the field. Unfortunately, the trail of money moving out of the country went cold after *supposedly* being exchanged by the Espinosa cartel. The clock on the wall just outside my cubicle indicated 16:00 EST, I was tired and ready for a break. A flick of a speed-dial button on the phone auto dialed my house so I could speak to the recording of my own voice. "Hi Honey, it's around 4PM and I am leaving the office now, I'll be home in a bit. Call me if you need me to pick up anything. Love You." I hung up and grabbed my sport jacket.

The clandestine NY office had to be relocated after the September 11 World Trade Center attack, to another undisclosed location. The ride from my office took about forty-five minutes or longer, depending on traffic. As I exited the Midtown Tunnel my phone rang. "Good evening, Agent Owens, this is dispatch central. We have a call for you from an unknown party saying it is a matter of national security; may I patch them through?" Could I possibly say no? "Make sure to record and trace this call." "Of course sir, connecting now, go ahead."

"Hello Jack, please don't say my name, you know who this is. I have some vital information I want to trade with you."

"Why would you call me, there is no information I would trust from your mouth."

"I know where Raul Espinosa is and how his operation works. I can give him to you."

"The United States government does not make deals with terrorists."

"Perhaps not, but you can and then do what you will with the information. This is a burn phone that will indicate its origin as your home address. Here is my number, 555-555-3243. Call me from a secure unmonitored phone, what I have to tell you is for your ears only. Then you can decide its value and future. The number is only good for another two hours. I am waiting."

The phone call dropped. Two clicks echoed from the phones speaker, "Sir the trace was a no go; I'm sorry sir. The transcript and recording will be sent to your secure drop box." I thanked the operator, "Please classify for my eyes only." "Of course sir."

Thursday afternoon traffic was unusually light on the Long Island Expressway heading east. I passed my usual exit getting off at the following one, Exit 52. I pulled into the brightly lit Premiere Diner parking lot, and drove around back to find a spot. Using a secure and encrypted connection to the secure VPN and then to my drop box to retrieve the transcript, I dialed the number. I was anxious and conflicted. This evil person had lied about everything since the day I first met her while in college. She destroyed and ultimately had my best friend killed. She tormented my wife back then as well, and tried to kill both of us a few years ago. Calling her could only be trouble; what can of worms will be opened? Besides, there might be some security protocol I am breaking. Nonetheless, I dialed.

The phone rang four times before I heard the connection click and her voice say, "Hello, Jack, I've been expecting your call." There was a few seconds of silence before Jack spoke, "Why would you think I would listen to anything or trust anything you say?" "You called me back, Jack – you must be curious. I can give you Raul Espinosa, my contacts here have been watching you and your family. My old friend Katie has done quite well for herself but she is involved in a dangerous game." I took a breath, "Get to the point before I hang up on you." "Jack, the point is, my own people are a greater threat to me than your people are. Putting them out of business saves me *and* your family. It is a win-win situation for you, me and the US government." I had to ask, "What is it you want?" "Not on the phone, I will text you a location here in Canada. Meet me, and I will send you home safe and sound with an abundance of information. Enough to help Katie close her case, get you your bad guys, and in return, keep me safe from my own people. You will also need to grant me full immunity from all pending prosecutions. I want to stop looking over my shoulder. Respond to my text in one hour, after that, the phone is history and so am I."

We hung up and I sat there for a while evaluating this predicament. A couple from the diner got into the car next to me, breaking my deep thought process. I headed home to my family.

Chapter 21 – Ready To Travel

When I arrived at our house, Mrs. Owens was not at home. The nanny had made lasagna and it smelled quite good. I thanked Rosa and told her to go home; she looked tired. My boys are full of energy and could wear out a marathon runner. "Good night Rosa, thank you." "Good night Mr. Jack, see you tomorrow." She is great, and we are so lucky to have her for the boys. I checked on my little guys. They were so innocent and at peace sleeping in their cute little racecar beds. Without hesitation or thought, I texted back to Jane agreeing to meet her. I hoped to land sometime late morning. I also told her I expect a text with the number to call, to arrange our meeting place; somewhere public with many people around.

A text alert dinged on my phone; Katie was on her way home. I love getting texts from her. She can be coy at times, but her text messages take "Poetic License" to the limit. Tonight's was tame. "*Hi my handsome and mysterious husband, on my way home. Tired and hungry but not too tired to skip dinner for some play time. I miss you. See you in twenty. I'll look for you in the kitchen, if not I'll find you in the boudoir.*" I envisioned all sorts of possibilities, and then shook it off. She better not have been texting and driving. Dinner smelled delicious, thanks to Rosa. When Katie arrived home, she found me in the kitchen and had a disappointed look on her face. "Honey, I told you we can have it all, dinner and… I'm your 'hoochie coochie' man." She laughed, we both laughed. I took her in my arms and gave her what we both needed most, a good hug.

My wife checked on the boys and then joined me back in the kitchen. "Those boys are so adorable when they are sleeping. I had to resist waking them up." I made sure to smile, indicating that I understood where she was coming from. Time with them is so limited during the week. Mornings were our family time. The boys were up early and we were too. Breakfast together was tradition, as often as possible. Anyway, we ate dinner and made small talk about our day. Katie got a little hyper as she told me about her meeting with Jason and Michelle. I asked her, "So it looks like your situation in the office, with Michelle, is ok now?" Katie leaned back with a sigh and a smile, "I suppose so; we will see." After a moment of silence and almost to herself, "So odd, everyone avoids the *'friend'* thing. They are so competitive for a team that has to work so close together." I smiled, thinking back to my training days at Langley. Even the women I slept with, other trainees, kept it strictly friends with benefits, and like Katie's situation, the *'friends'* part was questionable.

We cleared the dishes from dinner, and I had to decide how and what to tell my wife about my business trip plan for tomorrow. "Babe, I need to call Martin about some business stuff, I won't be long." Katie pouted then smiled, more of a sly grin, "Don't be too long." And she winked. She is so sexy.

The call to Martin Shaw, Director of the CIA's NY office, and my new boss was short. After informing Shaw of the latest developments regarding Jane, and my tentative travel plans, he responded "No." Followed by, "You are not to go on this wild goose chase. She is a fugitive assassin not a CI." We use CI for 'confidential informant'. But, in fact, an assassin is what she is. "OK boss, you are right as always, I will take tomorrow as a personal day to take care of some family business." He told me not to cross the line, or in this case the border, or my job would be at risk. Unfortunately, he and I do not have the same relationship or understanding that I had with Kevin Sorenson; who, was my next call. I also conferenced Senator White in on the call. They knew I had to go, but raised major concerns. John suggested calling Marcia Gainsworth.

Marcia and I partnered together to thwart off Jane's planned assassination of me and my wife. It was a dangerous operation that almost got us killed. Jane escaped, not unscathed, but nonetheless alive. She fled

110

to Canada and it has been almost five years of peace since, without the threat of Jane. Now she has crawled out of the evil hole she hid in, to taunt me again.

I made a call to Marcia, knowing this discussion could be a long one. Her message machine picked up so I just said, it was important and I would call her again later.

Expecting Katie to be fast asleep, I made my way up the stairs quietly to find she wasn't. I had a lot on my mind, including the fact that I could be killed tomorrow. This did not make my grand performance easy. It is amazing how the power of seduction can change one's thought process. It is the very thing that has brought great men, such as world leaders and kings to their knees.

As my wife leaned into me, kissing my lips passionately, the earlier stressed parts of my body forgot the perilous future awaiting me. She worked me slowly from atop and as I looked up at her I kept thinking how different my life would be if she was not in it. How much I love her and how incredible she is. I reached up to caress her breasts, but she took my hands and pushed them down, commanding control. She moved more aggressively now as she kissed my mouth, and bit my lip gently. I moaned, signaling that time was running out for me. She responded similarly and we both crossed the finish line together.

"I have to head north tomorrow, Canada, to follow a lead." I decided not to lie, but to leave some minor details out. There was no reason to worry Katie. Besides, it would lead to a disagreement, something we hardly ever have. "Is it dangerous?" "No, just routine follow up." OK, I lied, but for a good purpose. "Will you be home for dinner?" Her words slurring at the end; she was almost out. I told her probably not and kissed her on her neck and various other places. "I'll call you during the day and let you know my ETA for home." Not sure if she heard the last part, it probably didn't matter as she had my routine down at this point in our relationship. I held her close all night. Some part of me feared it might be my last chance to hold her.

Chapter 22 - Marcia Gainsworth

Marcia and I have been keeping in touch and trading information that helped both of us with our cases. We both worked on anti-terrorism across various borders.

I waited until Katie was out for the night, then went downstairs to call Marcia. I did not expect the reaction that I got. Marcia was dead set against my going to Canada. "You know it's a trap. Her goal has always been to take your life. Why would you think that has changed?" I repeated to her what Jane said to me on our short phone call. "This is foolish Jack; don't stir the pot." I told her that I had to go. Marcia told me, "I will make some calls to see about a surveillance team." Knowing this would be a losing battle, "I'm afraid Jane will get spooked, she is good at what she does, and perhaps even better than us." "Ok, Jack, no surveillance team, just me. We work well together and I am more than familiar with her abilities. You know I have your back on this; text me all the information."

Marcia became my most trusted confidante next to John White, and she is a very experienced field operator. I had a GPS tracking device the size of a thumbtack that I clipped onto the pants pocket inside my right pants leg; a place Jane would never see. It transmitted the GPS codes to Marcia so she could track and find me if needed, according to our plan.

Booking a flight, literally hours before wasn't cheap, but what the hell. My insurance would more than take care of it, if it came to that. The 7AM US Air flight out of Islip McArthur on Piedmont Air stopped in Philadelphia then continued to Toronto. A two hour direct flight now became five hours. Had this been ordained by my office, a private company jet would have been arranged. Since that was not the case, and, I suppose if I am fortunate enough to need a flight home, it will take equally as long or longer.

I returned to my bedroom and snuggled close to my wife. Her body was warm. I wanted to wake her and tell her what my plans are and who I have to meet with. A selfish thought that I would not really do. We never held anything back from each other. This she would understand but might not ever forgive. I hoped that was not to be the case; after all, when she married me, she married my job as well.

No alarm needed to be set; sleep never happened for me. I held Katie all night, her warmth made me feel safe. She smelled so good, I just wanted to take in as much of her as possible.

At 5AM I quietly crept out of bed; and after silently dressing, shoulder holstered my firearm and grabbed three extra clips of .40 caliber ammo. I would need to register with airport security and the TSA. They would also need to notify the pilots. Since I trusted no one, especially pilots, this made me uncomfortable. It is the law, and I hoped that not arranging this in advance would not be an issue, since time was a major factor for me.

It took over twenty minutes and a ton of paperwork, but I finally made it through security without a hitch. I had also mentioned the names of some upper echelon HLS officials which may have helped to move things along.

Marcia made her own plans, hopping aboard a government plane scheduled to drop equipment off in Toronto. A stoke of lucky timing for her, and a three hour time saver. Her plane was on the ground by eight AM with her loaded backpack and two pairs of fatigues, a choice to match a variety of landscapes. She had no idea where to go once there. Waiting for my tracking device to come online was the next step. Marcia found a little bistro, ordered coffee and waited. She had no idea when I would arrive.

Chapter 23 – A New Day

Jane woke up each morning tired and stressed. Ever since she delivered her twins, her body never fully recovered. Her nights were sleepless, to say the least. If she had a little luck to get a few hours of unbroken slumber, her unconscious time occupied itself with dreams of the past, present and future. Had she been familiar with the Charles Dickens '*A Christmas Carol*' she would have expectations of ghosts taking control of her sense of time and space.

The guilt of giving up her babies, of not being able to love them, haunted her. She still had anxiety over what she allowed to happen to Michael. Jane wanted something she could not have. The ability to love and care about another person. In her heart, she knew the twins lives with Marne and Ron would be better than she could possibly offer them. Most importantly, they were safe from the evils of her own people. Then there was Pete. If there was one person in this world she could trust, it would be him. She knew that he did not fully trust her, or believe the stories she told him about herself. He did however, cover for her during a deadly incident in his bar where the only possible suspect was her. That situation, a rare one, Jane actually saved innocent lives, destroying only the evil ones.

The people she thought of as her own blood and faith disappointed her. Supposedly, they were all children of Allah; mind and body as one for one purpose. Her confusion and frustration over their attempted betrayal seemed far more detrimental than the threat of the infidels they swore her to destroy.

"Today is the start of a new day." Jane continued to chant this to herself as she readied to begin a new regimen of mind and body training. She had to get back into shape. Birthing Janel and Mikael did things to her body she never expected. The tight wall of steel, her six pack was gone. Her mind became too relaxed and her sense of paranoia, which kept her alert and safe, more a memory than a trait these days. Today she will change all that. She was determined to set her derailed life back on track.

The refrigerator contained all sorts of items, most of them, a physical trainer's nightmare. Jane decided to throw it all out. Part of the fresh new start. The food mart was not far from her place, she will get over there later and stock up on fruits and vegetables and lots of protein items like fish, chicken, and eggs.

First things first; exercise plan, she thought, that's easy. "I will just do what I always did." She had no idea how hard that would be. Jane was still Jane, and anything she focused on doing always got done. Pain resulting from effort never presented an issue for her. Determination and a goal was all she needed.

Jane reached for a note pad that she kept in a drawer in the kitchen, almost cutting herself on one of many deadly knives she had distributed around her home. She wrote a list of exercises. She started with morning sit-ups, pull-ups and push-ups, preceded by various stretches. Her afternoon routine included free weights for arms and upper body strength and hundreds of squats. She wrote in bold letters, "Drink Water." After a brief rest, a five mile run. This surely would be a process to build up to. Jane psyched herself to get started. For once in her life she had no real commitment to anyone. This was for her.

Yet;

Something was missing, the frustration was unbearable. She thought the intense exercise would take care of it. Jane needed a release.

She dressed like she did in her college years. A low cut button down silk blouse tucked into her pleated pencil skirt looked awesome. By her standards, she was still out of shape but by most others she was incredibly perfect. Older by a few good years, her looks did not diminish. Jane set out to test her seductive powers. She needed to rebuild her confidence in that essential area. Jane drove two hours into Toronto leaving her car parked at a municipal self-parking lot two blocks from the Four Seasons over on Yorkville.

The lobby was beautiful. Jane had never been in this place before. She carefully assessed the layout and focused in the direction of the hotel lounge. She needed to look like she belonged; like a registered guest. These places often employed undercover security to catch high-class prostitutes on the prowl for rich businessmen. Jane met the latter part of their concern.

The reception desk, made of all marble surrounded by tall dark wood pillars was truly elegant. Her excitement was building. "Control, Jane," she repeated to herself as she smiled and walked past reception. "Hello miss, are you enjoying your stay?" Jane continued walking, pausing for just a moment, "Very much so, everything is so lovely; Thank you."

The dBar area as they named the chic lounge area was filled with mostly business men and women. The chatter was loud and it irritated Jane. *Keep calm, Jane, this is not your first rodeo.* Her mark had to be a married man, not a player, one who had no intension of cheating on his wife. Otherwise, there would be no challenge.

It was just after 5PM and the happy hour crowd was building. Jane looked around at the variety of suits, male and female. It seemed that there were very few if any couples. There appeared more to be the casual business affair types, though. There, in the corner, two chairs and a table, only one chair occupied. She moved in closer noticing the wedding ring. Her mark was quite handsome and on the taller side. His dark gray suit matched her attire. *Hmm, this could work*. Jane stood a few feet away looking as if she needed a place to sit. The empty chair had a stack of papers on it. He did not look up. *What is wrong with this guy? Wait, he just glanced at me. He's trying not to let on that he noticed me*. "Excuse me, would you like to sit? I can move these." He reached for the papers. "Oh, no. Please don't bother. I'm fine." "No bother." It was working, Jane was bursting with anticipation. Then it happened. Text book perfect. "Damn!" Papers went all over the place. The guy was on his knees trying to get them in order. Jane dove right in. "This is my fault, I am so sorry. Please, let me help." She got down on the floor shuffling papers. Their eyes met, the scent of her erotic perfume aroused his senses. With his papers back in order, somewhat, she sat in the now available chair. The handsome businessman or lawyer, he looked like a lawyer, asked, "Please, let me buy you a drink, it's the least I can do.

They made small talk as they had a few drinks. He was married, two young boys. Jane told him about her husband Michael and her two children. She explained to him that her meeting was cancelled at the last minute and that the hotel did not have a room for her. "Wow, it is late. I need to try to catch a flight home to New York." Jane stood and almost lost her balance. "I guess I'm a light-weight. I need to sit down or lay down." The gentleman caught her arm, "I have dinner meeting I need to get to and it is too late for you to catch any flights tonight. You can lay down in my room until I return. I have connections at the Omni Toronto, I will see about getting you a room there for tonight."

His room was nice, not a suite or anything but elegant just the same. "I'll be two or three hours. I'll find a place for you to stay and get you there. Please, call room service and order dinner if you are hungry." Jane actually felt guilty at taking advantage of this guy but she had to do what she needed to do – for her.

"Thank you, you are, well..." She grabbed his suit and pulled him close locking her lips to his. She felt him tense up and eased off a bit. "I am so sorry, I don't know what came over me. It's just that you are..." He pulled

Jane close and kissed her hard. She pushed him away just a little, "What about your meeting?" "What about it? It was just cancelled too." He took her hand and led her to the bed, "I know this is wrong but, it feels so right."

At one point sex got a bit rough and Jane almost lost it. She placed her hand on her lover's throat pressing him hard into the bed as she rose up and down on him. She had rage deep down that needed to be set free, her subconscious sending a message, "*you can end this now Jane.*" Then she caught a glimpse of her children's sweet little faces and thought, "*I can be strong, forceful and compassionate. I can be in control always.*" She released her grip and stilled on him, "Now!" They both found another kind of release.

"I had no idea; that was - incredible." Jane kissed him gently on the lips. "So were you. We can each be the other's secret fantasy." She then said, "Thank you. I'll catch a cab to the airport." Another harmless lie as she would walk to the municipal lot and get her car. She looked over her shoulder as she exited his room, "You might consider a little makeup." Jane pointed to her own neck and smiled.

Chapter 24 - Betrayal

Jane hit the trail early the next day, around 4 AM. She had an easy drive home from Toronto and felt recharged and ready for the day's events. She wanted to be pumped and alert when she met with Jack. The fool flew commercially, which made it easier for her to track his movements and time his arrival. Just as she returned to her cabin her phone rang. She was sure it was too early for him to be there. Besides she did not text him her contact information yet.

"Yes; who is this?" Jane answered cautiously. "It's Amy, don't worry, I am on a burn phone. I have information for you." Jane had no problem being the old Jane, curt and to the point. No wasted words. "Go ahead." "Agent Gainsworth boarded a company plane this morning, destination, Toronto. She has tracking equipment and weapons. I thought you would want to know." Jane started to build anger, the old Jane way. She felt dangerous and it felt good. "Ok, I understand, I will take care of it, do not bring anyone else in. She is mine." There was no need for further conversation, so Jane started to say goodbye; then she said, "Wait!" Amy was her contact to the American cell that engaged her years ago. They were Jane's enemy now, and so was Amy. Jane had an idea, a use for Amy, for her own agenda. The traitor would never know she was helping to defend against her own people who claim to be acting by the word of Allah.

Amy replaced her own twin shortly after the takedown of the Yemen camp, killing her in the back alley of her apartment building as she discarded her trash in the dumpster. Amy, or T2, as her previous Yemen leaders referred to all the replacement operatives, lived the American version's life all this time. She remained loyal to the cause and available for projects as needed. For the most part she was used for her communication with Jane, and as the go-between for other American and Canadian cells.

Amy's call raised an urgent concern that had to be dealt with. Jack already broke their agreement. She should kill him with no delay, but she had to remain calm and sensible. He might be her only solution to the other problem she faced. There would be plenty of time later to deal with him. First, she had to take care of the meddling bitch Jack involved.

"What? Is there something else?" Amy seemed irate and Jane would have none of that. "Yes, I need you to go to Jack's residence. Find a way into his home to keep an eye on his family. Stay close to his wife Katie and her twin boys. If Jack becomes a problem I will need them as an insurance policy. You need to be there in an official capacity. Do not raise any suspicion or she will alert Jack. She is smart, and no stranger to our operations." Amy was also playing both sides of the fence and may need to have Jane's confidence for chance she might be instructed to take her out. "I'll figure something out. I will send you the new contact number for a phone when I get it." Jane said, "Good, whatever you do, no harm is to come to those boys. If you need to act, take care of business and make sure to clean up. Bring the boys to me immediately." Jane figured, if all else failed, she would send Amy to paradise and offer the Owen's boys to the cell. She would pass them off as her own. Jane was not thinking completely rational at the moment. She never considered that Amy might suspect Jane's treasonous intentions. She hoped she saw Jack and Marcia's trip to Canada as a fact finding mission in search of Jane.

Chapter 25 - Watching Katie

The time crunch was on. Amy Saunders needed to figure out a way to get from DC to NY fast. She needed to request personal time off, at least a few days. As she walked out of her office, she bumped into agent Ken Walker. "Sorry Ken, I almost knocked you over." Amy knew the effect she had on guys when she smiled in her shy kind of way. Ken kept a straight face, he found himself awkward around Amy. He liked her and she knew it. "What's the hurry?" Amy showed more of a grin this time, "Lots to get done." "Me too, heading for Long Island, last minute protection detail in the morning." As he said it, Ken realized his mentioning of that information might not have been a good idea. "It's a favor for Marcia, on my own time, so no need to mention anything to the others." Allah surely was guiding this situation in her favor. "No problem, Ken; say, do you want to grab some dinner? I could use the company tonight." It seemed obvious that Ken was stressing between his obligation and his attraction to her. "Never mind, another time, you must have a lot to do before leaving tomorrow. Besides, our superiors would frown on any social meetings." Ken seized the moment, "Dinner would be nice. We don't need to tell anyone, or ask anyone's permission."

Ken showed up at Amy Saunders apartment as agreed, 7PM sharp. To add to his awkwardness, Amy opened the door in her partially visible night gown showing through a very sexy low cut silk robe. "Hi, Ken." She forged an embarrassed look on her face, "I'm running late as you can see. I thought cooking for you might be more relaxing, I hope that's ok."

Amy poured several glasses of wine and soon they both were feeling the effects of the alcohol. Neither had any intention of eating dinner. Any awkwardness Ken might have had, the wine took care of. He dove right in, ravishing Amy. She liked him, but had no interest in him past the job Jane had tasked her with. First they made love on the couch. The guy had the stamina of a horse on steroids. Round two started in the hallway, both already naked. He held her from behind and repeatedly pushed himself into Amy until she could no longer take it. "That's enough! My god, did you take something in anticipation of this evening?" Ken laughed, not the laugh of a shy guy. He turned her around and kissed her and led her backwards toward her bedroom. Another hour, and they both finally found their release.

Overheated like a car engine in the middle of the desert, Amy lay on the bed waiting for Ken to come out of the bathroom. She figured he would be tired, euphoric and easy prey. After a few short moments the door opened. It was dark in the room except for a narrow stream of light shining in from the window. As Ken approached the bed, the moonlight illuminated his body, highlighting his readiness for another round.

"Holy mother of... Allah, forgive me!" Amy sprang out of the bed, toward Ken. She moved like a wild cat, thrusting a short stiletto type knife into his chest. She pushed his large body onto the bed while continuing to push the knife blade further into him. His last thoughts were not why, but where, did this plastic *drop cloth* come from? Then all went dark.

His body lay cold, wrapped tightly in the industrial plastic wrap. She needed to call her handler. A cleaner would be sent to take care of Ken. Like her other desert family members, his death had no effect, good or bad on her. Ken was simply a casualty of war.

Amy had her plan set and needed to drive the five hours to New York. She would arrive just after breakfast. Jane would be happy and more trusting. First the call to her boss.

Chapter 26 - Insurance

Jane figured the vicinity of the airport was a good place to start her search for Marcia. In the back of her mind, she envisioned doing all sorts of horrible things to her; torturous things. Payback for the part she played in foiling Jane's well thought out attack on the Owens family. Jane started to replay the events of that night four years ago then stopped herself. Focus, Jane, focus. She checked all the incoming flights from DC and fortunately only three flights showed for the morning, all coming into the same terminal. The second flight appeared to be a small jet with no markings. She figured it must be a government transport. There she was, the sneaky bitch. Jane followed Marcia as she strapped on her heavy looking backpack and picked up a duffle bag. She thanked someone in uniform, then headed for the rental car area. Jane watched as Marcia got on the Enterprise bus.

Jane smiled, thinking this is going to easy. She waited at the exit of the Enterprise rental car lot for Marcia, and followed her to a little bistro ten minutes from the airport.

She watched for a while noticing that Marcia looked at her phone every five minutes while sipping a cup of coffee. The time to move had to happen now, before the agent connected with Jack. Jane made her move.

The bistro was not crowded and the morning temperatures turned out to be mild. Marcia made it easy by taking an available table outside. "Do you mind if I sit here, there are no available tables?" As Marcia looked up, several considerations engulfed her thought process. *There are plenty of tables, yes I do mind and...* By the time she recognized Jane, it was too late. "Hello Agent Gainsworth, or do you still fantasize that you are Katie Claire Owens?" Marcia was taken completely by surprise. How could Jane have known she was in Canada? "Please do not make any sudden moves, I have a silenced .22 aimed at your gut." Marcia kept her hands in plain sight, complying with her assailant's command. "I'm sure you are the one with the wannabe Katie issues." With her free hand, Jane took out a cigarette pack and placed it on the table. "Take this and place it in the top pocket of your vest." Marcia did as told. The device had some weight to it. "What is this?" "That my friend," Jane laughed, "is enough plastic explosive to send you and twenty friends to infidel hell." "You are pure evil!" "No, good old fashioned smart. I hold this trigger and you can move about freely. With a good five hundred meter signal, you can take off and I can patiently wait for a crowded moment." "Why are you doing this? And how did you know I was here?" Jane started to answer, stopping herself, "Enough talk, time is short; we have to get moving. Get up! You can drive." Marcia did as instructed and walked toward her rental car. She said to Jane, "Oh, I get it, you parked illegally and your camel was towed. Jane ignored Marcia's sarcasm.

Marcia had a pretty good sense of direction, a skill of great importance in her line of work. Even as the driver, the circuitous route Jane took her on had her confused. Any surveillance team following them would certainly have lost them in the turns. She said to Jane, "You really are a paranoid bitch." Jane continued to ignore Marcia's remarks, but let her confidence show by smirking. They arrived at an abandoned warehouse that Jane had prepared ahead of time. Marcia guessed that it had been an old packaging company by all the paper cutters and storage bins and label makers. "Over there, in that office to the right." Jane pointed to a steel chair that was bolted to the floor. The room looked like a cheap medieval torture chamber. "I like how you decorated the place." Jane found no humor. "Sit in the chair and shut-up." Marcia stood in place, not moving. As Jane approached, she rushed Jane, knocking her to the ground. Jane still had the remote detonator in her hand. Marcia screeched, "Go ahead; blow us both up!" They each took turns kicking and punching each other. Jane, one handed, pulled

Marcia's hair so hard that a huge chunk came out. As Marcia reacted to the pain, Jane roundhouse kicked her in the kidneys knocking her down and out.

When Marcia regained her senses, she found herself in the chair. Both hands and feet were tightly zip-tied. Jane sat in another chair about two feet away, just staring at her; she had something in her hand. At first Marcia thought it was the detonator; to her relief, Jane flipped it open and texted something. She then placed the phone in her pants pocket returning her attention to her captive. Marcia spoke, wincing in pain, "Never imagined anything existed as low as what you are. What is this all about?" Jane got up and kneeled directly in front of Marcia. She placed her hands on her captives' thighs and leaned in close to her face. Jane took in her scent which now consisted of perspiration and a little fear. "You like women don't you?" Marcia should have been shocked at the out of place question, but at this point nothing made sense. She kept running all the possibilities for who and how she was compromised. "Fuck off." Jane grinned as she stared into Marcia's eyes. Tauntingly, "Do your tough guy colleagues know of your ungodly sexual preferences?" Jane leaned in close again and kissed Marcia's cheek, then on the lips gently. Without warning, Marcia bit her lip causing Jane to push back quickly. Marcia spit in her face. Jane responded with a swift punch in her nose sending blood splattering everywhere. She was about to continue her assault when her cell phone buzzed. I had landed and responded to her message which contained the GPS location of the warehouse. "Saved by the phone, lucky you." The lights were turned off and the door closed. The message had said "ETA twenty minutes." Jane looked at her watch, it was almost 2PM.

Chapter 27 – Canada, Oh Canada

I drove my rental car, a Jeep Grand Cherokee, down the broken road to what appeared to be an abandoned warehouse. My stomach was in knots. There were no cars visible, at least not out in the open. It was real creepy but I had no choice at this point. OK, I had a choice to run and not look back. *No, that would not be manly*.

The entrance door was partially opened and squeaked loudly as I opened it further and walked in. I was in what appeared to be an old reception area. The double doors to the warehouse area had been removed and I could see a dim light shining far back into the dark enclave of the building. Ok, so I admit I was tense at this point. Perhaps I was a little bit scared and a whole lot apprehensive, but onward I went. The air was cool, the heat probably was off for years and the metal walls and roof did not help. I called out hoping Jane did not pick up on the trembling in my voice. "I'm here, let's get this, whatever we are doing, done." The echo rang out loud and tinny.

Meanwhile, back home, my wife had no idea what was about to go down. The doorbell rang three times;

Katie looked at the clock which showed 8:15. She wondered why Rosa did not use her key.

"Good morning, Mrs. Owens. I'm agent Saunders. I work with agent Marcia Gainsworth. Katie already had the 'I don't know you so I don't trust you' look. "Marcia asked me to look out for you." As Amy spoke, she realized that Katie may have communicated with the other agent, Ken Walker. "Actually, this was Ken Walker's detail, but a family emergency came up and he asked me to cover until your husband was home safely from his assignment." Katie smiled and gestured for the agent to enter her home. "I remember you from a few years ago. You worked with Jack; you're ATF?" Amy relaxed, the hard part over, she would take control of the situation when called for.

"I was just getting ready to go to work. The boy's nanny will be here any moment to take them to day care. Do I need to keep them home?" Jane did not prepare Amy for these options. If T-1 Amy remained close or worked with Jack, as her twin must have done she might have known more about the family's daily routine. "I think you can go about your day normally, there is no known threat; this is just a precaution Marcia wanted to take. I am here unofficially, as a favor." Just then, Rosa came in, using her key. Katie made the introductions with little details. Rosa understood both her employer – friends occupations and minded her own business; most of the time. "Why don't you go to work, I will stay with Rosa and the boys."

So, back to my situation. "Hello Jack, you look good, better than our last meeting. Come into my office so we can sit and relax." Jane led Jack to another office two doors down from where Marcia was bound and gagged. The room had an old and dusty (well everything was dusty) desk with two chairs in front of it. There was a love seat on the wall to the right of the desk and just left of the doorway. Jane gestured to the love seat, "Shall we?" She dressed seductively just as I remembered she did during our last encounter several years ago. I had to stand my ground, "I think the chairs are a better choice." Jane frowned and said, "Now Jack, we are not in college anymore, we have both matured. Trust, Jack; it's about trust." Jane gestured again as she sat. I hesitated and then sat next to her, leaving as much distance as possible between us. She still owned the *look,* very seductive. She appeared different now; older but still incredibly gorgeous.

"So, as agreed, I assume our meeting is confidential between the two of us?" "You made that clear on the call yesterday." "So no one knows you are here?" Jack paused, "I made arrangements in case I don't return." Jane held a small stick-like object in her hand. I tried to fight the urge to ask... then she pulled the Jane move.

"Take off your clothes. It's about trust, Jack. I'm not sure I can trust you yet." She moved closer and placed her hand on my thigh, slowly moving it upward. "Do you trust me – Jack? I need to be sure you are not wearing a wire." Jane is the most dangerous kind of killer. She is absolutely beautiful, oozing sex, yet has this innocent look about her. The complete and ultimate form of deception. I stood up and unbuttoned my shirt. "You stay seated – stay right there." After proving no wires or recorders existed on me, I got dressed and sat in the chair, which I pulled closer to the couch where she remained seated.

Jane wasted no time explaining everything to me. She told her story about her two kids and the threat to them. She also exposed Amy as a double agent and her threat to her and to Jack as well as the US government. "I can give you Raul Espinosa." An hour had passed and Jack was numb, his worst fears, information he already assumed, now became reality. "Why are you telling me this?" "I want four things, actually five. I want Amy Saunders out of the picture; she has to be dead. Complete immunity for all past offenses in the United States and in Canada. I want Canadian citizenship, a new identity, and I need two million dollars so I can take care of my children and their guardians." I was surprised, and surely did not expect these demands. "Jane, you are one of the most wanted terrorists in the world. I cannot, nor can anyone make a deal with you for any reason, no matter how valuable the information is." Jane leaned forward getting closer to me, "Raul is funding an organization that will succeed in destroying the western world as you know it. Your government has no choice. I am the key to breaking them up. It is a win-win for all of us." Jack stood, "I have to go; you cannot be trusted." "No, Jack. You are the one who cannot be trusted. We had an agreement and you broke it." She held up the object in her hand. "This is a remote detonator, follow me or we shall all meet our maker." She walked ahead of me to an office two doors down. "You are the one who broke our trust. Thanks to our common enemy, I found her." I turned ready to take Jane down but she held that remote and I knew she would not hesitate to push the button. When Jane unceremoniously pushed open the office door, I was stunned to see Marcia bound to the chair. She looked like she had been badly beaten. I was certain my blood pressure would burst my arteries.

"It's about trust, Jack. Without it, we both lose." She walked over to Marcia and pulled out a knife, I started toward her but she again held up the remote. I watched as she cut the plastic cuffs and removed the small cigarette pack like box from Marcia's vest pocket. Jane lowered the remote and put it in her pocket along with the explosive. She backed away from Marcia.

"Take agent Gainsworth home, she will be fine. I will wait for your call. I will make a complete statement about everything, the whole operation and give up those I know about. Oh, one more thing..."

Jane made the call to Amy letting her know that her job was complete and she should return home. I heard her say, "Everyone is safe and OK?" Later I would get the rest of the story from Katie who was unaware of the danger she and the kids were in. Jane's remarks and Katie's update was all I needed to understand that Jane had set up an insurance policy in case I didn't cooperate.

Amy Saunders was relieved that Jane had called and told her to go home. Not that she had a problem taking out the kids or anyone; that is what she was bred to do; she had gotten accustomed to the privileged life. Privileged by her standards, not ours. She started her car and headed back to DC. Her cover was safe for now. So she thought.

Chapter 28 - The Deal

The thought of Jane as my ally seemed almost unfathomable. After all, our history and the knowledge of the atrocities she committed in the past does not allow for a trusting partnership. Then again, the fate of our country might lie with who controls the information she offered to provide. I wondered at what price this would come.

I traveled back to DC with Marcia to make sure she was OK, and to help explain what we had both gone through. This was sensitive information, and I could not be sure at this point who to trust. I called Senator White and asked him to meet me in DC. His influence would be instrumental in keeping both of us from being arrested ourselves. Operating without jurisdictional approval is a violation which is treated most seriously. Even with my past involvement, it was a big risk.

We met with the director of HomeLand Security and other high ranking military officials. The President gave his approval for us to meet Jane's terms. He would speak with the Canadian Prime Minister to work out the Canadian side of the deal. I would never know if later they took care of her in other covert means, but that would be out of my hands. For now Jane became a *legitimate* asset.

As for Amy, our newly discovered traitor, Marcia wanted to deal with her personally.

Amy returned to her office and started reviewing some cases, trying to look busy when Marcia knocked on her door. "Hey Amy, what's going on? I heard you had some personal time yesterday." "Just some family business, how about you?" Marcia smiled as she sat herself down in the chair on the side of Amy's desk. "Same here." She figured both could play the game, but time was wasting away. Amy looked at Marcia's bruises and realized she had been played by Jane. Marcia pulled out her handgun, pushing the muzzle into Amy's gut. "Keep your hands on the desk and make no mistake, I *will* pull the trigger if you so much as bat an eyelash." At that same moment, two military guards with automatic weapons drawn, entered the office aiming at the traitor.

"What the hell is this? Are you crazy?" Marcia stood, motioning for Amy to do the same, "Amy Saunders, alias T2 from Yemen. You are under arrest for crimes against the United States." "I want a lawyer." Marcia took some pleasure as she spoke, "You don't need a lawyer where you are going. Say "Hello" to T2 William."

This time, Jack had official status to pursue any and all leads with his agency, HLS, and military backing. His call to Jane was short and to the point. She would be brought to the United States on a government transport the day after tomorrow to begin her debriefing and to confirm her arrangements after the mission was completed.

Chapter 29 – Katie Claire

    I remember the first time I met my wife. William, the real William, dared me to make a move on a cute girl sitting at the bar. He bet me twenty and anything else that went along with my success. I had a lady killer reputation; failure would not be possible. I made my move and acquired company for the evening and a twenty.

    William made his own moves; not part of any plan or bet. He played hero to a beautiful young lady in distress over a stupid billiard game. We noticed her earlier; smooth moves and drop dead gorgeous. I can still imagine her slender body with perfect curves as she leaned over the table to take an impossible shot. Ok, I've matured since then but that is a memory I will keep stored. By the way, she is even hotter now; (*just for the record*). Anyway, the jerks she competed against were supposed to be her friends. But drunk as they were, things got heated. You see, Katie was something of a hustler. She grew up with a pool table in her home. She considered her dad as good as any pro, and Katie learned the game from him. They played almost every night after dinner. That night she played for a round of drinks. Her opponents turned out to be sore losers. One big hunk, more so than the other two.

Katie Claire had the aura. When she moved, people paid attention. This night William paid attention, watching her as she cleared the billiard table, one ball after another. I walked over to tell him I would be leaving; my new friend in tow. Meanwhile, the sore loser had just started verbally abusing Katie. William had the guy in a choke hold. The guy started turning blue. Might have been the drinks, but I'm pretty sure he was almost out for the count.

William saved the girl, and got the girl. Almost immediately they were together all the time. It isn't like I became the third wheel. They were a couple, but we all remained very close friends. I considered William more of a brother, than a friend. I really liked Katie. She was the perfect girl. I never thought of her in any way except as a friend, except as William's girl.

It wasn't until after William had been replaced by his twin brother Carlton, and Katie leaving Atlanta broken hearted, that I realized how much I missed her and cared for her.

One night, two years later, I found out Katie was working in NY and went to visit her. A lot of questions bothered me about what had happened to her and to her relationship with William. At first she seemed reluctant to talk to me or discuss her past. She finally agreed to meet me for a drink. At some point I touched her hand, and it was electrifying. After a few drinks, things relaxed, and we danced a little. When she left, we kissed, a friends kiss. At that moment I knew that I was in love with Katie Claire Evans. I had always been in love with her.

We shared something we could no longer speak of with anyone but each other. William's death had brought us together. I believe my brother is smiling upon the two people he loved most.

William, I miss you. I promised you I would take care of Katie, and Katie takes very good care of me. I accept that no one could ever replace you in her heart, not even me. We have a special kind of love, it is deep and sincere. You are, and always will be with us, heart and soul.

Chapter 30 – Out with the Truth

Katie looked tired sitting at the dining room table. She was going over some legal briefs when I got home. She smiled, glad to see me home safe and sound. Evidentially, she had no idea that agent Saunders was a "T2." She and I used that term frequently when discussing the covert operation from a few years back that almost resulted in our demise. I decided that telling her the twin imposter basically had our children as hostages would ruin what should be a good night. I decided to leave that part of yesterday's story for another time.

Jane's information all pointed to a tribal group in Yemen. I had flight arrangements for the following morning on a military transport carrying medical supplies and food destined for Ethiopia. From there, I had to make my own travel plans. A team would be waiting from our attaché's office in Yemen to provide local transportation and protection. Once again, no one from my office except my boss knew what I was doing. A few analysts from the Carolina office and my old boss, Kevin, are my only contacts. The senator and his team in DC, along with Marcia also stayed involved. They were my resources to get things done quickly if needed. All this could not be happening without the President's approval. The only opposition we had, came from the Vice President, whose opinion was that I might stir up trouble in the Middle-East. The VP seems like a good guy, but there were times during the Yemen Camp take-down that I had an eerie sense about him. Then, too, he raised questions and opposition. I sometimes wonder if *he* had a twin. Researching that would more than likely stir up trouble I had little time for now – but someday...

"So, tomorrow I have to fly out again on business." Katie did not look up, "How long this time?" I told her I wasn't sure, "Maybe a few days." This time she looked up, "I ate already; are you hungry? There is some mac and cheese with broccoli." Yum, my favorite, I love veggies. I declined, informing my wife that I had a late lunch and wasn't hungry for food. "Why don't we go upstairs? Are you almost done?" Katie did not make eye contact as she asked, "Where are you going, Jack?" "Honey, you understand that if I tell you I have to kill you." She did not find that amusing. Katie used to have a sense of humor. I can't imagine what happened to dry it out. "Where, Jack?" Ok, so now I am in trouble. I married a woman too smart, she is a tough one. So I took a deep breath and readied my side arm (just kidding on the last part). "Yemen, to chase down a lead." I caught the look of death as she drew tears. "Katie, I will have a team there working with me and protection. This is a friendly visit."

Katie is a very smart woman. My wife has a good sense, and just enough woman's intuition. She quickly put together Canada and Yemen. "You met with Jane! Are you out of your mind? How could you?"

We spoke for over an hour and I told her as much as I dared, without breaking some law that could get me imprisoned. She begged me not to go, but in her heart she knew it was my job, and nothing would change the inevitable. I still believed, for my own sake, that not telling her about Amy Saunders was still a good idea.

To my utter disappointment, but not unexpected, my wife was clad in sweats, and reading more briefs when I got up to our bedroom. "I checked in on the boys, they were sleeping snuggled in their blankets." "You know, Jack, you have missed most of their soccer games this season which is almost over. You are away almost every weekend." I promised her that when this was over I would take some time off and take lighter cases. I would spend more time with my family. "I love you guys more than life itself, I hope you know that." Katie did not respond.

The alarm went off at 7AM just like every other morning. I rolled over and held Katie tight. "I love you." She held my hand tight. "I love you too, please be careful; we need you."

Dressed and ready to go, a car waited for me out front to take me to the airport. I had to take a puddle jumper to Stewart Air National Guard Base where the transport was leaving from. The flight took about twenty-five minutes once we were in the air. The winds were gusty, and our plane was held on the tarmac for about twenty minutes. All in all I could have drove the ninety miles in less than two hours.

The military transport plane seemed huge as I stood next to it, but once inside it was small and drab. The cabin area held only twelve seats, definitely a no-frills flight. I guess the rest of the plane was like a big warehouse for storage. Fortunately I was the only passenger, so I had enough room to spread out and sleep. Something I needed desperately.

"Good morning, Mr. Owens; and welcome. I hope you are able to find comfort during today's flight. My name is Captain Agnes Moorhead (not the actress, she's deceased), I am co-piloting today for Captain Andrew LaSalle." She was cute in a military way, her hair cut short with bangs. It fit her face perfectly. I figured I could have some fun with her surname; *behave – it's a long trip.* I told her to call me Jack and I will call her Agnes. "That is fine Mr. Owens, and you may refer to me as Captain Moorhead." Damn there's that name again…. "Our flight time is about sixteen hours. This is an old and heavy ship,

149

she rocks and creaks a bit." *Great, I hope the ship doesn't sink.* "We will make one stop for re-fueling. No one will be allowed to leave the plane, customs issues, as I'm sure you are aware." I asked, "What time is lunch?" She pointed to a built in ice chest and returned to her seat in *first class*.

Chapter 31 – Gods Creation

God's creatures can be amazing. The scruffy camel stood very still allowing his well accustomed body to cool down in the sweltering heat. The blazing hot afternoon sun reflecting off the glass-like sand brought temperatures above 100 degrees. His big brown eyes, unaffected by the strong glare bouncing off the sand, scanned the terrain. He hoped to find a waterhole or any vegetation that contained water.

Just five days ago, he was part of a caravan crossing the western part of Yemen along the coast of the Red Sea. The Zaraniq tribe he belonged to celebrated their victory with two of their tribesmen winning the Camel Jumping contest for the third year in a row. Most of the live-stock were accustomed to the commotion of hundreds of crazy humans ranting and raving over the ridiculous sport. The newer, more recently acquired camels, would get frightened and try to escape. They would either be lassoed or shot. One of the humans caught his foot on the saddle as he soared over the rows of animals, shifting it to one side. This created a laceration in his hump and blood dripped copiously down his side.

That evening, they removed his saddle and treated his wound. The desert winds picked up and a low howl echoed through the tents. The handler forgot to re-attach the wounded camel's tether to the tent post. Normally, by instinct, the animal would try to pull away but this time his restraint no longer existed. The Camel wandered aimlessly away from the camp into the darkness.

He grunted loudly as he contemplated what direction he should proceed toward. His instincts told him to head straight, following the shadows of the dunes and in line with the striations in the sand. To humans, they are mesmerizing and often produce mirages of an oasis where no water could ever exist. These lines that the previous evening's winds so perfectly created became the desert creature's map for survival.

Several days into his journey, the tepid air began causing the animal to heave, as dehydration began its ugly wrath on its body. He continued on, despite his health issue, until he finally found his waterhole. Truly an oasis in the middle of a vast dry desert. He blinked his eyes and pulled his dry and crusted tongue back into his mouth. Salvation lay just ahead.

Surprisingly, he did not encounter any humans. This area of desert, just a few miles off the coast of the Red Sea, is popular for caravans and western sympathizers. The large waterhole had become popular for tourists as well. Locals knew to stay away, thereby reducing the risk of any conflicts. The greedy local tour guides however, would bring paying customers looking for adventure here, neglecting to advise them of the risks.

His feet dragged in the hot sand but he continued on, knowing that the refreshing cool water would save him. He would also fill his body with reserves so he could continue his trek.

The click startled him. His senses perked up, but it was too late. The blast tore apart his body, sending it, along with the desert sand, high into the sky. From a bird's eye view, it looked like a sand storm starting up. Vultures and other desert scavengers quickly descended upon the remains, which lie just feet from the beautiful Oasis.

Chapter 32 - Yemen

It took a while to get accustomed to the rough air. This old dog needed to be taken out of service (the plane, not me.) After about two hours, I fell asleep. I slept right through the refueling stop. Although, I think I woke for a moment when we hit the ground and I banged my head. Maybe I was knocked out. Either way, it worked out for the best. We arrived around 5AM Ethiopian time.

I was met by a US Attaché, Morris Hinsky, or something like that. Jet lag got me down a bit. He briefed me on my connections in Yemen and invited me for some breakfast. With two hours to kill before my flight into Aden, I graciously took him up on the offer. Besides, real food, even in this part of the world, has to be better than government rations.

Breakfast consisted of a dish of Kinche, as well as *Engual be Siga* which is basically scrambled eggs with beef; I hoped the kind of beef that came from a cow. Surprisingly good, I have to admit. The conversation remained business-like as we went over my itinerary for the next leg of my trip.

Arrangements with local trusted security agents and a guide had been made. My meeting with the tribal leader in Ma'Rib had to be planned with strict confidentiality. The area is daunted with stress. The oil pipelines are constantly under attack. Al Qaeda puts pressure on the Tribes, the Tribes beg for help from the government and no one can trust the government or each other. I must be crazy to follow a lead here with no real promise of gaining valuable information. Jane might be setting me up. Then again, she could have taken me out in Canada with no risk.

My new friend, of little conversation, gave me documents needed to pass security checkpoints. These are special government papers with special symbols indicating that the proper "*fees*" had been paid, ensuring safe free passage to our destination. "Your name is Jack Smith." How original. Interestingly, Mr. Hinsky made no mention or promise of safe return.

So, if my description of the air transport was less than interesting, then I need not bother with the next part of my trip. I was provided with a six seat twin prop, and a pilot who did not, or would not, speak any English. The flight took just over two and a half hours. My stomach turned inside out several times due to jarring turbulence, and I worked hard to keep the "Breakfast of Ethiopian Champions" in its place. Things finally smoothed out as we flew over the ocean to make our decent into Aden. I wish we could have flown directly into Ma'Rib, but that airfield had too many eyes on it. Aden is a rather interesting seaport city, located just where the Red Sea flows into the Gulf of Aden. This city's history as a seaport dated back earlier than the 5th century BC. Most people are familiar with the Port of Aden as a result of the horrendous October 2000 Al Qaeda suicide attack on the USS Cole. Some of those same bastards were involved in the 9/11 terrorist plot. Those horrific actions took down both New York World Trade Center towers, as well as the Pentagon, with the downing of AA flight 77. My heart aches just thinking about those events. This part of the world can be so beautiful and peaceful with so much history. It is amazing how a few small-minded groups of people can destroy something that is so special.

The next part was the hardest. I knew of the issues getting to our destination. When the Yemen camp was taken down years back, our troops flew in directly to the location, parachuting to a safe area with good tribal connections. From that point, they had a short distance to traverse. For me this would not be the case. Every single mile of the two hundred mile trip was extremely risky. My stomach remained in knots.

My driver was a local by the name of Abdul, and my guide, a German fellow named Klaus. He worked at the American embassy doing this stuff on a daily basis. He had gotten used to us spy type guys and spoke as little as possible. There were also two heavily armed Humvees assigned to escort us. Names of the inhabitants unknown. I was glad to have them shadowing us.

I had plenty of time to study the maps. The plan to stay on main roads agreed with me. As a rule, main roads offered the best chance of a safe trip. It also cost the most. I think my papers indicated a pre-paid discount. Taking local roads part of the way proved a shorter distance, and a huge time saver, but offered more risk of attacks and roadside bombings. Pay or die? I always go with pay. So it looks like we grab the N1 out of Aden to the 215 merging into the 621. Then we take N6 into 5621. That is about three hours into the trip and almost halfway. We just started, and thinking about the distance makes my butt ache. The N17 leads into the N5 intersecting with the 515, and baby we are there. I made note that the 515, albeit the long way back, is a good alternate route if needed.

About an hour into the trip, we hit our first stopping point. Two uniformed capital soldiers asked for our papers. They kept us waiting in the intense heat for almost twenty minutes before sending us merrily on our way. That seemed easy. Hours later, although it seemed like days, we made it to the N17, which indicated the three quarter mark. We were almost there. As luck would have it, the fun had just begun.

Do they celebrate the Fourth of July here? I have to tell you they skimp on quality, Grucci would be disappointed. Only one rocket, and not much in the way of a colorful show. From the direction it flew, it looked as if it was fired from less than 100 meters away. The good news is that they either missed on purpose, or they were blind. The bad news is they had rockets aimed at us. We stopped, and everyone remained in the Humvees. Our protection detail remained quiet as well; not much they could do in this situation. Any action would provoke another rocket launch; one that might not miss its target. Our drivers looked around, perhaps contemplating possible alternate routes of escape. I asked our driver, "What if we make a run over to the left? It looks like it will bring us back a few miles but we might be able to shake these sand rats." I realized he might have taken offense to my nick-naming our aggressors but if he did, he did not let on. "You want to die? They are not so smart, but also no so stupid. Those are not ant hills, they are land mines. All possible routes are controlled by hidden IED's that will blow us up. This is normal and expected traveling these parts. Do as they require and we will be fine." Sure, pay or die. I wondered what his cut was for this deal. Our guide probably notified his buddies. Later tonight, he will probably park this piece of shit in his garage and drive to dinner in his late model Land Rover.

We waited about five minutes before a band of five soldiers approached from the west, on foot, carrying large automatic weapons. We were ordered to exit our vehicles and stand on the driver's side, lined up. The soldiers in the two vehicles behind us did not comply, causing some yelling from our hosts. Abdul and Klaus conferred and Abdul spoke in the local language to the soldier who appeared to be the leader. I asked Klaus what was happening.

"Abdul is explaining that the protection detail will stand down but not exit their vehicles. He is explaining that they will act if any aggression toward us takes part." I asked, "What's to stop them from radioing their buddy to send a rocket our way?" "These guys are soldiers, they are shaking us down; that's all." "So much for the safe passage." Klaus shrugged his shoulders.

"Papers! Show papers!" Each of us pulled out our papers, they all had diplomatic status. Me, I was listed as a press agent. "Noo good!" Why me? Abdul spoke to him again. "We have to pay him 21490 Rial." I asked, "How can we afford this crap? Tell him no!" I yelled my answer and I am sure the soldier understood. He did not look happy. "Mr. Smith, it is only one hundred dollars US. We must pay him." "Oh, wait a minute, that's all I'm worth?"

The "toll" paid, we continued our journey with no further delays. We finally entered the N5 and almost immediately picked up an escort. This merry band of drug smugglers had bigger guns than the soldiers we encountered earlier. Abdul spoke with them confirming they were to escort us to our meeting.

Chapter 33 – All Roads Lead to Afghanistan

This guy, my contact, had the longest beard you ever saw. It was literally a bat's nest. I bet he had soldiers to carry it or had to load it in a wheelbarrow or something. We met in his office, which was the typical debacle of tents connected to each other. Abdul introduced each of us, since he had to be our translator. We all made the formal greetings, "As-salamu alaykum," "Salam." We all exchanged one form or another of the cordials and sat to smoke a peace pipe; *oops, wrong story, sorry*.

I am not sure what I should have expected, but our new friend wasn't very friendly and at one point I considered my escape plan. To my surprise, his English was perfect, his grammar better than mine. "Mr. Smith, welcome, I am sorry for the earlier deception but I needed to wait for my underlings to leave us. I spent nine years in the States on and off. Five contiguously while at Columbia. I met my wife there as well. We both are degreed in foreign policy. My masters is in business and finance." I couldn't resist. "Must be an asset in your current business operations." "Mr. Smith, we all have our reasons for what we do and how we do it. You yourself should understand that in your line of work. The end result of what we do is all that should matter." I had to agree with him, I smiled and nodded.

Our host sat and gestured with his hands, "Shall we begin?" My newest and most long distance CI (confidential informant) went on to explain their way of life and how they operate between the local governments, and the Al Qaeda presence. He made it clear we share a common enemy, without exactly saying it. I was getting antsy as time was running out for us to make our departure. The topic I was there for did not appear to be on the agenda. My stomach began to knot.

Servants entered the tent structure carrying trays of food and beverages. Our host stood without warning. "Please, everyone, enjoy." I gave the evil eye to Klaus who appeared to be as surprised as me.

"Mr. Smith, would you accompany me? There is something I would like to show you" *OK, here we go*. We walked out of one tent structure to another, and then another. If he left me there, I would be lost in this maze. "Smith is such a common alias, I am surprised you got this far using it with no questions. Not so original, if I might add." Everyone is a wise guy. "So; your wife is a lawyer?" "Actually a prosecutor, she puts the bad guys away in prison." He smiled, "I have done my homework on you; your family is to be respected. Your wife is lovely." Ok, I

162

figured we are breaking the ice here. "She is fantastic, but as you are aware, wives can be tough to deal with. You know what I mean?" I paused for a moment, then continued. "Of course you do, how many do you have?" "Three, three lovely wives. Trust me I do know what you mean. But then again, I also am afforded the luxury of being with one who is in a good mood when the others are not." Now I smiled and said, "Ever have a bad run with all three?" "Never, they are aware of the consequences. It would be OFF WITH THEIR HEADS!" We both laughed.

My new friend did not trust anyone else in the room, not even my people. The information he confided to me, would get him killed, and for a price many would betray him. His information hung Raul Espinosa out to dry as the main contact for the drugs. I had more of an interest in the money part of it. "My friend, the only money I can explain, is the money I am paid by him. It is for the drugs I broker, that are exported from Mexico, which in turn goes to him. A piece of that cash goes to paying taxes to our mutual adversary." I said, "But the drugs you supply turn out money he sends back to them to finance training camps and weapons purchases." "I am sure this is true, but I have no knowledge of how that works between those two parties. You will need to speak with Mr. Espinosa regarding that information. I am sure with what I just told you, he will work with you for a deal."

163

He handed me a small device the size of a smart phone. It was a USB "Passport" drive. The device was encrypted, so, without the proper code, it and the data it contained was not accessible. "With this your beautiful wife can, what is the expression? Hang him up to dry." "Ok, yes something like that." We could have had this conversation on the phone but that would not make sense. It never works out that easy.

I had what I needed and just wanted to get the hell out of dodge before the *sand storm* hit. "Excuse me, Jack." One of my CI's assistants knocked and entered our private meeting space. He took him aside and they got into some serious discussion they obviously did not want me to hear. I was so tired, I let my eyes close for a moment to de-stress. All I heard was whispering in the distance.

"Mr. Owens, no worries, we are alone now and completely safe. You can be Mr. Smith when we return to my other guests. Before that, I have something for you, a gift from me to you, to secure our new friendship." He walked over to a curtain I had not noticed earlier and pulled it open. "These are my two nieces from wife number two's brother. They are a gift to you. When you are satisfied I will retrieve you." Before I knew what was happening he was gone and I was naked on a black satin sheet covered round bed. The women were beautifully exotic and sultry. They worked me hard, each competed to satisfy my manly needs. Katie would understand; this was business. To refuse would be to insult my host and could get myself and my team killed. This was 'taking one for the team.' Besides what happens in the desert, stays in the desert. Right? No! That fantastic moment with those beautiful women was just my mind messing with me. I would never cheat on my wife; she, is my fantasy.

"My friend, Jack, we are friends now so may I call you Jack? We should get back to my other guests." His abruptness startled me out of my reverie. Damn, it was so real for a day-dream. As we walked back, we passed two women arranging flowers, unusual in the rural desert. They wore veils and head covering but I swear they were the two from my dream. It was so real I think a bit of guilt will haunt me.

After some small talk, we put down the peace pipe and made our way, our long way back to Aden. There, a plane waited to take us back to our Ethiopian base. Another transport was waiting there to take us the rest of the way home. Driving at night is dangerous, but so was sleeping under the roof of my new ally. I hoped our pilot in Aden was aware it would be very late when we arrived.

Chapter 34 - Back in the USA

The trip home was a non-event. We paid another toll somewhere around Dhamar. We did not haggle over the three hundred dollar equivalent requested. These guys smelled so badly, the camels held their heads up as high as possible to gain some fresh air. We just wanted to move on. The transport that had flown me to the land of paradise, had completed its delivery of donated goods and US government supplied food and medicines. They were kind enough to wait for us to return. Perhaps kindness had nothing to do with them waiting, and was more of an order from the top. When we arrived at 4AM and awakened them, their lack of smiles told a story we did not care to hear. An hour later we were "wheels up" and on our way home.

The airport clock indicated that it had been a long day, showing 7:15AM. My internal clock was messed up. We left at 5AM, which I think is like 9PM the day before in New York. The flight was like ten hours. I needed a week to sleep. Rather than going home to shower, I went straight to my office. There is a gym available to us in our building with facilities. I enjoyed a long hot shower and soap; something I was much in need of. Traveling abroad, soap seemed to be an unknown object of which no one cared about. *I cared*.

"Good morning, boss." Director Martin Shaw looked a lot better in his crisp suit than I did in my worn and creased sport jacket. I was clean, my clothes, not so much. "My God, Jack you look beat. How was it?" I sat slumped in the chair facing his desk as he sat himself down. "Covered a lot of terrain in a short amount of time for a little bit of information. I made a new friend over there, but as we both know, these friendships last until the next threat or payoff happens. We need to act quickly."

Martin conferenced in Kevin Sorenson and Senator White and I detailed my conversation with the tribal leader. We copied the data drive and sent the original down for analysis and further backups. All agreed to allow the Manhattan DA to use part of the information to bring down Raul Espinosa, as long as we get to interrogate him first.

We all agreed to meet tomorrow afternoon for another, more formal session. Included would be our teams, and the FBI along with the ATF. I asked for Marcia to be present as well. Arrangements were being made for Jane's peaceful extradition to the United States. Her debriefing would be done by a member of each team, recorded and observed by the others. An analysis of her information, as it is repeated, should help us to determine its validity. After all that has happened, this might prove to be the most prodigious break in the past five years, since the Yemen take-down.

Early afternoon approached quickly, and it felt like midnight for me. Exhausted and disheveled, I headed back to Long Island, grateful for the light traffic. The drive only took about an hour, which is fairly good time, even at eighty plus. I got home around 3PM to an empty house. Rosa must have picked up the boys at day care and taken them to the park since it was such a nice day out. Did I mention how great Rosa is? The boys love her and we trust her. It's about trust these days, especially in my line of work. I think Jane used the "Trust" line on me. Anyway, our nanny treats the boys as her own, and has developed a nice group of other nannies to mingle with. The kids have all become friends. Everybody is happy. Life is good.

I showered again, put on comfy sweats, and tucked myself into bed. Ten seconds later it was lights out. In my dreams, the plane rocked back and forth. I fought off air sickness. The image of the stone-faced copilot pointing to the trunk filled with crappy rations repeated itself over and over again inside my head. In my dream, I heard little voices yelling "Daddy! Daddy!" I sat up in bed, dizzy and with borderline nausea.

"Daddy! You're home!" In stereo, the best sound ever, now that it is reality. I hugged and kissed my boys and called down to Rosa. "Hi Rosa." "Hola, Mr. Jack, we had a nice day at the park. Do you need anything or can I go? I have a doctor appointment this afternoon." I thanked her and wished her a good afternoon. "Come here you guys, let's watch some *toons*." The boys and I snuggled in bed watching their favorite cartoon shows while waiting for Mommy to come home.

Katie and I call each other randomly during the working day, or night. We long ago agreed that both our demanding jobs made it difficult to operate our personal lives on any particular schedule. In my line of work, expectation of timely communication can lead to disappointments and concern. So no promises are made, we just call when we can, or want to. In other words, I had not called Katie today.

Katie's Prius pulled into the driveway; the headlights reflecting on the house gave her away. The boys had fallen asleep, each dominating a side of my chest. I carefully moved them onto our pillows and went down to greet my wife.

"Hi Honey." My arms up for the hug as she entered, her arms filled with packages and her attaché case. "Jack, thank god you are home." I took the packages from her, taking them into the kitchen and placing them on the counter. "Yum... something smells good." "Take out; I would have gotten for you too if I had any idea you were home." She seemed annoyed. Perhaps our communication agreement is one sided. I took her in my arms, noticing she had tears in her eyes. "I'm ok, this was not a dangerous trip." Katie is no fool, she was well aware of how dangerous traveling in those desolate areas could be. "I'm sorry, I should have called you." Katie smiled, "There's enough for us to share."

We ate, and drank half a bottle of delicious red wine. Katie moved the boys to their own room. God bless them, they can sleep through anything. I watched as she undressed and put on a robe. "I'm going into the shower; it's been a long day." Katie left me sitting on the bed as she disappeared into the bathroom. I sat there, contemplating if she might need some private time.

No words were spoken, none were needed. I stood behind my wife, holding her close, soap dripping everywhere. The room was steamy, the water soothingly hot. We made love, washed each other and spent more quality time in bed, speaking only singular words, making sweet sounds. We slept holding each other.

In the morning I was up first, lying in bed thinking about my day to come. The clock showed 5:30 AM. Katie's hand gently took hold of mine. "I know we agreed, but I worry about you every minute of every day when you are on assignment." Our hands still making contact, I took hers and kissed it, holding my lips to her delicate skin for a long moment. Even her hands, first thing in the morning, smelled so sweet. "I know, I love you and I am sorry that my job causes so much stress on this family." "It's ok, I knew what I was getting into from the beginning. You are my knight in shining armor. I will always worry." We had a half hour before our day had to get started. These moments are why our water bills are steep. "I need to shower, you stay right there; I'm locking the door." I laughed, "You are locking a door to keep a CIA spy from getting to you?" She gave me that look… "Ok, I have to get ready too. I have something to show you over coffee. Don't take too long."

"Oh my god, you are the man, how did you?" I showed the copied and edited data disk to Katie. I told her that with this, and my testimony, Raul Espinosa and his notorious east coast associates were hers for the taking. The data disk contained dates, names, bank accounts and other information tying him personally to the money exchange, into the billions of dollars. I actually would not have to testify due to my covert status; the judge would

171

be given confidential written testimony to corroborate the authenticity of the information.

"Good morning, Rosa. Today is going to be fantastic. See you tonight." Seeing Katie this excited made the risks I took so much more worth it. We kissed our boys and left together in separate cars. We both expected to have an interesting and exciting day.

Chapter 35 - Katie's Home Run

"Good Morning; Happy Monday." If Katie Claire Owens had any hesitation no one would notice. The information she obtained would rocket the case against Raul Espinosa right into Federal Court, and she would bring it to them. *Wait, imagine the stylus of a record player (remember, a big flat disc that spun around and the needle that pulled the sound off the vinyl tracks) slipping across the disc and the horrendous sound it would make.* What was she thinking? She is part of a team working for a local jurisdiction. Her boss, the Manhattan District Attorney, would bring this information to the proper authorities and they would hunt Espinosa down and bring him in for trial. But it would be Katie, or rather my information, that would unlock the case against him.

In an effort to mend fences with Michelle and prove she could be an equal member of the team, my sensible wife took a leap of faith. Katie knocked on Michelle's office door, "Good morning, can you spare a few minutes." Michelle looked up and actually smiled. At least she was trying. "Sure, what's up?" Katie sat herself down at the chair to the side of Michelle's desk and opened her brief. "I have some invaluable information that I thought you should see. Jason needs to see this, but

I wanted you to have a look at it first. We should bring it to him together." Her face questioning, I continued. "You know; you and me, as a team effort, might add some additional credibility to the information."

"This is unbelievable! Are you aware of what this means?" Excited, Katie burst out without thinking, "We have Espinosa's balls in our hands and we can squeeze them until he chokes." Michelle had the expression of shock, she looked frozen for that short moment and then; they both broke out hysterically laughing.

"Come on friend, we need to get this case moving along." Wow, she used the rare and unexpected *friend* word. Katie and Michelle headed straight for Jason's office.

The "Dynamic Duo" as Katie and Michelle jokingly called themselves, reviewed the information with Jason. He then called DA Johnson out of a meeting. They had evidence; names, dates, contacts in several states. The amount of information on the data disk would fill a room if it had been on paper. They had him on extortion, counterfeiting, drug trafficking and, worst of all, human trafficking. The mood in Katie's office that day went from busy and confused to excited and motivated. Calls were made, and federal warrants issued. My office, specifically my boss Martin Shaw, received the call first to verify that the encrypted data they could not see would be available for a federal judge to review. Martin referred them to me and I agreed based on several predetermined stipulations. I get first crack at Espinosa after he is arrested. The Manhattan DA gets the collar and their day in court, and then the Feds get to hang his ass. All departments agreed on sharing this takedown and working together in a joint effort.

Finding Raul Espinosa took all of six hours; five of them involving red tape. My data, courtesy of the Sheik, gave them the location of Espinosa's extravagant vacation home in the Colorado Mountains. The Feds and their private plane swooped in without notifying the local authorities, taking down his private empire in a flash. They took him to an undisclosed federal detention center here in New York, where I was very patiently waiting.

"Raul, my name is Jack Owens. I am here as an official agent of the United States government. You, my friend, are in some serious trouble." The slime-ball stared his dark eyes at me and belligerently informed me - "You have nothing." I stood up abruptly from my chair and banged my hands on the metal table. He jumped, almost breaking his wrists, which were chained to a hook on the top of the table just in front of him. I noticed some blood splatter from where the chains caught his skin. "We have everything! There is enough evidence for three jurisdictions of government to bring you to trial and convict you. That is, if you are lucky and don't find yourself in one of my prisons. You understand what happens in that scenario; you cease to exist and we use special techniques to get information from you." Raul didn't seem intimidated by my interrogation. "This is fucking America; I want my lawyer now!" I had to be more convincing.

The interrogation room had the conventional one-way mirror, but there were no cameras. Only my people had access to the viewing room. We had all day, but just today, to get what we needed. I opened my attaché case and pulled out a small case containing a syringe with a very large needle. "For all intents and purposes, this room we are in falls outside any American jurisdiction. This is Sodium Thiopental, commonly known as truth serum, an *almost* lethal dose. I apologize in advance, as this dosage will cause you extreme pain throughout your body. Something similar to hitting the ground after falling from a six story rooftop. It is not my intention to kill you; that would most certainly get me into serious trouble. There is limited time for me to get the information I need from you." Now Raul looked intimidated.

"Wait! What do you want from me?" I pushed a little serum out the needle tip for effect, and placed it on a hand towel on the table making sure it stayed in his line of vision. "Tell me the names and locations of your Al Qaeda contacts. I want to know how and when money is transferred, and how much. Provide me with the money trail all the way back to its origin." Thanks to my trip to Yemen, I already knew the origin to be Afghanistan.

"I want a deal; immunity. No jail time." I shook my head, picked up the syringe and motioned toward the mirrored window. There was a loud buzz and the door swung open. Martin Shaw entered, along with a huge military officer in fatigues. "This is my boss, and this young man is our enforcer. You are out of time, in a few moments you will answer my questions. You will not care about any deals. This medication *will* make you talk, and the pain will convince you to do it quickly." Martin nodded and the enforcer walked behind Raul, placing him in a choke hold. He completely immobilized Raul. I again pushed some serum out of the tip of the syringe. The odor of the chemical had a putrid alcohol smell that was sickening to us, but worked its magic as we hoped it would.

"Wait! OK, no death penalty; it has to be off the table from all jurisdictions. Federal prison, private cell and anonymity so I have a chance to survive." I looked at my boss; he nodded and motioned for his man to release Espinosa. I pushed a pen and pad over to him, checked his feet restraints and released his hands so he could write.

"I want everything, in detail, or no deal." I held up the syringe, "And no second chances."

Our little show worked, and we got what we needed. My job was just going to start now. Katie and her office, the feds, they had their man and he would see his day in court. The most notorious kingpin of drugs, and sex slavery is finally off the streets. I had enough information to follow the money trail to another Al Qaeda camp which was controlling cells here in America. Another milestone against the war on terrorism.

Chapter 36 - About Our Day

Friday night is pasta night at our house; my favorite food in the whole world. We both arrived home at the same time. Both bursting to tell the adventures of the day.

I asked, "Where are the boys?" "Rosa took them to see the new Disney movie with her niece and then out for burgers at Chuck E. Cheese. We have a good two hours." We looked at each other, no words were necessary, and headed up stairs leaving a trail of business accessories, shoes and various articles of clothing.

Katie went first, we never did this before. Mixing sex with business talk might add a new twist to our relationship. She said to me, "What a fantastic day. You are my hero. I am sure you are everyone's hero at the DA's office." I kissed her neck as she removed the last of her sexy undergarments. "Erik looks really good for a successful political run. Michelle, who knows? But, right now we are good." I worked my way down south. "Oh, that's good, really good." On my way up I replied, "Indeed, today was a win-win for everyone. Everyone except Espinosa and his motley crew." Katie asked, "Do you think it will make the papers?" "I doubt it; I hope not. Word will leak but the more official, the harder for us to round up the cells. I expect a federal gag order will be issued if it hasn't been already. We all should hear of it in the morning." Katie made her move on me finishing with a solid push onto the bed. She climbed aboard. "Oh Lord." My wife smiled down at me, "That's what they said at work." My hands grasped her firmly around the waist and held her steady. "I hope not in a similar setting." "Business and pleasure mix only with you, my love." "Damn straight." Enough talk, I took control as we changed positions. This woman is a sex goddess.

"Quick get dressed; Rosa just texted that they are on the way home. We have, like, ten minutes." I threw on sweats and retraced our messy trail down the stairs, picking up various items on the way. Katie took one of her famous three minute showers. Obviously, I did not join her.

We spent some time with our boys and, after tucking them in, settled down and ate our pasta. "So, now what?" Katie's tone changed and she was serious. Her face had worry on it. "Now, I use the information of a life-time to follow the money trail. I will be traveling next week. No set plans yet. We are meeting on Monday. The analysts are compiling all the information." "You are an analyst, Jack, not a field operative. What about us?" Katie keeps telling herself, and me, that *I am just an analyst*. "Things just evolved, you knew this from the beginning."

Katie pouted, she understood and just needed to vent. She is scared, sometimes I am too. "I will be going into Afghanistan for two, perhaps three days. Thanks to Raul's information we made a contact there who will talk for the right price. He is in a situation where phone calls and travel are always under suspicion. We need this to be a face to face meeting." "But." "Katie, I have to do this. Raul will make contact for us as prospective drug brokers with a huge market. I need to be sure myself that the location is the main source." Katie did a complete one-eighty, changing the subject. Our conversations never went this way. I'm sure she was too close to the whole thing. "The boys have soccer tomorrow." I smiled and took her hand, "Can't wait to see them tear up the field."

Saturday turned out to be warm, and the kids were having a great time. These are the years of innocence. The game is fun, win or lose. Soon that will change and it will be about the win. All this is preparation for the real world, the world adults live in. These tender years need to be treasured.

The parents each take turns bringing cookies and fruit for the kids to snack on during half time. The adults make small talk. We discuss sports, world news and our jobs. I suppose I am the only one who lies to everyone else about what my real job is. *"So, Jack, you're a business analyst? What kind of business?"* "Oh, spying, *assassination, protecting the world from evil."*

It rained all day Sunday. The family stayed home and spent quality time together. The boys and I built cool objects with their Legos. They became obsessed with these awesome building blocks after Katie and I took them to see the "Lego" movie. Those Lego people were scary. Right after the movie we had to find a Toys-R-Us store and buy the Basic Bricks Deluxe package. There were aisles upon aisles of really cool building sets; then I saw it. I wanted the Coruscant Police Gunship but Katie stopped me at the register. She told me, "We are not here for the big kids." Anyway, we played and Katie did a little work; then we all watched the Disney channel together.

Chapter 37 – Prep For Travel

We flew Jane into New York's Kennedy International Airport via a special military transport. Her accommodations were nicer than mine were last week. Fortunately, Tuesdays are quieter than Mondays, and traffic on the Belt Parkway turned out to be lighter than I expected. The government plane will be the same one to fly us into France, where we will catch a domestic flight to Kabul.

Jane exited the plane like a Hollywood celebrity. We had afforded her some credit for traveling expenses. Her hair was cut shorter than I have ever seen it; just above shoulder length. Jane looked sassy, actually professional. She was as beautiful as ever. The transport crew stopped dead in their tracks in admiration. The pencil dress she wore reminded me of the college years. Katie dressed like that. Back then, Jane molded herself after Katie in many good, and many evil ways. Apparently, she retained some of the good qualities.

"Hello, Jack, nice to see you in a calmer environment." She may be stunning to look at, but when you stare deep into her eyes you see the burning rage. She extended her hand, which considering the surrounding audience, I accepted. "Hello, Jane, I hope you had a decent trip so far." Oh-oh, here it comes; Jane leaned in and kissed my cheek. I refrained from pulling away, keeping it friendly for appearances. A military aide interrupted our loving reunion, "We have a car ready for you." Our flight scheduled for 7PM, we had time for a game plan session. We reserved a meeting room at a local airport hotel. Kevin Sorenson, Senator White, Martin Shaw and two CIA analysts from my department were there, waiting for us. Also, General Armstrong sat in, representing the eyes and ears of the President. I figured if a military strike like the one we initiated during the Yemen Camp situation was needed, he was the man to make it happen. The drive took five minutes. "You look good Jack. It feels weird being on the same side for a change. Maybe I will let you buy me that drink I so rudely denied you back at Emory." Trying to do the smart thing I ignored her. Jane always worked her prey before the kill. I hoped to survive this deadly trip. *Fear not the extremist hiding in the sand, but the fair maiden walking by thy side.* Ok, I made that up.

My CIA guys swept the room for bugs and other devices, declaring it secure. After the formalities, we got right down to business. I knew this was going to be difficult for John, seeing the bitch that destroyed his son's life, both his sons.

The senator, in turn with General Armstrong, discussed our travel plans, timing, risks and exit strategy should things go wrong. Oh, did I mention there was no exit strategy? Our success depended mainly on Jane's proven ability to con. If she decided to betray us or we were somehow exposed, a drone, some twenty thousand feet above us will nuke the compound and Katie will be spared a costly burial.

"Jane, you will need to allow us to implant a tracking chip in your back, where you cannot reach it. This is a condition of our deal." The senator seemed adamant. I had no idea that he would pull this on us. My guess is that he had gotten pressured from the powers above our pay grade. I might have been able to keep things in perspective for Jane, had I been given prior notice of this crazy stunt. Jane looked like a tigress backed into a corner. Her demeanor changed; she leaned back in her chair, eyes cold as ice. "Not going to happen, we have a deal and I need you as much as you need me. I have no reason to run." Jane had the look of death in her eyes and the beautiful Jane became the scary one. In my mind I heard, "*It's about trust, Jack.*" As much as I hate her, even though I could put a bullet in her head and have no regrets, I did trust her for this event. I needed her to keep me alive. "That's enough! Jane and I have an understanding, she will behave and live up to our agreement for both our survival. Besides, they will check for surveillance devices. It could get us killed." Jane looked at me, and for a moment I saw that *trust* in her eyes. The General, who was standing in the corner stepped forward and nodded to one of his security men who approached me, placing me in a half nelson. The senator began to object but was halted by the General. "This woman is a high level terrorist who may or may not be playing us. We are not going to take the chance that she will turn on you; or run." The other soldier held Jane's head, pulling it down into an almost obscene position. The General himself inserted the chip just left of center in her back. She did not even wince. After the antiseptic and bandage were in place they released both of us. "My apologies, Jack." The General stepped back to his corner.

Jane's anger seemed less than expected, a trait of deception I feared most about her. Our backpacks were taken to the plane ahead of time; Jane's probably having been rummaged through several times. We headed back to the airport, ready for another fun adventure in Sand Land.

Chapter 38 - Afghanistan

Our flight left on time, 7PM sharp. On board with us were two creepy goons. They were not in uniforms. I was pretty sure they were not spooks. My guess, plainclothes military or NCIS. The General sent them along as a protection detail to make sure we got close enough to our target destination. They will help defend against roadside attacks, but once we hit the *badlands,* we would be on our own.

So, I was back in Ethiopia for a refueling and a forty-five minute stretch of the legs. I should have stayed here from last week's trip, maybe save on some jet lag. Although, the food might have done a number on my stomach. Jane unbuckled her safety harness and said, "I am going to the ladies room. Erratic flying and peeing do not work well for me." I had to agree, especially on these smaller transport planes, not the smoothest flights. Those were the first words she had spoken to me since we left the states. Jane looked down; I could tell she was in pain from the chip they inserted in her back. That thing just might get us killed. I had to wonder if the military guys cared more about getting Jane back than preserving my life. *Damn them.*

"Wait, I'll go with you. I need some steady ground myself." "Don't worry Jack I won't disappear on you yet." I didn't like the "yet" part and neither did our two bodyguards. I waved them off, "I got it guys." On the way to exiting the plane, I grabbed a small pouch from the galley containing first aid supplies. The bathrooms in the airbase terminal fortunately were for individual use. As Jane entered the one with a stick figure and skirt picture, I pushed in behind her. "Wow, Jack, out of country and you change your stripes. This is going to be an interesting trip." I didn't smile, "Hold that fantasy for when you are alone, this is business, lean against the wall." I positioned her face forward in front of me. "This is going to hurt." Oh, the fantasies if one was listening on the other side of the door. No further explanation or instructions were needed, Jane cooperated. I removed the chip and placed a tight bandage with antiseptic over the wound. Jane proceeded to fix her top while I turned away. "Now you're shy? Thank you, Jack." "I did it to save us both from getting killed. Keep it in your pocket until after our chaperones are gone. Then don't forget to lose it."

Jane opened the bathroom door, "Coast clear." Of course, as I followed her out, a young female private turned the corner catching us, and flashing a smile. Great, she had a story to tell her lunch buddies. Who am I to set her straight and ruin her fantasy? I guess she kept what she thought she saw until we were out of there and in the air, lest I might have found myself in a cell next to Jane.

We boarded the cozy transport and took off to our next and final destination for today, Kandahar International Airport. The flight took another six hours, and with the time difference of three and a half hours, the jet lag had us exhausted and wired at the same time. I managed to get a little rest though, dozing on and off again. At one point I dreamt that I was walking in the desert and ran into a talking camel. He said to me, "What the hell are you doing back in *Asscrackistan*!" Then he walked off. I abruptly awoke, thinking to myself how politically wrong that was. Dreams can be so bizarre. I think it was between noon and 1PM local time and almost a day later when we finally arrived.

Adding one more to our team, "J" met us at the terminal. He would be our driver, and translator if needed. I did ask his full name, and after his response which would take up three pages on my pad, "J" worked for me. I asked my ambiguous counterparts from some branch of our government security forces, "Can we trust this guy whose name we can't spell or pronounce?" They assured me he was one of us. He and Jane made some small talk, which made me nervous. Apparently her English is better than her native Arabic language. I thought the Afghans spoke Dari or some other dialect.

"Jane, speak English only." She smiled politely which in her language is "F-Off."

We took thirty minutes to take care of personal needs, reconvening at the customs exit. Arrangements were made with the "Islamic Republic of Afghanistan" government to get us through as diplomats, even though none of us actually had that status. We were on a fact finding mission for one of the big oil companies. What a story.

The driver insisted on getting paid in advance. This way after he drives us into an ambush, claiming engine trouble, he can escape. He had a Durango SUV capable of transporting seven passengers. A decent vehicle, although I doubt it ever saw a car wash. I said to Jane, "Good job with the camouflage, the sand covering will blend in with the surroundings." Jane ignored me. Seems she and Katie have some things in common.

Budgets as they are, our time allotted for this mission had limits, and our chaperones had strict instructions to extract us when the clock stuck twelve. I suppose one minute later, adjunct CIA spy Jane becomes terrorist Jane again, and all bets are off. This is crazy and I had to wonder what the hell I was doing.

We left the airport with our less than presentable driver and proceeded to head into the deep caverns of hell. I wondered how Jane really felt about this. This could have gone one of two ways, actually three, but I discarded the death part. Jane will realize her homesickness and turn on me. After all, there was no tracking device and no threat to her any longer. Or, she will realize how much better off things could be for her back in the States and help complete this fact finding mission. Then there were her estranged kids making the latter scenario more likely.

Chapter 39 - Playing in the Sand

We drove several hours south on A1, heading toward for our destination, the Sangin District in the notorious Helmand Province. This region is one of the most dangerous areas our forces have had to deal with. Officials of one government faction or another stopped our vehicle twice for "tolls," but other than a few payoffs, we were OK; so far. The driver estimated a four hour drive time, plus stops; so we planned on six hours. I might be paranoid, but I am sure "J" knew the toll collectors. They looked alike, perhaps his cousin or brother-in-law. He, for sure, took us on some out of the way detours so they could stop us without any legitimate government forces intervening. It's all part of the game, and we had to play along.

As early evening approached, we reached our first planned stopping point. The time had come for Jane and me to part ways from the others. They would turn back and camp in a safer area, close to allied forces. For them, it meant the bad people would stay clear. For us, we headed into even more dangerous territory, and had to take the risk for appearances. Our cover had to be believable. The agreed upon story went as such... Jane recruited me for smuggling drugs and she would use her share for funding local cells which she legitimately had contact with. Her story had better be believable; our very lives depended on it. We had hired protection, our driver and guards. They were not part of our plan, so we had to make an excuse to leave them and travel on our own. The story sounded so crazy that I didn't believe it myself. We figured that was why they would believe us. I would seem pretty stupid to them and had to ignore my pride for the good of my country.

Our trek mapped out about five miles to our rendezvous point. The arranged time for 7AM local time seemed like a good idea during the planning phase of this operation; now 7PM would have been a better choice. Unfortunately we did not have a tent or much of anything to keep us warm. "Maybe we should head back to our team for tonight, we will freeze to death out here." Jane didn't look at me as she said, "It's too late and they might be observing us. Rousing suspicion is not a wise choice. We are fortunate that we made it this far without blowing our cover. We avoided reprisals from other entities out here as well." "So you propose sleeping under the stars – we are not Eskimos, even they have igloos." Jane started digging through her back pack. "We have no other choice, so *man up* tough guy." She pulled out matches and held them up. "How about some firewood? That alcove back there looks like a good place to settle in for the night. It will block the wind and cover our backs. We can take turns keeping lookout." I sighed, "Great!" and went on my way to find fuel for our fire. I too, can speak without looking back, "Aren't you afraid the fire will draw attention?" I sensed Jane's smile, "The bad guys are all at home or in their caves snug as a bug and warm." "Not all the bad guys."

We each had a blanket and a heated vest. These military grade undercoats worked fairly well, and the batteries lasted five to six hours. We would need to wait as late as possible before activating them. I built a blazing fire, which in hindsight might have drawn more attention than we wanted. We ate soup and some Mountain House meals out of a pouch. I checked my watch which displayed 2200 hours. "Ten o'clock, lights out for one of us. I can take the first watch." Jane said she wanted the first one, and I was tired, so there was no disagreement. "Wake me in two." I doubted I would sleep. Not that I didn't trust her; I didn't. In fact I feared her in so many ways. About an hour later, I was out, exhaustion winning over fear.

I'm not sure what woke me; possibly the cold as I was shivering. I sat up to find Jane still awake and alert. She looked so innocent, her face glowing in the light of the fire. "Hey your turn, get some rest." "You have another thirty minutes, you will need them. I will wake you." I figured I could take a few more to get psyched for my turn at watch. It must have been ten minutes or so when I was awakened again. This time I was not shivering. Jane had lay down next to me, her warm body pressed close into mine. I started to get up but her hand which was around my waist took a firm hold on me. "It's about trust, Jack. We are OK and both need the rest. Our bodies and the vests will keep us warm, the batteries will last longer." I'm not sure what details I will divulge to my wife about this mission, but this part will be stricken from the record. Innocent as the situation may have been, some things are best left unsaid.

It's amazing how forty-five degrees of night air can feel like ten below freezing, and then by 5AM it's already a warming sixty. The sun radiated off the sand and stone surrounding us. I sat up realizing Jane was not next to me, nor anywhere in sight. I had to fight off panic from ensuing. This god-forsaken place we had gotten drawn to, has a reputation as one of the most violent and dangerous areas in all of Afghanistan. The Taliban presence is strong here, with many individual factions running amok. The police and government officials are corrupt. There are many reports of young children being abducted, armed, and forced to participate in militant actions. Reports of sexual abuse and torture throughout the region are constantly being reported. U.S. and allied forces have had a difficult time securing this area. I think we have had more casualties here than in any other region in the Middle-East. Now I sat here alone, and possibly lost without Jane.

I started rummaging through our bags for the GPS equipment, relieved to find it in its protective case. "Hey, you're up. I did a quick surveillance of our surroundings. There is a waterhole not far from here. It has fresh water we can use for drinking and washing. Then we can be on our way." Jack tried to hide his moment of hysteria. "You know, that was stupid going off on your own?" "Easy, Jack, you're not my baby sitter." She grabbed her stuff and started walking westward. "Are you coming? It's on the way. We have enough time for a quick clean up. We may not have another chance before getting back to safety." We hiked about ten minutes. The terrain was getting rough as we climbed. The altitude of this area, just over twenty-nine hundred feet, made hiking a bit difficult. The terrain changed as we travelled, getting a bit greener, hence the waterhole and probably other sources of water. It was a beautiful site, an oasis in the middle of rocks and sand. I found a smooth area and put my things down. Jane was already undressing. "I'll go first, you stand watch, and be ready. This is the opium capital of the region. The Taliban is the least of our worries out here." I held my .40 caliber handgun firmly, in a ready-to-fire position. Jane had undressed completely and headed into the waterhole. She was a dangerous distraction. A secret weapon of the most dangerous kind. I was not attracted to her, not in the way most men were. I knew her too well to find any sexual lure. Yet, there was no denying her profound beauty. I carefully observed her while not forgetting my responsibility as lookout. "Jack, we are probably OK if you want to join me." She was a tease, and enjoyed taunting me. I didn't respond and turned away as she walked out of the water, dripping wet and glistening in the rising sun. "You have to go in, it is so refreshing. It might save you from heat stroke. It will be brutally hot in an hour or so." I handed her my firearm and walked over to the water, pulling off my clothes quickly, with my back to her. I trusted she would respect my privacy and not pull a Jane move on me. Perhaps my mind lost control and allowed a little fantasy to cloud my sensibility. The cold water brought me back to earth. The night air put one hell of a chill into this water. It did feel good.

We started what I hoped would be the last hour of our journey, which would put us at the meeting location right on time, 7AM. As we made our way to our destination, the foliage became thicker. Jane grabbed my shoulder signaling her concern for intruders. I listened carefully and heard the sounds of feet crunching gravel. We hid behind some large rocks, peering over them to see some heavily armed men lead a group of young women and children down the path. I noticed that each female had one leg tied to another, children too. They were slave labor, I assume, for working the opium fields. Human trafficking of another kind. These guys are known to work them until they died from malnutrition, heat exhaustion or beatings and sexual abuse. I wanted to open fire on the bastards. Jane sensed my frustration and held my shoulder applying pressure as a reminder to stay silent. She whispered, "Any noise, especially gunfire, will bring the entire band of thugs down on us. They never take prisoners." We waited until they were far down the road and made sure there was no other group behind them before we continued on our journey.

As we turned past a large cluster of mountains, actually large boulders, we entered a clearing and a small hostel of tents and other makeshift structures. Jane pulled out the GPS. "This is it, we are here." As she said this in a whisper to me we heard the click of automatic weapons. There were at least a dozen armed men aiming at us. We raised our hands. Jane greeted them in their language and mentioned our contact's name. I only knew him as Hakim.

Chapter 40 – Not My Fault

They led us to a small tent that stood alone, away from the other parts of the makeshift compound. As we entered, I looked over my shoulder to see women and children, apparently part of the operation, silently keeping themselves busy. Evidently, the band we encountered earlier must belong to this motley crew. It made me sick, the thought of paying money to these culprits. Possibly, it was the water.

"You two are very brave to have made this trip, and fortunate to have survived. I was concerned for you." I had to say it. "Were you concerned so much that your band of slave drivers would have cut us down if they discovered us?" "Ah, Jack Owens, I have heard much about you. Please give me some credit. My people were aware of your impending visit. They had instructions to offer you water if needed, and direct you to my camp. This is our territory and no one enters or leaves without my permission; no one." "Then why all this covert stuff and why couldn't we drive here?" He did not smile, "I trust no one and our deal was for no surveillance." With that, two men entered the tent. "Please remove all your clothing so we can put the *trust* issue behind us." We did as requested, all modesty aside. As I expected, they scanned and probed every part of our bodies. The guy who checked me must have been a dentist, he knew how to probe with dental tools. I have to say he was gentler than my hygienist. "What is this?" they found Jane's incision. I figured the truth would be best. "My people tried placing a tracker in her, I pulled it out. We are on the level, and a deal is a deal." We got dressed and started our discussions. We got names, and places, and a full detail of the operation in Mexico where Al Qaeda cells worked the drug and money exchanges. We also got the connections in California and New York.

Hakim handed me a satellite phone, "Please acknowledge my cooperation, so I may get paid as agreed." Our deal was arranged with a Sheik, who would transfer funds from a Turkish bank on my approval. "As soon as my bank calls with the transfer information being cleared, you will be free to leave. My men will drive you back to a mile before your origin point." I had to ask another question. "How do you know our origin point?" Hakim, if that was his real name said, "We have been watching you since you left the airport. This is my territory, no one and nothing moves without my knowledge and approval." No shit.

We were driven to the start of our hiking position and sent on our way. That was easy. So far things worked as I had hoped. Jane behaved and we were heading home with enough information to raid the cells and end the threat of terror. At least for now.

We started our short hike down the mountain to the road, were we would rendezvous with our team. Jane spoke first. "I held up my end of the deal, I hope you will too." "I will make sure you are taken care of and your kids are safe, we already took care of part of the threat to them. You know they are better off if you stay away. You will always put them at risk." "That is not true, Jack; that is why I did all this, to make it safe for them and for me to be near them. It's not my fault I am like this." She went on for the duration of our walk telling me bone-chilling events of her childhood; about the torment and abuse, physically and sexually. She told me about Michael, her one true moment of intimacy. I found myself almost pitying her, but then shut it down; she tried killing me and Katie. She took part in the murder of my best friend. She may be trying to repent or be bullshitting, it really didn't matter. "Katie, as it turns out was the only other person who actually tried helping me as a friend. I do regret my betrayal to her. I was jealous of her and William, I wanted what she had. I wanted to understand, and to be able to love someone. I could not even comprehend what it meant, let alone feel it." I wanted her to stop talking. I felt like she was conning me again. "I will make amends through my children."

The extraction point looked clear. We waited until the set rendezvous time of 10AM. Our transportation arrived on schedule and we were off to the airbase and then home. Not a minute too soon.

At the airport, we thanked our driver for his help, and for not blowing our cover and getting us killed. My CIA team member also reminded him that payments would be made to him in three installments over a three month time period. We did this to make sure he did not betray us after we left and to help him hide the money. The team also had surveillance on him and his family. Our lack of trust in him ensured the integrity of our arrangement, and at the same time would keep his family safe from any unexpected retaliation.

The air transport was waiting for us, and took off almost immediately after we arrived. I slept solidly for most of the trip to Turkey, where we refueled and picked up two Washington guys in need of a ride home.

I dreamed of Katie holding me in bed. Her warm body next to mine. She made me feel secure. Then my dream got a little intense, Jane was next to me in the desert. I felt guilty. Maybe my dream meant something. Maybe I had to come clean to Katie. The old Jane would make a point of telling her, and twisting the truth to make it look bad. No, Jane is different now. I do not trust her but, I am sure she will not interfere with me anymore. I think we are past that. If Katie asks, I will not lie. Otherwise, why make her feel jealous or raise concerns? What happens on a mission stays with the mission. I woke as the plane's wheels hit the runway. We were home, *sweet home*.

As we exited the marine air terminal, two heavily armed soldiers approached us. "Jane Austin, you are under arrest for crimes against the United States." I protested, and had the riot act read to me. The shorter of the two giants quietly confided to me, "You really pissed off the General. Something about a tracking device and not taking any chances of losing her." Jane looked at me, her eyes on fire. "Remember your promise, Jack. Remember your promise." The fire in her eyes died down, she looked sad and vulnerable. "Listen, she is a valuable asset, do not let anything happen to her. Can I have a moment?" They stepped about three feet away, both holding their firearms at the ready. I took Jane's hand in mine and whispered in her ear. "I will work this out, you need to fully cooperate and do not give them any reason to hurt you. It will be a few days. After we take care of the cells, I will come for you. We need their guard to be down." I could tell from the look in her eyes that she believed her fate had already been determined by the American leaders. She was sure they never planned on letting her go after the mission was completed. She tried to say, *"Tell my children that I do love them"* but no words came out of her mouth. She looked lost and broken. Jane placed her hand over mine which was still holding her other one. "Good bye, Jack."

Chapter 41 – Alex

He thought to himself, "She is beautiful." Alex liked her and fantasized what it would be like to make love to her. Perhaps this would happen right before he would cut her throat. She wanted to be friends. His job was to gain her trust and get information. If things went wrong and a hostage was needed, or an assassination, his real training would finally be put to good use. Allah is waiting for him in paradise. First he had work to do. His part in the jihad to complete.

"Good morning; I have donuts." Katie brought in donuts for the office, two dozen Krispy Krème in assorted flavors. In a good mood, Katie remained hopeful her husband would be home today as promised. She placed the boxes in the kitchen next to the coffee maker and headed to her cubicle. Alex stood in the hall holding his cup of coffee, reading a brief. He watched as Katie waved to him and disappeared into her private space.

"So; is it ok if I touch these walls, or are they moving you to the corner office?" Katie wasn't sure if Alex was being smug or just messing with her as a *friend*. "I doubt any office at all, and you can touch whatever you want," she paused and smiled, "Except me." Alex laughed, "Wouldn't want that husband of yours to be jealous and come shoot me. Just kidding. Are you free for lunch?" Katie did not like any jokes about Jack. No one knew what he did for a living except for her team working this case. Even joking, it seemed inappropriate. Yet, she was trying to gain a comfort level at the office. "Who is going?" "You, and me, and whoever else wants to; I will ask Michelle." Katie accepted and excused herself to do some work, laying the hint for Alex to take a hike, in a nice way.

Alex Ritter, born to a Croatian father and American mother in Brooklyn NY, went through an identity crisis while in college. Conflicts in Bosnia and other local areas near the region brought out American hostilities over the oppression and horrific atrocities occurring over there. His father, a non-practicing Muslim, took the opposing side to America. Eventually, political adversity in the home caused his parents to divorce. His father returned to Croatia. He was away at school during most of the family crisis. His father's subtle political views embedded in his subconscious made him curious. He joined the Young Croatian's club, where he started a new form of education, or re-education.

Al Qaeda recruited Alex early on into one of their cells. He found a connection and something to believe in. In his mind, his father would be proud of him. His induction started as a slow process. Alex finished school and got his law degree. His Imam encouraged him to embed himself somewhere in government where he could serve a positive purpose. He would soon be called to serve Allah. A few weeks earlier, that call had come. His jihad handed to him. Katie would be his target. They wanted Alex to get close to her. They knew about the infidel, Jack, and his earlier involvement in Yemen and now through Alex, they knew about Jack's attempt to foil their source of income.

In need of a cover. Alex made a successful play for Robin. He figured it would be easy. Besides, she was cute and expendable. He needed a character witness to throw off any suspicion of wrongdoing. If he moved too quickly, and raised suspicion of his interests in Katie, Robin would serve as an alibi. The timing worked out well. Robin broke up with her loser boyfriend a few months earlier and they were already very friendly in the office. Alex invited her out for drinks one night and then dinner the following weekend. Robin expressed her surprise that they had many similar interests. Alex did his homework and fabricated what he needed to spark the relationship. They dated casually, taking it slow. Robin liked him. Besides, what could be better than a perfect gentleman with a promising career? Wisely, he asked her to keep their relationship a secret to reduce office politics from interfering.

Dating Robin made Alex feel as if he was cheating on Katie. He thought he might be losing it; Katie could never be his. She is a target for his jihad, that's all. Still, he found it difficult not to think about her in a sexual way. Robin initiated the closer intimacy that he seemed slow to introduce into their relationship. He realized she needed more than he was willing to give. He only needed a week or two more. He had to endure and submit to her desires, to keep his cover. If Robin got too pushy, he would have to make her go away. This thought turned him on.

On the night before Alex would make his move on Katie, he had dinner with Robin. They were at her apartment. "I made lasagna and Caesar salad. Would you please pour us some red wine?" They ate and made small talk about the office. Alex tried pushing Robin for information. As usual, Katie's name came up. "You know Alex, I love Katie. She is great and I know you guys are friends, but it seems weird that you bring her up so often when we are together." Alex told her she had to stop being paranoid and jealous. "I do not like jealous woman and you have no need to be so. You are a beautiful and sexy young lady, and so smart. I am a lucky man to be with you." He could tell she was annoyed. This was their first real argument. After they finished dinner and the bottle of wine, Robin took Alex's hand and kissed it. "I'm sorry

Alex, I can be so silly sometimes." "Come here," Alex commanded her. She obeyed, seemingly turned on by his assertiveness. They passionately made out. As Alex kissed her mouth and neck, he found himself thinking of Katie again. He pushed her against the wall, hard. Her head hit the wall and sounded like a crack of thunder. She was stunned. Alex ripped open her blouse and performed his assault on her using his tongue. Her head hurt but her senses were more concerned with what was going on lower down on her body. As he worked his way up, he forcibly turned her around pushing her face firmly against the wall that she just hit her head on. He entered her from behind. At first she was shocked. Robin never had rough sex before. She was frightened. The man behind her is a stranger. In some odd way, this turned her on. They climaxed together, and Alex immediately pulled out and stepped away. She was confused by his actions. She had no clue he fantasized that it was Katie he had just been with.

Alex assembled his clothing, and once dressed, walked over to Robin, who just sat on the couch looking frightened and sad. "I'm sorry Robin, are you ok? I don't know what got into me. I just wanted you that way. I was so turned on." "You frightened me, Alex. It's as if you were someone else." Alex gently took her hand in his, "For that moment, perhaps I played someone else. We were two other people for each other. It certainly seemed to turn you on. Didn't you like it?" Robin, perceptive and smart caught his remark. Maybe *he* wanted to fantasize about someone else but she didn't. Married couples, together for thirty years maybe, but a new relationship. He should be thinking only of her.

"Sweetie, I'm tired. The wine and your amorous assault has worn me out. Do you mind if we call it a night?" Alex was relieved, "I thought we would snuggle, but I understand. On the weekend, we can hang at my place, and I will light a fire. We can relax, and I will make love to you ten times, any way you want, and anywhere you say." Robin smiled; "You better bring the blue pills buddy, I have expectations." Alex fixed his reckless actions from earlier that evening. Robin had no idea what Alex could be capable of. For tonight, she remained oblivious - and alive.

Chapter 42 – Keeping It Social

Plans had to be made quickly. Too many loose ends were hanging over us to wait any longer. We had to take down the cells now. At least the ones here in the US that were responsible for the horrific acts of violence against humanity, for the sake of funding terrorist factions.

Following the same successful game plan, the senator offered his home in North Carolina as a secure place to convene for our meetings. The meeting was set for Monday. Rebecca White planned a nice lunch for the mid-day break, and of course, plenty of goodies for the morning session. Lots of coffee was consumed. Some of us could have used something stronger to spice things up.

Katie and I took the boys and flew up early on Saturday to spend the weekend. John and Rebecca are longtime friends. Their deceased son William and I grew up together as best friends and college roommates. Back then, my wife and William were dating. Unfortunate circumstances related to the Yemen Camp *take-down,* also lead to his demise. Through some magical connection, and despite all the bad, those tragic times brought Katie and me together. As for the Whites, we are friends, but more so, we are family.

"Oh my goodness, look at your two beautiful boys. They've grown so much." Rebecca hugged Katie and then me before taking the boys' hands and leading them off to spoil them. John had not come down yet, so the two of us stood there like second fiddles. I said, "Ok, so we know who rates first nowadays." Katie kissed my cheek, "You're jealous, grow up." We let ourselves out to the back porch. "This is my favorite part of their house. These gardens are so gorgeous. Mine don't even come close." Katie always loved it out here. When she was pregnant with our boys, she would spend weekends here with Rebecca. We lived closer and I traveled a lot. Having our boys' God Parents close was a blessing. I told Katie, "Your gardens are beautiful too. We have a great home." The fact is, this felt like home to us more than our own home. Perhaps someday, as the boys grow older, our new home will hold a more important place in our hearts.

"Hey kids, you both look fantastic; I guess New York agrees with you. You too, Jack." I knew he was referring to Katie. We exchanged hugs and kisses, well, just hugs for me. "Jack, you have a nice tan. The desert treated you well, I'm glad to see." "I lost five pounds hiking during the last trip; and aged ten years from the last two trips to the Sand Lands." He smiled and reached for the cooler; "Beer?" I took a cold one. "Katie, how about you?" My wife, the little angel, graciously accepted the Senator's famous lemon raspberry iced tea.

John and I schmoozed over this and that, avoiding any real shop talk for now. Katie told her story of success taking down Raul Espinosa. "I have to thank my macho husband for his fantastic *intel*. Oops, now I sound like you guys." *I blushed*. "It would be great if everyone could know how the information was obtained. I don't like taking so much credit for your hard and dangerous work." She looked at me, her face expressing modesty. "I love you honey; thank you."

"Vroom, vroom." The twins each ran past us with toy airplanes in their hands. I immediately thought they flew better than some of the transport pilots I had flown with recently. Rebecca was right behind them, pleading for them to slow down. I assume for their safety, as well as her own. She looked beat up. "Boys, slow down!" Katie hardly ever yells, at least not at the boys. She was concerned for Rebecca.

As always, the weekend planned for us was sensational. John and Rebecca are wonderful hosts. The Carolina spring weather had been perfect. New York still has that leftover winter chill, but the air there was warm and inviting. The flowers were already in bloom. John and I managed to steal some quiet time here and there, away from our families, for business talk; a sort of jump start on Monday's meeting.

We found ourselves in John's office, which is off the great room that overlooks the patio and pool area. "How about a snifter of cognac and a Cuban?" I asked, "Aren't they illegal?" "Of course not, my boy. Found them right on the shelf in my favorite liquor store." He smiled; I got the joke. We smoked a delicious Montecristo and sipped the cognac. "These are rare moments," I said. John agreed. "Peace and tranquility is what I wanted for you before the storm hits." I didn't want to ruin the moment, but had to ask, "Have you made any contact with Carlton?" John looked sad. Carlton is the senator's first born of his twins, by one minute. He had been declared stillborn, and taken from his family. He, in fact, was a healthy baby who was kidnapped by Al Qaeda operatives as part of a devious plan to overtake the United States government. The surviving twin, William, grew up alone as an only child. I met William here in the Carolina's when we were both small children, and we became fast friends. Like brothers, we were inseparable. Then Carlton, who was raised Muslim, in Yemen of all places, came back to the US to replace William and seek his life in politics. The plan was for him to infiltrate our government at the highest levels. Anyway, there is a lot to that story and the past is the past. Except, that Carlton, who impersonated

William for some time, caused a lot of pain for his family; as well as Katie and me.

"I get reports weekly. They have not broken him yet. You would think after years of interrogation he would give up and talk to us. I suppose I should try again." My heart breaks every time we have this conversation. William and I were like brothers. I have no connection with Carlton, known as T2. "Should I go and see him? Perhaps some talk about William's and my experience as brothers might strike a nerve and make him have some feeling of kinship." John shrugged his shoulders, giving no indication of his opinion about my idea. I followed with, "I don't want to make things uncomfortable; we can talk more about this at another time. Maybe after we finish with this mission." "You're a good guy, Jack. You know how much Rebecca and I love you and Katie and the boys. You do whatever you think makes sense. Besides, he was moved to an undisclosed location; undisclosed, even to me." We left it at that.

The rest of the weekend was very enjoyable. Rebecca played grandma to our boys. They adored her. They also saw more of the Whites than their own grandparents. My dad passed two years ago unexpectedly. I take comfort knowing he got to spend time with his grandchildren, and his passing was painless. My mom is in an assisted living community and doing well. In her later years she chose not to travel. We try to visit as often as possible. Fortunately, Katie's folks, now living in Arizona, visit once or twice a year and we try to get there once a year as well. They are gadget people and have a new iPad. They "Face Time" video chat often with Katie and the boys.

Chapter 43 – Marcia

Marcia Gainsworth, workaholic, spent her Saturday in the office. She had a ton of paperwork to catch up on and a federal trial to prepare for. Amy Saunders will have had her day in court, and then off to the catacombs of hell. As one of the most highly regarded agents at Homeland Security, Marcia moved up the ranks quickly. She started out at Langley, where she first met me during boot camp. Marcia remembered me as a feisty recruit fresh out of college. She told me that I carried on as if I were still in high school. "You had the looks and charisma that attracted women." During the surveillance and attempted take-down of Jane a few years back, she was brought in to work with me for the undercover operation. I didn't remember Marcia from the CIA training, but she immediately recognized me. Marcia told me she recalled my "subtle and smooth moves amongst the other female trainees." When she brought up Langley to me, I was a little embarrassed and concerned that we may have had an intimate relationship. She told me that those could not be regarded as relationships. Her reply said it all; "Oh, my God, no!" Her cold remark embarrassed me. I was hurt by her apparently revolting thoughts; that we were together at some point, back then. At the time, she did not tell me that I should not take it personally; that she was not interested in any man.

Later on, Marcia fessed up. In some odd way, she was, and still is, attracted to me. She told me she "Loves me like a brother." I knew my friend kept a watchful eye on me, like a sister should. This was not the case earlier on, when after a few weeks at Langley, she was offered a transfer to HLS. She saw the opportunity to break away from the pompous CIA recruits, and took it with no regrets. Now she gets to work in both worlds. She loves her job, and the variety of unique associates she is exposed to.

Marcia grew up in Auburndale, Florida and went to the University at Gainesville. As a student of political science with a second major in criminal law, she had a full schedule. Besides taking sixteen plus credits each semester, she belonged to two study groups.

During her second semester at Gainesville, Marcia met her first love. Anne Marie shared two classes with Marcia and at Marcia's suggestion, joined one of the study groups. One night while cramming for a test, the girls fell asleep in Anne's dorm room. In the morning, they awoke body to body as if subconsciously, they both recognized the attraction. Anne made the first move with a smile and a gentle kiss. This was Marcia's first same-sex encounter, although she had known since junior high school of her attraction to her own gender. "What are you doing?" Marcia asked softly, but did not move away. Their legs entangled with their faces just inches apart. "I, I thought it felt right, I." Marcia returned her kiss, not letting Anne finish her sentence. Their relationship lasted through the first semester of their junior year. One day, Anne abruptly told Marcia that she had met someone else. She had met a senior who had already gotten accepted into medical school. "He is handsome, smart, and really gets me." Marcia was in shock; there were no warning signs. "What do you mean, *he* really gets you? Does he know about you; about us?" Anne, in tears, apologized and pleaded with Marcia to keep their relationship just between them. "People are not stupid. We were intimate around campus; you have to tell him." The two woman never spoke again and avoided each other as best as they could.

Marcia had a few relationships over the years but never found "the one." Her job made it difficult to have any type of long term relationship; and, her situation left her with fewer opportunities. Female agents had to work harder and act tougher, so her strong personality and tough attitude raised no questions. That is the way she preferred it. She felt that if her co-workers knew of her sexual preferences, it might compromise her ability to succeed in the field and advance in the agency.

Stress was building. All agents were required to see company therapists, and she was sure hers knew the secrets causing that stress. However, they never spoke of it. Something else added to her anxiety. Her concerns for me and my new alliance with our nemesis, Jane. Almost every night, dreams came to her. *Marcia would be walking down a dark street, rain poured down on her. Two people just inside an alley are passionately making out, undisturbed by the wet weather. As she walks past them, she sees the flowing reddish blond hair partially covered by a floppy rain hat. The woman is rising up and down as she and the man, whose face is now partially revealed and looks like me, make love.* Marcia is jealous; how could this be? *As the woman seems to climax with the man, in sync, she moans loudly. But then, something is not right; she sees fear in his eyes.* At that point, each time, Marcia wakes up. She is wet from her own orgasm. After getting up and going to the bathroom, she has no trouble immediately falling back to sleep. The whole process is partially a sleep walk. The dream always continues. *Marcia is in her building now, following the two lovers as they enter an apartment, perhaps hers. Next, she is watching them make love in her bed. This time she does not see the woman's face, only her gorgeous hair flowing down her perfect naked body. The woman is on top, and the man who she uneasily admits is me, has his eyes closed as they go at it. All of a sudden, there is a high pitched screech. It sounded like something like out of a Hitchcock thriller. The man's eyes instantly open wide; the woman is gone, but her laughter is echoing in the background. I am lying there covered in blood, my throat sliced open.* Marcia does not wake up, but that is the last thing from her dream that she remembers when awakened by the morning sun.

The therapist told Marcia that she needed to open up, and disclose the contents of her dreams. Until she did so, the nightmares leading to her stress could not be resolved. Marcia could not, would not, talk about her dreams. She would never be allowed to work an assignment with me again. Certainly not one involving Jane. She will need to work this out on her own. She needed to see Jane dead. Then perhaps the nightmares would end.

I know all this because she confided in me one night, over the phone, while discussing a case. She told me that I was the only person, the only man, she could trust. I was the only person she could openly talk to about her personal situation.

Chapter 44 – Carlton

His head pounded. They never stopped asking questions. "What is your name?" "William!" "No! Your name is Carlton. You are a US citizen turned traitor and terrorist by enemies of the United States and the free world. What is your name?" "William! I do not know who this Carlton is." In truth, this T2 operative did know that he was not really William. In fairness, not that he deserved it, he only found out the real story shortly before they sent him here. "They" would be the Al Qaeda leaders who ran the desert mockup of a real US city, and raised him as a liar and a terrorist. It wasn't fair what they were doing to him; imprisoning him like a wild animal. They all lied to him. His whole life, he thought he was someone else. None of his friends were even real.

"Why don't you leave me alone?" It's not my fault." Carlton, the real William's identical twin brother, sat in his six by ten cell. He saw daylight for one hour each day and was allowed light exercise during his free time. Prisoners in the concrete camp never socialized. If Carlton had the chance, he would kill them all. Reality being what it is, that is never going to happen. He could not even kill himself. Nothing was left to chance by his captors.

Starvation; he tried but they force fed him until he gave up his protest.

"What is the mission, what is your jihad?" "To become politically involved. To gain knowledge of your government operations. To influence political outcome." "Who else beside the girl called Jane and the one called Sarah did you work with?" "No one else. There is no one else."

Carlton known as William's T2 went through the same questioning almost every day for the past 4 years. His answers are always the same.

Senator White stopped visiting Carlton, exhausted and stressed with anxiety over the whole ordeal that lead to his other son's death. Rebecca could never bring herself to visit her first born.

"Bring me Jane. I want to see Jane. Is she alive? Does she know I am here?" Carlton did not know where "here" was nor did anyone else. Not even the Senator at this point, knew his estranged son's location. "Call my dad; I will talk to him. I can help you with information. Call my dad."

His chants fell on deaf ears. It had been too long. Any information he might provide, even if true, would be useless at this point in time. His psych evaluations indicated that he was beginning to break. His mind, while intelligent, had no real social interaction for most of his life. Now, after four years of solitary, he was a completely lost soul. He sat on his bed, head in hands, then he laid down flat on his back. His eyes closed tight, he allowed himself to daydream of the days back in Yemen.

"Hi, William, can I walk to class with you?" Sarah was his best friend. She looked out for him, and always reminded him to be careful not to anger the leaders. He trusted her. Jane, on the other hand, was different. Colder, and all business-like. She did have an awesome smile. She was beautiful, a different kind of beautiful than Sarah. He thought he loved Jane. Jane was supposed to love him back. They, the actors, always said it to each other in the movies. It seemed to make them smile when one told the other, "*I love you.*" To Carlton it was only words. He never understood what love really meant. It was an emotion he never experienced growing up. Now that he is remembering, she never actually said it to him. Then there was his wife. The arranged marriage back in Yemen. Maybe that was all a lie as well. No one will miss him. "Allah, I do not know why you have allowed me to endure so much torment, and for so long. I have done everything true to the jihad; True to you. I am ready. Please, I beg you to take me to Paradise." He said this quietly, as he lay still on his steel framed bed.

224

His last thoughts were of him and Sarah walking to class on that last sunny day. Carlton drew his last breath deep and exhaled slowly and completely. He felt calm and peaceful for the first time in years. Darkness fell upon him; he stopped breathing. Only his soul knows where it ended up after leaving this world.

Carlton was found lying on his back. His eyes wide open, and face expressionless. The guard who found him, remarked, "I looked into his open eyes, they were cold and soulless." The coroner determined the cause of death to be a heart attack.

Chapter 45 – Consortium

The peaceful weekend ended all too quickly for them. The dream-like environment evaporated too soon. The blue-water pool, newly blooming flowers, quiet conversation and beverages of comfort left the Owens family and their hosts feeling cheated by the dawning of Monday morning.

My old boss and current mission teammate, Kevin Sorenson, was the first to arrive. The doorbell rang at 8AM sharp. We were in the kitchen enjoying fresh brewed coffee and croissants baked by the renowned Rebecca White. "Good morning everyone! Am I the first to arrive?" We all exchanged the usual informal greetings and added another setting to the table.

Katie finished her coffee and came over to me with a big mushy hug. "Rebecca is driving us to the airport and Rosa will pick me and the boys up. I already called work to let them know I will be in after lunch." She kissed me and smiled, that smile that needed no words. "You boys play nice and keep the world safe." Katie hugged John liked she would never let go, and saved another for Kevin. "Take care of my man."

A few minutes later, the General arrived with a team of techies. "Good morning. My guys are setting up signal jammers to ensure no one is using a boom mic or any other surveillance equipment. That looks really good. May I?" The General referenced the coffee which Rebecca promptly and graciously poured for him. I couldn't resist, "So, are you military or CIA? Because, I think you are showing signs of paranoia, which we have the dibs on." The General did not laugh, and dryly said, "Never can be too careful."

I watched as our wives left, smiles quickly became expressions of seriousness. John spoke first. "Gentlemen, let's get things rolling here." By now the rest of the teams had arrived. I think there were six military and four CIA analysts. The Vice President sent the Chief Of Staff to be his eyes and ears. The data I had brought back from Afghanistan gave strategic locations of cells controlling the flow of money out of the country, as well as to funding of homeland terrorism. One cell is located right here in nearby Connecticut, the other operated in Nogales Mexico. The latter being the main hub for drugs and human trafficking, bringing in millions of dollars each year. Connecticut is the corporate office of the operation, handling transport matters and bookkeeping per se.

"Jack, why don't you fill us in on the locations and your take on the situation." The senator motioned for me to take the floor as he stepped back a little. "Good morning, everyone. As you all know, my team and I traveled into Al Qaeda territory in the Sangin District last week. We recovered the data you now have in your possession. With this data, we have successfully cut off a major drug, sex slavery and money laundering operation. The Raul Espinosa cartel has been shut down and their kingpin is in custody." Everyone in the room remained quiet. "The Manhattan DA has a rock solid case to hold Espinosa and various members of his gang for trial. Espinosa will then be hauled off to federal court where we hope he's issued a death sentence for crimes against humanity, treason and terrorism. It was through his interrogation we gained information from the Afghanistan informant." The Chief of Staff motioned to speak. "Go ahead sir, we are keeping this informal so please..." The presidential representative did not stand, he just sat up straighter. "Mr. Owens, it is our understanding you cut a deal with Espinosa allowing him to avoid the risk of a death sentence. I also have information that you made other deals with the known terrorist and confirmed murderer, Jane Austin something or other." I love how professional and informed this guy was. No wonder he is in the top spot in the White House staff. "Sir, you sound like a reporter. We did what was necessary for the greater good. The deal we cut with Espinosa will not change his convictions, just his sentencing. Each of these villains will get their due, in good time." The General chimed in, "The military agreed with this plan. Without these two resources we would not be meeting here today. Jane is another issue that Mr. Owens and I need to have a conversation about. It seems her tracking device has malfunctioned. However, she is currently in *protective* custody."

I asked, "May I continue?" I didn't think there would be any objections. "So, if you look at the notes, we plan to hit both locations at the same time. These locations are electronically connected by sophisticated satellite systems. Any occurrence in one will immediately alert the other. We need to be cautious, as the Mexico location has many innocent people who could end up as collateral damage. Many of these are woman and children. I will let General Armstrong lay out the tactical plan."

"Thank you, Agent Owens." The General spent the better part of two hours going over all the strategic plans for the ground assault in both locations. Each take-down will combine CIA and Military forces. An unusual combination. I bet the FBI feels really left out. My team would join up with a black ops team in Mexico. Our approach will be from the east. The compound had heavily guarded access points with mountains to the north. My job was to use the names I acquired during my visit to Afghanistan to gain access to the compound. My new friend from the desert will need to make an introductory call via satellite phone to clear me as a safe business associate. Convincing him to do this took some effort as he had concerns of retaliation. I reassured him there would be no one left to retaliate against him. I also had to promise more money to compensate for future revenue losses. Once inside the compound I had to place a small device anywhere that it would not be detected. This device sends a signal to a satellite that directs the drone we plan to fly overhead at twenty thousand feet. The drone finds the signal, what we call the hot spot, and fires directly at it. The rest of the teams had to get as many innocents out before the place is leveled. We had all the *intel* we needed and so the "take no prisoners" plan was in effect. We had a mere six minutes to find and evacuate all innocents. If we remained anywhere within the compound after six minutes and one second, dust we would become.

Connecticut was a whole different game. The cell's operation was located in an industrial park with many legitimate businesses and thousands of people. The FBI and ATF would be called in to handle this. I heard talk of NCIS as well. A second meeting tomorrow is planned for that venture. They had no problem going in undercover, as delivery men, and taking the operation down. Unlike

Mexico, quiet and peaceful as possible. Prisoners welcome.

The rest of the meeting moved on to discuss protocol, risk management, budget and all the basic stuff we go over before each operation. I found it difficult to concentrate. I kept thinking about my promise to Jane and how I would hold to it. The powers to be above me most definitely plan to renege on her deal. I shouldn't care, she might not deserve her freedom but a deal is a deal. As she reminded me more than once, *"It's about trust, Jack."*

Chapter 46 – General Harold Armstrong

Talk amongst the troops remained the same month after month, "Why are we here? This is not our war." With morale on the decline, there was talk of desertion. As one of the youngest officers deployed overseas, the General, back then Colonel Armstrong, knew that gaining the respect of his men would be challenging. He also knew, that as a Colonel, his responsibility was to ensure the plan of action for the troops under his supervision were carried out. His Brigadier General furnished a list of priorities and districts of importance that needed to be secured. Also provided, was a manual on keeping morale up, even if the truth and cause of actions had to be embellished for the soldiers' own good.

His men traversed jungles with no paths, and maps provided limited information as to where hot-spots and targets existed. Every step forward could be their last. He had seen men blown up by hidden booby traps. Bodies ripped apart by shrapnel. Young men, boys of barely 18 years old, torn apart. Every so often, reports by President Johnson, information that the troops would be going home, would be exchanged by his men, rumors heard from other troops' blather. But when asked, he would simply reply, "One can only hope. There are no confirmed reports that I am aware of. We will have to wait and see what happens." What he really wanted to say is, "*If there was any truth to these rumors, don't you think as a Colonel I would be informed of this firsthand? Don't you think I would be the one to tell my boys they are going home?*"

The air was oppressive, the humidity unbearable as they moved through the dense brush of the triple canopy jungle. The area they just left had been cleared and announced to be safe passage. What they did not know was that a lethal chemical called "*Agent Orange*" had been used. Years later, thousands would suffer horrible aftereffects and many would ultimately die from its poisonous components. The General often wondered if he would fall to that fate as well.

They saw the battle of Khe Sanh in 1968. It brought them through some of the most beautiful parts of Vietnam. Unfortunately, war turns everything ugly. We lost a lot of brave men there. Trenches served as burial pits as mortars and bombs rained down on our troops. General William Westmorland ordered aggressive bombing. At times we suffered air strikes from our own planes. "Friendly Fire," as it was called, was the ultimate oxymoron. As the North Vietnamese troops advanced, panic ensued in Saigon. A mass exodus occurred by the local inhabitants, fearing execution by the aggressors. It was a total boondoggle.

That war produced a psychological phenomenon never seen before. Pegged as a war the United States had no place in, draft dodgers made their way up north to Canada. Men faked being gay, sought out medical treatment for illnesses that did not exist and outright refused to report when their draft number was called. In fact, many protestors publically burned their draft cards. Their mentality was, "Jail over war."

His troops consisted of a mix of dedicated men and "conscientious objectors" fighting a battle they did not believe in. As his troops marched into Saigon carrying heavy rucksacks and munitions on their backs, he saw despair even among the loyalist of his men. He called his loyalist captains and other cadre into an emergency meeting. A strategy for boosting morale was created. Colonel Armstrong went to each and every camp to speak with all his men. He made them aware of their duty to their country and the importance of solidarity and allegiance. They had a job to do, and no matter what, they had to do it well and with honor. He also told each and every young man that his door was open to them, anytime.

These young men who were removed from the comforts of their homes, towns, and families needed a father figure. A tough but a compassionate one. The effect was immediately recognized and word spread of his ability to rally and motivate his troops. Other leaders of all ranks started to work more closely with their men in an effort to emulate Colonel Armstrong.

As President Nixon started to actually bring our men home, Colonel Armstrong stayed until the last of his men had been brought back to the States. He received many honors and advanced in rank as he served in two more wars.

I heard the Generals story over dinner one evening with John; Senator White. Although I have no great love for the General, he deserved my respect. The actions against Jane made no sense, and then they did. No one had the intimate history that I had with her. General Armstrong's paranoia was reasonable. I needed to be accepting of the cautious nature of my peers.

Then again, I had to do what was needed to be done in my quest to *save the world* from the evils of terrorism.

Chapter 47 – Enslavement

Anita lay quietly on her side. Her body pressing into another's backside. Thirty woman and children packed like sardines in a foil can with a motor and wheels. They were dirty and hungry.

Three days ago she left school as soon as the final period bell rang. Earlier, her eleventh grade teacher told her she made the Honor Roll. Anita could not wait to get home to tell her parents. A car stopped and asked her for directions to the nearest gas station. The young couple looked innocent enough. She had heard of kidnappings becoming more prevalent the past few months. Anita grew up safe and innocent. She trusted people.

Before she knew what happened, she was subdued under the influence of chloroform. She awoke in a dark cell on a dirty bed. Her hands and feet tied to the bed posts. They raped her several times over two days and made threats of death to her and her family. By the second day she had become numb to everything. She was broken. "You belong to us. You are nothing but a mule and a whore. We know about little Juanita and Gomez. He is what, three now? Do what is asked of you and no harm will come to your family. Disobey, and one member will be tortured and killed for each time you do so." That night she was allowed to bathe and eat a small bowl of rice and chicken. Soon after she finished her meal, a guard came to her cell; she was sure he had been one of her attackers. He tossed a dress on the bed. "Put that on and be ready, you are going out." She did as told. The guard drove south to a place in a very bad part of town. "Go in there and do as you are told. I will wait here for you." Anita got out of the car and entered the building. It smelled bad, like death. She could hear yelling, screaming and crying. She began to panic. A woman greeted her and told her to stay calm, "Everything will be OK. My, you are pretty." The woman handed Anita a glass of water and a pill. "Take this; it will ease your nerves." Ten minutes later, the room began to spin; she had lost all sense of reality. People, men came and went. She remembered only tiny bits of what happened while in the house of horrors. When Anita came out of her stupor, she was naked and bloody. She cried, then went numb again.

Back in her cell, she understood the reality of the situation. She would never see her family again. These animals have stripped her not only of her clothes but of her dignity and soul. They succeeded in reducing her to nothing.

Chapter 48 – Spying on Katie

"Has anyone seen ADA Owens?" Various people in the office shook their heads or said "No." Some mumbled with jealous undertones, something like, *"She is special; maybe she took a special day off."* Alex told them not to be rude. "She is special, and a fantastic asset to the DA's office." He held his anger at the remarks that followed, he sensed they were now directed at him. Robin, who had just returned from an early lunch with her brother, caught the end of the riff going on. "What's up Alex?" "Nothing, Robin. I'm just looking for Katie." Robin put her jacket on the back of her office chair. Her office being a very nice concierge desk with lots of fancy phone equipment. "Katie called in late this morning. I expect her in the office about two thirty." Alex must have seemed confused to Robin as he did not have to ask… "She spent the weekend in North Carolina. She took an early flight this morning. By the way, Alex, how was your weekend?" Alex thought, *just fucking great!* "It was good, quiet; the way I like it." What he really wanted to say is thanks for the information. Katie and North Carolina means Jack and Senator White talking business. He wondered if Katie knew any of the agenda. His information on the Owens family indicated an intimate marriage consisting of more than sex. He was assured husband and wife shared sensitive information that could be valuable to the jihad.

Alex had a sick kind of fascination with Katie Claire Owens. On one hand, he was tasked with spying on her to learn everything about her and her family. Soon he would be asked to interrogate her. His other side wanted to do bad things to her. Sex was part of it, but he wanted something more. He wanted to torture her. Something about her made him have these urges. Feelings he never had for anyone else. Dr. Freud might suggest that the subject's underlying aggression resulted from desires he could never fulfill. Alex laughed to himself realizing there was nothing subconscious about his desires for all the things he had planned for Katie.

As Alex cleared his mind to focus on his job, the ADA job, Katie walked in. She always smiled; that alone pissed him off. It was becoming harder each day for him to play act as her co-worker and more so as an ally in the office. Katie waved hello to Alex as she made her way to her cubicle. He had to get the ball rolling, so he followed her to her private office space. "Hey Katie, did you want to go over those briefs now that the other case has calmed down; perhaps over lunch?" Katie frowned, "Calmed down is not a reality, just in a short hiatus until we get a trial date." "You have a point, but at least the paperwork and evidence is all set and the hard part is done." Katie lightened the frown, "That is true, I suppose. About a lunch meeting; my afternoons are crazy the next week or so." Alex gestured with his hands in disappointment, "Maybe a drink after work? We could wind down and take care of business at the same time." The frown of further disappointment returned, "I'm sorry Alex; my boys, my husband's availability is not dependable. His work has too many last minute late nights. I'll see if I can clear some time toward the end of the week if that is ok." Alex pointed at Katie, "You got it girl." She knew he was disappointed. She felt guilty and called out to him; "Wait a minute, what about tomorrow night? Jack is working from home, and if not, I can ask the boys' nanny to stay a little later. We can grab a quick drink and go over the briefs then. There are two outstanding cases that are going cold, right?" Alex confirmed and said he would bring any files needed. They agreed to meet at McCabe's, four blocks down on 3rd.

That night Alex planned his rendezvous with the target, Katie Claire Owens. He would start the evening casual. He would watch for her to leave the building, hopefully by herself. As soon as she cleared the line of sight for anyone near the office, he would run up and join her. They would start toward the pub but he would remember he left his wallet at home which is on the way. Alex used another Jihadist to pay cash for a small flat two blocks from the office for this part of his plan. Once he had Katie in the apartment, he would secure her and then make his way quickly to the pub to establish his alibi. Earlier that week he scoped out the routes from the office to the apartment and then to the pub and back. As per his earlier Google search of national databases, there were no surveillance cameras for the first part. As for his alibi, he would take the longer way home so he could be sure the cameras caught him heading away from where Katie would be found.

Chapter 49 – Intelligence

The RQ-180 Drone flew the open skies at twenty-three thousand feet in stealth mode. A similar remote controlled bird brought down the Yemen camp a few years ago. It had been used in several strategic and covert air strikes in the Middle-East with great success. Today, its target for surveillance was over Mexico, the borders along southern California and Arizona.

The eyes in the sky flew its figure eight patterns taking video and photographs of terrain, free standing structures and roads. The flight crew, sitting steady on the ground in a secret underground facility in Laredo, Texas, zoomed the eight hundred thousand dollar camera on every nook and cranny. They kept this going around the clock for three straight days. Two identical drones alternated every two hours. At the end of this project, as they called it, the drones will be brought down for maintenance and then loaded hot; ready for the next part of the operation.

The amount of data that can be scanned and matched today is incredible. A set of profiles are loaded into the computer, and the drone's surveillance equipment can scan items as detailed and small as a license plate on a car. Our programming for this operation included white vans, military vehicles, cars off to the side of the road and a thousand other criteria. All so that a machine can do the work of hundreds of military intelligence officers.

Tonight the drone automatically changed it course per its automated programming. The bird now followed the 14 into the 10 northbound. The team kept their eyes locked on the monitors as a caravan of soft covered trucks made their way toward what they assumed would be Nogales.

Tonight's operator, or remote pilot, kept careful watch over the radius of surveillance. The drone is programmed to abort and return to the command center if it reaches a pre-set maximum distance. The Global Positioning System or GPS sends an alert in case the drone needs manual guidance.

"This is Romeo-Mike-924-Alpha-Whiskey to Tucson command center." "This is Tucson, go ahead." Command of the drone changed over to the north post in Tucson. They were closer to the current location of the drone and better prepared should a search and recovery be needed. Both teams observed what followed.

A call woke Senator White. He looked at the clock on his nightstand as he answered. The display read 2:03 AM.

"Senator White, apologies for the early wake-up call. I thought you might want to see the images the drones sent back to us of a suspicious caravan heading northwest towards Nogales." The senator sat up, still in bed. Rebecca touched his arm as she often did when she sensed his stress level rising. "Give me a moment to transfer to a secure line and bring up my monitor. I will need the VPN link code for your station." John got out of bed and leaned over, kissing his wife on her cheek. "Might be awhile. Go back to sleep."

The road was bumpy and they bounced hard with every rock or pothole the vehicle hit. Their bodies were pressed against each other so tightly they could hardly breathe. The young girl tossed in the van two days ago and just a few hours after Karen was taken, cried. Karen whispered, "We are going to be OK. We are going to get out of this. I promise." The girl just stared at Karen. The other hostages made no attempt to communicate. They were broken, probably beyond repair. Karen got over her withdrawal. Her body still ached, but her head was clear. She would do whatever it took to survive.

"OK, Tucson Command, I will take that link code now." John brought up his secure VPN link to the command center's terminals and joined them, observing the images sent from the drone. The senator was sure his military counterparts were notified as well. Three soft covered trucks were stopped along an off-road path. One truck had the rear cover pulled open. About thirty woman and young children, mostly female were lined up. At first it looked like a relief stop, but they all stood still like statues. It appeared that large crates had been pulled off one truck and moved to another. The night picture was grainy but clear enough to get the gist of what was going on. John heard the team leaders in Tucson request a zoom and pan. The crates definitely held explosives and the women and children were there to cover it up in case of a stop and search. John again heard the command center chatter, "They are looking at us as if they know we are up there." On the monitor, the presumed leader of the convoy looked up at the sky as if to say *"Screw you, so what if you see us. What will you do?"* John thought to himself, *"We will do something. We will free those poor souls and take you down. Your day of reckoning is long overdue."*

Chapter 50 – Freeing Jane

Marcia went to talk to Amy at the Federal court house where she had been held since her arrest. The trial date approaching quickly, she was amazed the court appointed lawyers allowed her to see their client.

"Wow, you must have some connections if they let you come see me. Aren't you a material witness or something?" Marcia sat on the one chair allowed in the ten by twelve cell. Amy had been labeled as one of the highest profile terrorists currently in captivity. Marcia realized that was bull. The American public does not have a clue about the others. Her tiny cell is one of the few set apart from the rest of the small group of inmates awaiting trial. She had three strikes against her. She was a traitor to her country, sort of, since her true citizenship was still an item up for review. She also was a terrorist and at the same time, a law enforcement officer. This opened her up to the diversified group of inmates held here. There also are concerns of her own people taking her out to silence her. Marcia asked, "So, are they treating you ok?" Amy looked away, "Don't sugarcoat it; we were never *friends*. What do you want?" Marcia expected this type of response. "You were brought up in a false environment by extremists who stole you from your family here and abused you. They used you for their crazy, cruel and warped view on righteousness. All in the name of Allah." Amy looked away again, "You don't know anything about how I grew up. Those people were the only family I had. Call it what you like, but this is my life." "But Amy, you lived and worked side by side with me and others. We hung out socially. We became your new family. You fought against the very things you say were your life. People change. You apparently changed." Amy had her head in her hands, Marcia though perhaps she started to cry but Amy hid it well. "Talk to me; give me something. There is a lot going down soon and you could help make it happen with less casualties on both sides. You may truly have different beliefs than me, than your *friends* here. That is ok, but we are your friends. Help us. I promise, I will speak for you if you help me now. You haven't done anything that we are aware of aside from conspiracy." *Obviously they had no knowledge of her involvement with Ken or his disappearance.* "Things can go a lot easier for you, maybe less prison time. A chance to get out and live a better life. A free life." Amy turned her head wiping tears. She looked confused. "I don't know anything about any operations, never did. I received instructions to keep an eye on Jane and to report information on what was happening at our offices. Then Jane had me do this crazy thing that got me caught. She is the traitor." Marcia stood, "If you think of anything." She called to the guard to let her out. As the guard was about to hit the button to release the locks on Amy's polycarbonate infused glass enclosed box, Amy jumped up and grabbed Marcia's arm. "Wait!" Marcia jumped and the guard drew is weapon. "There is something." Marcia waved off the guard who looked like he pooped his pants. "There is one person who is a threat to the operation that I am aware of. Until all this happened he was infused into your society such as I was." Marcia sat back down. "His American alias is Alex Ritter. He works for the Manhattan DA's office. After Jack Owens' trip to Yemen, Alex had instructions to keep close tabs on Katie Owens, who works with him. It might be too late, but at this point my people are desperate to get information that will help ward off any invasion by your government. I am sure he plans to interrogate her." Marcia felt her body going numb. "Are you saying he has plans to torture her for information?" "It is probably going down already. You need to be careful, we all have instructions to take down captives before any infiltration can happen." Marcia stood and called again for the guard to quickly let her out. She told him, "Keep an eye on her, no visitors; no phone calls until I return!" She turned one last time and gave a slight nod to Amy and left.

Her first call was to me but I was not available; still in meetings for the big take-down. Next Marcia called the Manhattan DA's office, realizing as the answering service picked up, that they were all gone for the evening. Katie's phone rang four times and then went to voice mail. She had to think quickly. Jane could approach Alex. If Amy told the truth then Jane did not know about Alex. Jane could be an asset. Alex surely knew about Jane. To him she would be an ally. The government had Jane in lockup. Fortunately, she had also been taken to this federal court house. Her detainment here only temporary until they had a chance to move her to some secure place. A place where no one would be able to find her. Perhaps, back with her T2, William.

Marcia found her way to the operations area for the prison part of the courthouse. She held up her credentials, "Hi, I need access to the prisoner Jane Austin." The guard in charge looked in the computer and responded, "No such person, sorry." "Listen, this is a matter of national security, I need access to her now!" The guard ignored her. Marcia realized she was about to give up everything to save Katie. There was no time to make calls and go through the proper channels. She had eight years to full pension.

The guard never saw it coming, he hit the floor hard. Marcia took his firearm and after a few seconds found Jane's location. It was dinner time and there were few people around making it easier to navigate the corridors without drawing too much attention. Using the guard's ID card, she swiped her way through the small maze of corridors until she found her person of interest. Marcia flashed her ID to the officer guarding the only prisoner, Jane. He too never saw what hit him. The code to open the impenetrable cell a mystery, or not. The fool had it written on a pad next to his computer keyboard. "Holy crap!" She punched in the code and the cell door unlocked. "Quick, take his clothes, they will be baggy but less conspicuous than this orange thing. Jane quickly did as told, asking no questions. "Here, take my jacket." They exited the prison area and holding her ID, Marcia prayed that exiting the building would be as easy.

Marcia's car was right in front of the courthouse in the small parking area reserved for court officials and police. "Get in and I'll explain." Jane finally spoke, "Wow girl, you are awesome, and in some big trouble. I didn't know you cared so much for me. Was it our time together up north?" Marcia ignored her. "Did Jack send you?" Marcia replied, "Jack has no idea what is going down. He is not reachable at the moment. Katie is in danger. One of your operatives has her hostage and means to torture and kill her for information that you and Jack discovered." Jane just looked at her, still with a confused face. "You better drive, girl, before the troops swarm down on us." Marcia drove out of the parking area and straight to the airport. "By the way, I have no operatives, none in years.

What is going on?" Marcia explained the situation in as much detail as possible. "When we are done and Katie is safe, I will find you a place to hide until Jack can get you out of the country." "My deal was to be pardoned for past crimes. I am not going to look over my shoulder anymore." Marcia promised to do whatever could be done, but right now there was no time to discuss that.

They pulled in to the private airfield area of the Washington Heliport. The ATF has several reserved birds for emergency missions. She held her credentials again and grabbed Jane's arm, pulling her along. "Derek, thank god you are here. I need the biggest of favors, no questions asked. I need you to fly us to NY, Manhattan, right now." Derek looked surprised, "Marcia, you know I can't just grab a bird and take off. I need authorization, flight plan; all the proper protocol stuff. No way that I am getting into that kind of trouble, even for you." "It is a matter of national security!" "I can't." Marcia saw the look in Jane's eyes. Before Jane did something stupid Marcia drew her .45 caliber firearm, "Consider yourself commandeered; now you are off the hook. Let's get flying." They headed out onto the tarmac toward a small helicopter. "No, that one!" Marcia pointed to a military jet copter. "I remember you told me you certified on that one earlier this year. Show me how fast you can get us to New York City."

Derek fired up the rotors and we lifted off. This machine made so much noise we could not speak without wearing headsets. "Tower, this is Alpha One Zulu Two Seven Niner, requesting priority clearance for unscheduled emergency test flight." "Alpha One Zulu Two Seven Niner is cleared for a northbound departure. Climb and maintain at or below One Five Thousand Feet." "Roger, DC Tower." He looked at Marcia who took the seat next to him with Jane behind them. You better hope NY lets us land. We are all going to be arrested."

Jane did not get much rest during her brick and mortar confinement. She needed a power nap. A method of rejuvenation she learned while at Emory. In those days she had to balance her evil plans with late night college antics, studying and drinking. Power naps kept her going. The hum and sway of the helicopter made her drowsy. She closed her eyes for a few moments.

The water had a chill that made her bones ache. The darkness that usually kept her safe, now made her insecure. She could taste the water, it was sour and oily. She felt a bump against her back and as she turned, Sarah's body lay there bobbing up and down. She felt sad for her campmate. "Why did you do it?" She turned to her left, the splashing water made her vision blurry, but she recognized the voice before seeing the face. "I had to; for the Jihad." "No! There was no Jihad, only a plan to kill me,

252

and Katie." Jacks face faded into the dark. Jane called out, "Wait!" Her feet could no longer find the bottom silt to rest on and she tasted the water again. She deserved to drown, to die alone in the dark cold water. A hand grabbed her wrist, his face, Pete's face glimmered for a split second. "Are you OK, Jane?" First she heard the radio calls and the pilot speaking the unfamiliar language pilots and tower controllers spoke. The chatter so irritated Jane that she held her ears before opening her eyes. She sat up quickly and tried to smile. Marcia was looking over her shoulder with a concerned look. "Jeez, Marcia, just a power nap and a dream." Jane had ten minutes to herself and she was now ready for action. Whatever the message her mind was trying to convey, it would have to wait.

Chapter 51 – Perilous Friendships

Surprisingly, they had no problems entering the congested NY airspace, and made it there in under an hour. Marcia removed her headset and climbed off the chopper. "Tell them I forced you at gunpoint, I'm already in deep shit." Jane loosely tied his hands to the seat. "Please, give us two hours, sit here, then you can call it in." Derek nodded, indicating his agreement with Marcia's request. Amy had given Marcia the address of the apartment Alex used as a safe house. They headed directly there, paying the cab driver to move through traffic like he was a police authority. Jane was sure he enjoyed this drive all too much.

Alex checked his watch, very little time had elapsed between Katie being seen leaving the office building alone, and his arrival at the local pub. His alibi should be strong. The bartender asked if his wanted another beer. "No thank you, love, two did me just fine." Alex frequented the establishment enough for the staff to recognize him by face. The bartender tonight, fortunately knew his name as well. He left a nice tip for her. She would be sure to remember his time at the bar. "Seven forty-five, bed time for me. Have a good night." Alex waved to the owner standing by the kitchen entrance, apparently flirting with one of the waitresses.

Heading back to his captive at the apartment meant walking north up Third Avenue. He decided to head south, further downtown, for two blocks. Alex circled back on Second Street to avoid cameras picking up his direction. The detour took him twenty minutes of brisk walking. Slightly out of breath he entered the old brownstone building and made his way up to the second floor apartment.

Katie remained right where he left her, tied and gagged on a chair he bolted to the beautiful wood floor. He figured the landlord would be pissed. "Sorry, love, had to divert traffic. By the way, you looked great on the beach. Let me tell you some of the thoughts I had while watching you." He stopped himself, trying to stay focused on the task at hand. A renewed panic overcame Katie as she realized her sense of danger on the beach in East Hampton was valid. She realized now that if she had acted the first moment she perceived danger, she might have prevented her current situation. "Now we can get down to business. Here is how we play the game. I will remove the gag from your mouth. You need to remain silent." Alex picked up a ball peen hammer. "I will ask a question and you will answer. Feel free to elaborate with all details possible. If you speak above a quiet tone, or scream, I will break one of your hands. You get the picture?" Katie nodded, and he removed the gag. "What is going on Alex, what is this?" "This is me getting you to tell me what your CIA husband really knows. What the government pigs are planning." Katie now realized the events of four years ago were still in play. Jane was not the only terrorist operative out there. Katie pleaded with Alex, "You know what I know; he gave us all the intel he had on Espinosa. That's all there is to it!" Without warning, he backhanded Katie in the face, drawing blood from her lip and nose. Alex's face turned beet red with *rage*. She became horrified as he licked her blood off his hand. "I am no fool. I have been here long enough to know that two lovers, especially married, tell all. His dirty secrets turn you on – admit it!" "You are crazy!" Alex picked up a towel from the small table near them. "I have been watching you day in and day out. Do you understand how frustrating you can be? Smiling all the time. I have wanted to fuck you for months but I didn't. You are smiles, all the time. Your perfume sends my senses out of control. You wanted to be friends. Fine we are friends and I need information. Then, we can be friends with benefits. You and me." Katie was beyond horrified now, and could not find her breath. "Admit it, keeping those secrets is hard, telling me will ease your frustration. Afterward, we can make nice and you might survive this night." They both knew that Katie surviving could never be an option. Alex took the towel and gently wiped her nose and dabbed the blood from her mouth. Without warning he leaned in and licked the remaining blood from her lip and kissed her while inhaling her perfume. He stared at her for a moment then reached in and opened a button on her blouse revealing more flesh. "We can play this slow, we have all night. No one knows you are here. Without any warning, he abruptly yelled, "Just tell me!" Alex laughed like a crazy man, and put his finger to his lips, "Shhh, almost woke the neighbors." As if Dr. Jekyll and Mr. Hyde stood in front of her, Katie pleaded with Alex. She insisted that she had no other knowledge of anything Jack or his fellow agents were planning. His split personality never showed itself before. He seemed so even-keeled and nice. "You are lying!" He picked up the hammer and grabbed her wrist. "You spent the weekend in North Carolina at the home of Senator White. The one guy we both know led the raid in Yemen a few years ago. Jack goes to Afghanistan and then has this meeting. Do not play with me; talk!" Katie spit mucous and blood in his face and looked away. Alex put the hammer down and picked up the gag. "Maybe we need a break, don't you think?" He secured the gag extremely tight, it was painful cutting into the corners of her mouth. "You need incentive." He got off on how wide her eyes opened revealing her terror. Alex grabbed her left hand again and smashed the ball peen of the hammer, centered just behind her palm, below the knuckles. She screamed an almost silent scream, and fought hard not to black out as she heard, and felt, the sickening sounds of bones breaking.

Several minutes passed before he returned from somewhere, possibly the bathroom. "You should cooperate. Maybe we need to be less formal, get to know each other better first." Alex checked the gag to make sure it remained secure. "I am going to release you from the chair. Your hands will remain tied. If you fight me in any way I will break your other hand." He cut the ties from her feet and grabbed the rope binding her hands. He pushed her face-down on the small double bed over in the corner of the one room flat. At this point the pain had numbed her whole body. She had to survive. This crazy terrorist will get his. Jack will find her, he will make this *monster* pay.

Katie heard the jingle of his belt as he dropped his pants. His hands were cold as he pushed up her skirt and pulled down her thong. She hardly felt his tongue as it glided up her leg to her cheek. He started to mount her as everything faded to black.

Chapter 52 – Saving Katie

The knock at the door startled him. Something always interrupts him. He pulled up his pants and grabbed a .22 lying on the counter. He looked through the peep hole to see a beautiful strawberry-blond haired woman. "Can I help you?" "Alex? I am Jane. They sent me with instructions. Hurry let me in." Alex did not have a good feeling about this unexpected visit. He did recognize Jane from things his co-conspirators had told him. Alex's curiosity got the best of him. "Just a minute, I need to get dressed." "Hurry, let me in damn it!" Alex quickly fixed Katie's clothing and threw her on the floor, still unconscious. He pushed her under the bed and removed any evidence she was there with him. Jane waited not so patiently and considered kicking in the door. If she hadn't convinced Marcia to wait down the hall she might have. The door opened, "The infamous Jane. Come in."

Jane, with her keen sadistic sense, immediately recognized the signs of a struggle. She looked around the room, the one room space with little places to hide. Where was Katie? "Nice place. I like what you have done with it." Alex was not in the mood. "You came here with instructions, let's have it, I'm busy." Jane needed him off guard. She also noticed a tiny spot of blood on the edge of the little table next to a torture chair. It had to be one, considering it was bolted to the floor. Jane stared at Alex. "What?" "You are cute, I didn't expect, well I don't know what I expected." "You think I'm cute? What information do you have? I'm busy." "And I just escaped from a federal detention cell. I want revenge. You need my help. I have been deprived of *everything*. I'm hungry." She made a move on Alex who had become frustrated and riled up from his interrupted intimacy with Katie. He let her kiss him, yet something did not seem right. This was too easy and these things never happened to him. He felt played. He focused on the kitchen counter drawer where he stashed the .22. As they swapped spit, he maneuvered in the direction of his weapon. Then it happened; her hand took hold of his sex tool. OK, maybe his assault could wait. Jane took care of business like she always did. Her hand and body movements took him into another dimension. For that moment his jihad and his rage against Katie were forgotten. Distracted, Alex did not see it coming. Jane pushed her stiletto deep into his neck. His eyes told the story of disappointment and shock. "I guess this is not your lucky day." Jane let him drop to the floor. The thump his body made as it collapsed to the floor gave Jane a renewed sense of power that she missed. She went to the only possible hiding place in the room. Jane pulled Katie out from under the bed. She was semi-conscious, and in shock. Katie only knew Jane as an enemy; one of them, like Alex. She tried to fight off her unlikely rescuer. "Katie! Alex is dead. I am here with Marcia to rescue you."

Marcia finally reached me by phone. I called Katie's boss to help; he asked no questions. Fortunately Erik was home and able to meet them at the hospital. He stayed with Katie so Marcia and Jane could stay out of sight, avoiding the police for now.

The flight from the Carolinas took forever. Even though the doctor told me on the phone that aside from her hand injury, my wife was physically OK, I worried more about her mental status. Marcia explained what happened and how Jane took Alex down. Katie was my first concern, but we had to take care of Jane before the authorities detained her again.

My flight started the final approach into the airport. I could see the rooftops of buildings along the shoreline as we flew over Manhattan. I dialed my cell phone breaking FAA rules. That is what the official ID is for. "Hey Marcia, I spoke with John and arrangements are being made out of Andrews. There is a transport going out day after tomorrow." I gave her the details and instructions for Jane to remain quiet and out of sight until I worked out her situation. "Give her a single use burn phone and tell her to wait for our call. Find her a safe house until she can leave here." Marcia would have her own issues to deal with very soon. Her superiors would not take kindly to her handling of this situation or the use of unauthorized government transport. They will be pissed, especially since the Senator and possibly the VP calling them on her behalf. In the long run things did work out. If they didn't, she might have ended up as my partner at the company.

Katie cried when she saw me. I held her tight, causing her to wince. She had been beaten badly. Her hand in a cast, and shaking non-stop. My heart ached for her. "I am so sorry, my love. I will fix this so it can never happen again." Once again, I had failed to protect her. She may not have realized it, but I will never, be able to let it go.

When we got home, Rosa, our life saver, already had the boys fed, bathed and in bed. When she saw Katie, Rosa broke down and became hysterical. Poor Katie had to console her. I needed aspirin, or a few of Katie's more powerful pills.

We never spoke of the details of that night. The situation needed no spoken words. I knew what and why it happened, and Katie understood the same. I am putting my family at risk with every mission. The truth is, even though our situation was clear before we got married, reality has a way of making the truth unacceptable. At that moment, I feared for my marriage. I envisioned being alone without Katie and the boys. I decided right then and there that if I had to choose, being a Wal-Mart greeter wouldn't be so bad. In any event, getting out of the field would soon need to become my priority.

Chapter 53 – Assassination

The wire transfer was completed as agreed. This being the largest single payday the Sheik had ever received for doing so little. His brief meeting with Mr. Smith, AKA Jack Owens, netted him enough money to legitimize his businesses and sell them off. Although retirement is a word not commonly used in his realm, he liked the sound of it. Travel seemed like a fantasy. He had not left his compound in years, let alone the region. His only Western experiences consisted of his years of graduate school in the United States and some European travel with his wife soon after they married. He fondly remembered those days. Simpler days for sure. Money was tight. It took great effort back home to apply Western influences to his business practices. His efforts were not well received by the local people. He had to deal with hostility from rival business. Most of the profits came from business travelers and tourists in need of his services. The eighties were good to him. The nineties so-so. After 9/11, both revenue sources dried up almost overnight.

As a business major and experienced import export consultant, getting involved in the transport of drugs and other contraband came natural to him.

Through connections, he started moving "product" to the west. He did not directly know who he worked for, but later realized it was Taliban rebels. Eventually his entire operation turned into a money laundering network under the influence of Al Qaeda.

Business was good; profits were huge. His wife had to know who his business associates were, but she enjoyed the money, and all the attention it brought her. Neither of them regarded themselves as criminals. Unfortunately, his associates, overwhelmed with paranoia did not have complete trust in him. Al Qaeda successfully recruited several of his closest advisors as double agents. A kind of insurance policy that their best interests would be looked after.

The meeting with the western couple seemed odd, but not so improbable, as they were business associates from his other capitalist ventures. Surely no one cared what he did as long as he handled all his business properly. A tiny Al Qaeda cell consisting primarily of technical specialists listened in on everything transmitted over the air. They existed purely as a spy network similar to our CIA. Chatter had been intercepted alluding to Mexico, specifically the Nogales area.

The information came too late. An attack against them was in progress on two of Al Qaeda's most important locations in the western world.

The double agents quickly realized what had happened. Their Sheik had a meeting with a suspicious westerner not more than a week prior. It could not be a coincidence.

The hit squads moved swiftly. The information the agents sent to their leaders, they thought, would be well received. A reward for the valuable information about the Sheik's betrayal, well deserved. They did not expect to be gunned down in their sleep that very night.

"Greece is such a beautiful country, do you not agree?" They held hands looking out at the incredible Greek Isles from their hotel balcony. "My darling husband, what shall we do for supper tonight?" The Sheik smiled lovingly at his loyal and obedient wife. "I took the liberty of ordering room service. We can have an intimate meal out here. It would be such a shame to waste this fantastic view. Then we can see what else we can enjoy out here." His wife smiled and kissed his cheek. The knock on the suite's door startled her. "Allow me." He kissed his wife's hand as he stood; her smile toward his kindness was genuine.

The large rolling cart sat just inside the room adjacent to the balcony. The waiter poured the first two glasses of champagne for the guests. "Is there anything else I may get for you tonight?" The Sheik replied, "No, thank you, that is all for now." The waiter nodded and left the husband and wife to enjoy their intimate dinner.

"This champagne is delicious." His wife blurted out her appreciation of the fine beverage, and giggled. The Sheik had not seen her this relaxed in a long time. She looked lovely tonight, and he told her so. He could sense her eagerness to be intimate with him. This vacation is what they needed. "Life is good, my precious wife, and you are my love."

The tremendous explosion tore the balconies completely off three floors of their hotel. Numerous rooms were destroyed. The Sheik and his wife were completely incinerated by the massive blast. No other guests were harmed, the rooms damaged by the explosion empty; their occupants fortunately chose to dine out that evening.

Chapter 54 – Take-Down
Mexico

I met my team at Andrews Air Force Base at 7AM. The General's men were already there. I suppose the military's goal is always to prove they are better than anyone else; they probably are. "Good morning, everyone." The General had his men standing at ease, ready to board our flight into hell. They looked like little GI Joes (and one Jane, no relation to my terrorist feline), each one perfect in form. "Agent Owens, good morning; we had a 6AM rendezvous." Have I mentioned I don't like this guy? "You will have to excuse me General, the military transport you sent for me neglected to show up, so I had to board a commercial flight." He did not respond, nor did I expect him to. He picked up a stack of manila folders and started handing them out. Each folder had a series of codes and names. "These are individualized instructions for each member of this assault team. It covers everything we discussed earlier this week, in detail, along with other information you will need to be successful in your mission. I will be in communication with each of you through the comm devices. These units are undetectable and fit inside the ear so they are almost invisible." The General walked over to a camouflaged trunk and opened it. *Wow, inside was a lot of heavy artillery*. I had my eye on the really sub-compact Uzi IMI; The Israeli's favorite weapon. This magnificent firearm has been in use for over 60 years and still remains reliable. The General caught me daydreaming of a terrorist slaughter, Uzi in hand. "These are not for you. A weapon detected on your person will get you killed. Please hand the captain your sidearm. We will keep it safe until after the mission." I responded as expected, "Not going to happen and I am not going in cold." They all stared at me like I was a zombie who had no right to speak back to their high command. I thought better of my response and gave it up; saving a fight for another day. I was not nervous until now. Until I lost my only method of defense. Well, possibly, I was a little nervous before; after all, this was the most dangerous operation I have ever been a part of. Then I remembered my earlier encounters with Jane and the dusty trails of the Sand Lands of hell. Maybe this is no big deal. In and out, one-two-three. Please; Dear God.

The flight took under five hours. The C-17 Globemaster III military transport, like the one we took more than once to Ethiopia, did not have very comfortable travel amenities. It was loud and shaky, leaving my head aching the entire trip. All the nuts and bolts holding me together felt as if they were coming loose. At least this was a shorter flight. We landed at a small airfield in Mexico with a shack for a terminal. I think we were about five miles from the Nogales International Airport. The C-17 could never pass under radar so we must have had an agreement with the Mexican authorities for this operation. A lineup of Humvees waited for us just a few hundred yards from the aircraft. No time for pit stops. This operation was a "Go" from the moment the plane's hatches were opened.

Our staging point took twenty-five minutes to reach. All teams had their orders. I transferred to a pretty nice 2013 Grand Cherokee Jeep Limited. I guess that's the drug dealer's choice of ground transportation in this part of the world. Two of my guys came with me as my henchmen. The others moved in with their military counterparts, ready for the extraction of the hostages and other *innocents*.

The gate to the drug manufacturing plant, disguised as a clothing manufacturer, had six guards and a gate keeper. I stopped my vehicle a good distance from them and we got out. We approached slowly, hands out in front, posing no threats. "Buenos días señor, estoy aquí para ver al Señor Gonzales. Yo trabajo para Espinosa. Como ustedes saben, Espinosa ha sido detenido por las autoridades de Estados Unidos, estoy llevando a cabo su negocio ahora." I basically informed the guards that I replaced Espinosa while he worked out his legal problems back home. My Spanish is less than perfect, I expected that their third grade education would not notice. "Cuál es tu nombre!" This should play well, "Mi nombre es John Smith." In the drug world there are quite a lot of alias like mine so that should not be an issue. The guard yelled something, and I motioned my limited understanding. His hand movements cleared things up. I had to proceed solo. This I expected, but one could hope. Another guard I had not noticed earlier motioned for me to raise my arms high. He did a pat-down for weapons, finding none. He forgot to check my butt, his loss. You would think with all the smuggling, that would be a given. All things considered, lucky me, his hands did not look all that clean.

As I entered the compound through a series of gates, much like a prison, I noticed several trenches with lots of firepower. These guys were ready for a war. I hoped they were not prepared for the one we were bringing to them. The realization hit me as we drew closer to the entrance to what appeared to be the main building. I am not going to make it out of here unless I am convincing enough to make a deal and they agree to a second meeting. To succeed, I needed to find the main manufacturing area so I could plant the locator beacon and the drone can take it out. If God is with us, the hostages, consisting mainly of women and children, will be in a different building. Our intel told us that they moved these poor souls several times a day, like cattle being herded. Forced into slave labor and prostitution, the majority of the captives are children, mostly females. They also use them as drug mules under threat that their families will be tortured and killed if they run or fail a delivery. I had to wonder, if the rescue failed, would they thank god for ending their lives quickly. Would they find salvation in ending the torturous situation they were in?

The room they brought me into was lavish and very high tech in both its furnishings and equipment. Mr. Gonzalez, manager of this establishment, sat behind a huge mahogany desk. He had two henchmen, one on each side of him. There were three others in the room. All had AK47's and looked as if they were itching to use them. "Buen día señor John Smith, por favor tome asiento. Please sit, be comfortable." We discussed the finer points of supply and demand and agreed that doing business would be profitable for both sides. Mr. Gonzalez made it clear that he would need my real name and lots of other information if we were going to be partners. I agreed to furnish that, and copies of the last three years of my tax returns as well, if we moved forward. We shook hands, and I gave him a number to reach me to discuss our next meeting. "Señor, may I ask to see your manufacturing plant? I need assurance of quality and professionalism. My investors need my guarantees." I think he might have been insulted, and I feared this was the end for me. The big man made a phone call. "Por favor, ven a mi oficina y deje señor Smith a ver la fábrica; gracias." He hung up and smiled, "It will be my pleasure." My tour guide arrived less than a minute later. I guess they do not tolerate tardiness. "Sígueme, mantenga sus manos a los lados y tocar nada." He told me to keep my hands in plain sight and touch nothing. This guy looked more like his native language should be Arabic. I considered a test, but thought wisely and held my tongue for one big Adiós Hijo de Puta.

The factory was located somewhere else. We accessed the facility by taking an elevator down one level and then traversing a good amount of corridors. If I had to do this again myself, I would need a GPS. I think we traveled about a quarter mile in total. Our teams considered an underground plant. It made the most sense for an operation this big. By design, even I would never be able to show anyone where it is located from above ground. Probably not even from below, due to the maze of twists and turns it took to get here. I would imagine a wrong turn would result in death by booby trap. We arrived at an area that allowed a viewing of most of the operation. As I feared, no way would they allow me inside. Time was running out. I hope they had located the innocents and were ready to extract.

"Perdone, ¿dónde está el baño?" I held my hands low and made the face a woman makes as she crosses her

273

legs. He just shook his head in disgust. The bathroom fortunately had a stall and urinal. My escort followed me in. I held my stomach and entered the stall and started to close the door. He pushed back shaking his head. "I need privacy, bad stomach, mucho tamales." I closed and latched the door. Being talented I managed some gross sound effects as I extracted the tiny device from my rear. These guys would be proud of me. This guy, definitely from Sand Land somewhere, would not be so impressed. His suicide people plant bombs up their own asses all the time and blow up cafes. I removed the device from the prophylactic type balloon and placed it under the toilet tank. "Oh man, mucho bueno, gracias." I washed really well, and we exited back to Gonzalez's office. We agreed to talk in a few days. I would return home with good news for my people. He actually seemed like an OK guy for a major drug kingpin. I wanted to wish him a good trip but thought wisely and refrained.

Outside, the warm sun felt good. My armed escorts lead me to the main gates where my two associates waited. As soon as they saw me and I waved as planned, my guy remotely activated the device and the signal was sent to the drone. At the same time the other teams moved in to take the hostages. I waved to my escorts as we drove away. "Adiós, Amigos."

The sophisticated equipment in Gonzales's office started binging and bonging and his men moved into action. An electronic device, not one of theirs, had been activated. It took less than three minutes for his men to locate the device I literally pulled from my ass, and destroy it. Unfortunately for them the drone already had its coordinates locked on the target.

We got most of the hostages out, so we hoped. We will never know. The massive plant and everything up to three stories below was destroyed; vaporized is more like it. We used the same technology as in the Yemen Camp take-down. *Take no prisoners*.

My heart ached at the same time as I felt tearful joy. The lives of some forty human beings, mostly under the age of twenty and female, had been saved. Karen held Anita's hand tight. "I told you we would be OK." Anita squeezed her companion's hand in return and smiled with tears of joy and relief streaming down her cheeks. Today, language between them had no barrier. Their futures uncertain, they had the opportunity to redirect their fate. Interviews with the freed captives led to us finding and taking down smaller operations, mostly forced prostitution in Mexico and the western United States.

I called the Senator to update him, and then my wife, to let her know we were all OK and that the mission was a success. I think they both cried.

Connecticut

Such a harmonious plan as it had to be, the take-down of the Connecticut operation went as smoothly as one could hope. Both teams, Mexico and Connecticut had live satellite communications to allow our assault on each location to occur simultaneously. It was imperative that neither location had the opportunity to warn the other using their highly technical alert systems. Although I will never get the pat on the back I deserve, my trip to Yemen and ultimately Afghanistan proved crucial to the success of these operations. We would never have known about the unique alert systems these guys had. My new ally in the Sangin District came through. I now would owe him in return, even though we paid him a huge sum of money for his information. His calls to Mexico on behalf of the Al Qaeda side removed any doubt. I did assure him his risk was nil as there would be no one left to tell. At the time, I was not aware of the unfortunate situation that had befallen the Sheik and his wife.

The big man must have been looking over us on this crazy day because we suffered no losses and minimal injuries. Connecticut resulted in only two casualties. NCIS and FBI teams quietly secured all the surrounding businesses, moving workers to basements or far sides of buildings away from any potential exposure from blast debris. Evacuating the innocents might have resulted in tipping-off our bad guys. Air support, disguised as news helicopters, flew overhead watching for runners. The bad guys had two lookouts disguised as a concierge and an actual security guard. As the first line of defense and alert, each had to be taken out. Once the heavily armed teams of Navy Seals secured the location, the FBI and ATF teams rounded everyone up with no incidents. After they cleared the building, the bomb squad disabled the kill switches and remote access devices. The locations east and west, both had a self-destruct plan to wipe out all evidence and records. Those records are now in possession of the FBI. I expect a lot more, smaller take downs will result from the intelligence gleaned from this operation. With no organization and no manufacturing, evil will have to take a hiatus. America had a win-win day today, taking drugs off the street, and saving young women and children from the horrors of human trafficking. Ultimately, we achieved our goal to rid funding sources for local Al Qaeda cells.

Good news of a successful mission in Connecticut was relayed to us. I think another vacation is in order. Asking Katie where she would like to go would have been a nice gesture. The odds are, her response would be to say "nowhere." Then she would ask me to retire.

Strangely, if asked, I might actually consider it at this point. I should have called her again.

From thirty thousand feet above, the earth looks so simple. I have flown on a thousand flights, and each time as I look down at the globe below, I am in awe of the incredible beauty. If all the enemies of the world could see it from where I was, view it for what it really was, perhaps we all could get along. Looking down at the Grand Canyon, the most incredible artwork, viewed in full only from the sky with its gray and red carvings, I fell asleep. My dreams were so real, so vivid. Some are terrible and frightening, more so because they represent real situations of the past or the reality of the future to come. This dream picks up from my last awakened moments. Katie and I relaxing on lounge chairs at the base of, let's say, the Grand Canyon or Red Rock Canyon. The point is, this was a good dream. She glistened in the sun as I rubbed suntan oil on her exquisite body. She wore the same two-piece bikini as the last dream like this. Katie pulled her bikini top string letting it fall away. Her back was perfect. "Excuse me sir; Time to buckle up, on the ground in ten." *Damn it!*

Chapter 55 – Martinez

In the wake of the successful take-down of a major drug enterprise, Juan Carlos Martinez's wife began rallying in her husband's name for more reforms. She created her own consortium with other political powers that wanted the same things her husband fought for. Word spread throughout Mexico and others began to follow. The pressure on law enforcement resulted in an increase of arrests. People had a renewed outlook. This continued for some time. Eventually, as the money flow regained its momentum, the drug and sex trafficking picked up again. Law enforcement started losing ground, and eventually things reverted back to the old ways. Mrs. Juan Carlos Martinez was abducted while doing an interview with a news reporter. They found the journalist three days later bruised, but otherwise unharmed. He had been separated from Mrs. Martinez immediately after the kidnapping and never heard her voice or anything about her after that. An extensive search was made; no trace of her was ever found.

Chapter 56 – Pete

Her eyes opened slowly. He looked so perfect asleep. Jane did not realize at the time that Michael, the father of her children could have been her savior. Had fate dealt a different hand, she might have cared enough about him to change her ways. In fairness, Jane did not know any different. Her upbringing was similar to that of a lab rat. I suppose more like a puppy pit bull being reared to fight. All animals are born inherently innocent. Like the dog, if taught to kill other animals from infancy then that is all it knows. Remorse occurs only if one knows, feels, he or she did wrong. Jane had not dreamed or thought about her one and only in a very long time. She is free now. Free from the need to hunt and free from being hunted. I came through with my promise to her. The Senator and Vice President overruled the General's orders and upheld the original agreement. As long as she behaves and stays off the radar, no one will come looking for her. With my help, the threat to her children no longer remained. Still, Jane reformed? Completely? I can't totally believe that. Deep down there is a ticking time bomb. Tick tock, tick tock; one day she will reemerge and the world will once again be in mortal danger. For now I hope sleeping dogs can lie.

Pete always arrived at the pub two hours before opening time. He preferred to prep the small kitchen and take care of bookkeeping earlier, rather than later. After the trouble a few years back that left bodies everywhere and Jane MIA, he started leaving the bar with the rest of his staff at closing time. His comfort level better in the earlier part of the day.

Pete heard the back door open and reached for his shotgun. Positive that the door had remained locked since the night before, someone was about to get two rounds in their chest. "Whoa, it's only me. I see you never changed the locks." Jane stood there holding a key up for him to see. Pete squinted from the glare of the sun streaking in from the half open door. "Holy shit, girl! I almost fired both barrels at you!" She walked up to him, disregarding his freaked out anger, and pushed the barrel away. "How about a hug, my friend?" Pete looked good. He recovered well from that god awful night years ago. He cleaned up good, too. She stepped back and took a good look. "I suppose you have a girlfriend now or something?" "No, just better to look the part, good for business. What are you doing here; are you still on the run?" Jane helped herself to a beer and asked Pete to sit down. "There are only two people in the world I have ever truly trusted; actually, now three. There are only two people I ever had feelings for other than faking to get something from them." She held his hand tight. I want to tell you everything, I need to. Are we still friends?" Pete nodded, realizing how much he actually missed her. Jane added spunk to his place and brought in the crowds. "Of course, more than friends. You know how I always joke about your flirting keeping my business afloat? In truth, I was a little jealous." All of a sudden Jane realized he might actually care for her more than a friend should. She did not want to lead him on. She did not see him, in that way. He wasn't bad looking, his age, older though, did not bother her. His friendship posed an odd emotion. It should be the opposite, friends first is always better. She would need to ponder this one for a while. "I need a place to stay, can I hang here for a few days? I have so much to tell you." Pete looked away and Jane had the notion disappointment was headed her way. She couldn't blame him. Because of her, he suffered painfully and lost a lot of revenue. It took almost a year for that night to fade from his patrons' simple memories. The never-ending government investigation made headlines on the air and in the papers. He hoped the media would bring in the curious, but it didn't. These days, his pub is doing really well. He needed this income, this place is all he had. "Jeez Jane, the spare room in the back is now added storage. There is no place except the bar or pool table to sleep on. I'm not sure that will do." His head down, he looked like a sad puppy. Jane, the old Jane, would build anger and express hostility implying dominance and control. Instead, she just smiled; "It's OK, I understand." Pete relented and said, "I have a roll out in my living room. My place is small, a one bedroom cabin, but we could find a way to manage." Jane returned his smile and actually managed a slight tear. Her humanity, the new emotions she never experienced surprised her. She hugged Pete. "Thank you." Pete poured himself a beer, and they clinked glasses. "So now what?" "Who's running the bar?" "Me and Joni, a part timer waitress with three kids and a jerk husband." So, any chance you would let me fill out an application?" Pete stood, "Live together and work together? What next, we save on taxes and get married?" Jane just stared like a light bulb went off. Pete lost his smile, "Well, I guess I could use a partner, sort of; and security. From what I can remember of what they told me, you can take care of yourself and evidently me too." Jane smiled and resisted any further body contact offering her hand in agreement. She was relieved he did not ask about Michael.

The cabin, small as it was, appeared cozy and warm. When Jane and Pete came home after closing the pub, Pete lit a fire right away and poured two glasses of merlot. The living room doubled as the dining room; the kitchen, directly adjacent and open to the combined space. Convenient for a single person. The sixty-five inch

LED TV could be seen from anywhere in the cabin except the one bedroom.

Pete motioned for Jane to sit as he handed her the glass of wine. "Sorry, bachelor setup; one small couch and one hard chair. We might need to pick a few things up to reorganize and make it more comfortable for you. Just let me know if you are tired and want to go to bed, I will vacate… this is, your bed." Pete definitely seemed awkward. "You are the best, Pete. Thank you so much. I'm not shy. I'll tell you when it's time to call it a night." Pete blushed.

"So, I promised to tell all. Just to keep things honest, I cannot tell you everything, but what I do tell you, is the truth." Jane started out with the whole kidnapped at birth story. She told of the horrors of the camp in Yemen and of her abuse by a Sheik's son, and how she killed him. Jane left out parts so as not to scare Pete. Although, he looked freaked-out already. She also fessed up to her part in controlling William who was actually Carlton, the Senator's kidnapped son. Pete's mouth remained open showing his shock. "I thought you were an American agent?" "Not then, I am sort of now." She continued with her attempts on Jack and Katie's lives, leaving out the college days that lead up to that point. Jane finally got to present day and her travels with Jack, saving Katie and her partial pardon. "I am making you uncomfortable, I'm sorry, but you are one of only three people who know all this about me. My children are safe now. Their father, Michael, from that night at the pub, was the only love I ever knew. It has been almost five years. You, Pete, are the only other love I have known." She sensed his uncomfortableness, "I mean I love you as a friend. I can talk honestly with you." Pete looked disappointed. "Trust; it's all about trust." Pete finished the last of his third glass of merlot and stood. "It has been a long day." He opened a drawer in the credenza to the left of the couch and pulled out a big heavy blanket and two pillows. "Good night, Jane; see you in the morning." Pete left, looking disappointed in some way. Jane fell asleep quickly. She felt safe and slept solid until the sun woke her in the early morning.

Pete had a restless night until he admitted to himself that he had feelings for Jane; always had since he met her years ago. The truth about Jane bothered him but also intrigued his sense of adventure.

Chapter 57 - About Jane

Jane had no childhood. Yes, she was a child, but not like anyone we grew up with. As I said before, from birth, they raised her like a puppy pitbull. During the tender years, most young children learn to share, love, and be loved. Her trainers denied all of these basic traits. They did however, provide her with certain amenities children loved to play with. Malibu Barbie and Ken were her favorites. On TV, the toy commercials showed children playing and fantasizing family adventures with dolls and toy automobiles. Jane was encouraged to pull Barbie's head off and rewarded when she demonstrated running Ken over with Barbie's car. No one ever hugged her or told her she was pretty. If she instinctively showed any compassion for others in her *hometown,* or regret for doing something mean to someone by her leader's instruction, she would be punished.

During her pre-teen years, the leaders changed strategy. They praised her acquired psychopathic behavior as normal and rewarded her for it. They explained to her that others would never understand how special she was. Jane saw herself as being much above the other inhabitants of her hometown. William should have been considered a friend; she saw him as weak and lost any respect she had earlier on for him, as he became more needy, more in love with her. Hell, she didn't recognize love either back then. There is no way he did either.

"You exist to serve Allah. This jihad we are preparing you for is Allah's will." After all that has happened, where is Allah now?

Jane began to feel agitated, she took a deep breath and exhaled slowly. She saw a doctor on TV, Oprah or something, do it for a test subject. It looked fake, but she tried it anyway. It actually worked.

Michael cared for her and asked for nothing in return. Jane understood that as love. She was sad when he no longer existed on earth. This must have been love as well. She missed him. "*I must have loved him,*" she thought.

Jane spent a lot of her down time thinking out of the box, looking past the psychopathic breeding her trainers forced upon her. She thought, "I can actually trust someone."

Still, she was confused, but not really. Her kids were needy. They did not offer much to her. Yet the feelings she had for Michael, the trust she had with Jack, both of these alien qualities, she felt more so for her children than anyone else. Pete left her even more confused. He possessed both qualities, love for her and trust between them. She also had an increasing desire for him; sexually. And, he was a friend. Jane realized that what she felt for Pete, qualified as love... and, she loved her kids.

Free to move about, free to explore the feelings her oppressive leaders denied her. Jane had to make things right. If Allah is real and cared for her, he would allow her to live life free of the jihad she was born into.

Chapter 58 - The Kids

The days of spying were over. Auntie Jane is here for a visit. From what Jane told me later on, she had a really difficult time getting Marne and her husband Ed on board. She wanted a relationship with her kids. A family like relationship. Jane accepted that her children's parents are those two, but she had to have a relationship, and guardianship in case something happened to the *parents*. The idea of anyone else raising her children was unacceptable. Jane felt rage building just thinking of that possibility. No, this has to be dealt with now.

Jane showed up mid-day to speak with Marne. She expected the kids to be in daycare and Ed at work. She took a deep breath and knocked on the front door. Ed opened the door, "Jane? Interesting, don't you usually lurk behind a tree or something?" Jane just stared in his eyes for a second then smiled, "Not anymore." She gently pushed past Ed, "Where's Marne?"

They sat at the kitchen table and had coffee. Ed lurked in the background leaning against the refrigerator. He loves those kids. Jane told me later on, that he feared she planned to take them from Marne and him.

"Ed, honey, why don't you wait outside for the kids? They should be home in a bit." Ed said "Sure, whatever" and left the house. "He's a good man, Jane, and he loves those kids." Jane took Marne's hand, "I know he is." *Or I would have killed him already.* "And you are a great mom." Marne did not find comfort in Jane's words. She still expected the punch line, not to be good. "All the issues that stood in the way of me having a relationship with them have been taken care of. I still believe they are better off with you two. Auntie Jane works for me, but it has to be for real. Being a constant part of their lives is what I want most. I want to spend holidays with them, and you as well, if you will have me. I want to fill the role of a third parent, sort of." Marne was uncomfortable. She knew that Jane could be a dangerous sort, even though at that moment she was out of character and seemed normal. She had no choice and considered some of the advantages. "That is great, Jane; we will work it out. But we need to take it slow, and let them adjust to you being around."

The screen door swung open and the two little ones ran into the kitchen screaming. "Aunty Jane!" They ran to her with hugs and kisses. Jani grabbed her aunt's hand and pulled her to get up and come to her room. "I have a new dolly." Jane smiled, a genuine smile and said, "I think they have adjusted already."

After her visit with Marne and her kids, Jane went to see Pete. She arrived at the pub just after four to help Pete get ready for the happy hour crowd. The part time waitress who replaced Marne a while back, sometimes known as the barmaid twerp (Jane's description) already started setting tables. "Hey, where is he?" Miss Friendly pointed to the stock room. Jane walked in brushing her hair. Pete looked up, "Nice hair." "It's really windy out there, this afternoon. What's with miss personality?" Jane motioned toward the dining room. Pete looked out toward the dining area and shrugged his shoulders. "I get it, she doesn't like me. Did I kill someone she knows? Wait – she likes you." Pete did not look directly at Jane. "Pete, do you like her?" Jane actually felt jealous, something new she just discovered. "Of course not, at least not like that. She's OK and does her job, and she is easy on the eyes." Jane gave him the look. "I mean the customers like her." Pete seemed nervous all of a sudden. He turned to move a box of wine and as he put it down, he lost his footing and fell into Jane; His face inches from hers. Jane grinned, "Well, isn't this awkward?" Pete leaned in and kissed her. Jane felt flush. The kiss lasted two seconds before Pete pulled back but it seemed like ten minutes to Jane with a million crazy thoughts flashing through her mind. "I'm so sorry Jane. I, I don't know what came over me." Without any contemplation Jane locked lips with Pete and pushed him hard against the wine rack, almost causing an avalanche of bottles. Tongues battled and hands explored. "Done out there boss, what next?" As she finished her sentence, Pete's smitten waitress had her first disappointment for the evening. Mouth open in shock, she quickly turned and left the stockroom. Pete was still holding Jane around the waist staring into her eyes. "Your eyes are different. You seem to be more at ease. I like this new you." He gently touched her inviting lips with his fingers and leaned in, kissing her neck briefly. Jane's perfume tingled his senses. He felt so drawn to her and did not want to let go. "Now what?" Jane smiled, kissed his cheek and turned to leave. "We take it day by day." Pete, leaning on the small table next to him, "That's it? That's all you have to say? After we -"

"Fire the waitress."

Chapter 59 – Raul

The bell rang, indicating the end of the period. Math being his favorite subject, Raul always found numbers easy to work with. His next and last class of the day, fourth year Spanish, bored him. Growing up, his parents only spoke their native language. Both elder Espinosa's met and married in a small town just outside Tijuana on the Mexico side of the border. From poor families, his father had to travel into San Diego where he worked as a bell captain for one of the hotels. His days were long, due to the travel time and delays at the border crossing. Raul and his family finally moved across the border; his father obtained a work visa through his job. The gangs immediately vied for his allegiance, but Raul managed to stay clear of their influences. It was during his senior year that his father had a heart attack and died. The family suddenly found themselves with no income.

Mid-year, he left school to get a job. He did not expect it to be so difficult. A friend introduced him to a drug dealer looking to expand his enterprise. Raul had the ability to travel back and forth to visit family in Mexico with no problem returning stateside. The movement of drugs across the border seemed so easy. He made more money in one year than his papa did in his whole lifetime.

With his keen sense of math, and fluent English, as well as Spanish, he soon broke away to create his own drug smuggling empire. He did this in the name of supporting his family.

There were many woman in Raul's new life. He was a macho guy; the man in power. The woman flocked to him like a super-magnet to a steel plank. At home, one of many in Mexico, his wife and two year old son led a simpler life. His childhood best friend's younger sister always looked up to him. She was the one he wanted to marry and raise his family. She and his son were all that was good in his evil world. He kept them separated from his day to day dealings and tried to visit as often as possible. He did not ever consider her loneliness while he gallivanted and whored around expressing free will.

One day, one of his larger drug connections introduced Espinosa to a young woman who represented a new buyer. Adeen Jahar stood five-nine. She had the most gorgeous olive complexion and the smoothest long black hair pulled to one side and down over her left shoulder. This stunning woman had Raul's attention. "How much did you say you wanted to purchase?" Raul was still mesmerized by what he later called his apparition. "What will fifty million dollars buy?" "Surely you jest, as connected as I may be, that is way over my limit to purchase. We will need to start smaller, get to know one another." Her smile electrified the room, "It would be wise to do the deal as we request. We will front you half the money, twenty-five million cash up front. That should help with your buying power." Raul asked, "You can move that much content? You would have to compete with me." Adeen replied in a firm voice, "Actually, we do not want to take possession of the product. You move it using your usual resources and return our initial funds plus a reasonable percentage." She smiled, "Consider us your new banker." So began the new money laundering enterprise making Espinosa one of the most powerful cartels on both sides of the border.

Six months down the road, the new business relationship had grown into a billion dollar money swap organization. Who actually controlled the enterprise didn't matter. Raul kept getting richer, and Adeen provided a healthy revenue stream for her peoples' cause. Raul and Adeen formed their own relationship. Their bond strong and his trust focused only on her. The business friendship became physical. As planned by her leaders, she had him completely under her control.

Another of Adeen's redeeming qualities, her law degree. Although non-practicing, she maintained her Bar-credentials and made sure to declare herself as co-counsel. This allowed her to have longer, more confidential visitation sessions with her client. As his first trial focused on drug and sex trafficking, Espinosa's confinement was more lenient. His future situation during the trial for crimes against the United Stated will be much different.

"Hello Raul, how are they treating you?" He hated that she sounded like an attorney, cold and all business. "You look incredible, so professional." Raul leaned in, expecting her to respond likewise. She didn't, which furthered his growing frustration. "There is privacy to speak, but the cameras are active." His sexy lawyer moved to his left indicating he should follow. His eyes, transfixed on her own dark beacons, did not break for a second. He understood, they needed to face away from the cameras. "Why all the fuss? We have our deal; there is nothing more you can do for me except to give them a show that will have to last me a life-time." He reached for her again, forcing her to take a step back from him. "Stay seated and behave, we have but five minutes. I am taking you home this afternoon. "Don't ask any questions, just listen closely. When the action starts, hit the floor and stay face down until I get you. Then be prepared to run for your life. Failure is certain death for us both." She smiled, turned to the camera and back to Raul. "I love you, and may be considered a traitor to my own people for taking this risk; for jeopardizing the jihad. Follow my leads and don't screw it up." Raul Espinosa, King of his empire, had never had anyone in recent years dare to speak to him like that. She had balls, his balls, and he loved her. "As you say, my Queen. I am ready at your will."

Chapter 60 – Intimate Moments

"Have you ever thought about making the switch to the other side? Not right away but after you pay your dues at the DA's office."

We sat snuggled close on the couch in the family room. The television was on, with the volume off. I had turned it down because we thought one of the boys had cried out. After Katie checked on them she did not turn the sound back on. This became a common practice for us, leaving the volume off and the picture on. In some way we found this a convenient way to steal private time to talk about things. Any subject matter that may have gotten lost or forgotten as a result of our chaotic lives.

"So, have you?" "Have I what? Considered leaving a job I just started this year? A job mind you, and thanks in part to you, I am finally settling into and a part of the team. What's going on Jack?" I really had no excuse for what I was feeling. How do I tell her, I am afraid for her in this job? My nights sometimes consist of disturbing dreams. Dreams of her being chased by an angry convict she helped to put away. I know that in some twisted way this is about me. My guilt at putting her in this position almost every day. She worries about me. My incredible wife respects what I do, she married me knowing the risks of my job. She supports me and hides her fears – most of the time. It is my selfish actions that should be considered. Perhaps asking her the question, putting this spousal concern on her will prompt her to confront me, to force me to acknowledge my responsibilities to the family.

"I wanted to practice law since junior high school. I wanted to put the bad guys away. After all that has happened to me, us; that is all I want to do now." "But don't you ever want to be on the other side? Do you sometimes find yourself concerned for the defense? Perhaps the poor schmuck's lawyer is a dope and you are winning through his incompetence?" My wife did not seem all that pleased at this moment. "First of all, dearest husband, who would shoot first and ask questions later, statistically most of them are guilty. The defense spends so much time making sure the guilty are treated fairly. I need to be on the side that makes sure the guilty pay for their crimes in a way that they can be rehabilitated or kept safely away from society. Besides, defense attorneys make too much money. That would mess up our family budget."

Next came the question my subconscious really rooted for. "Look in the mirror Jack, you knew how I would answer. Is this about you, really?" She is so damn perceptive it makes me crazy sometimes. I told her, "Let's go upstairs." Katie made the face; *take no prisoners*. "No *anything* for you until we talk this out." "But K.C.," I sounded like a whining little girl. "We are missing Naked and Afraid, it's the season finale." "Jack!" "Listen Katie, I worry about you, and about me. You only need to worry about me. Besides, what's wrong with making good money? I thought about it; you could develop a viable defense practice, and in a few years when I am up for retirement, I would come work with you. Every good defense attorney needs an ace investigator. We could spend more time together, even work in some *afternoon delight*." I thought it sounded *sweet*. "First of all, No; Not a good plan. Second of all, us having time apart works for us. We don't smother each other like other couples do. We have stories to tell because our days are interesting and different." Katie would like me to retire and become something like a mall cop. Safe and boring. She took my hand. "You are my macho man. You make us feel safe and take such good care of me and the boys. I love our life as it is. I worry about you all the time. You still piss me off with some of the dangerous things you do. Somehow you pull it off and get the bad guys and come home to me. I love you."

Our discussion ended on that note. A good note it was, for now. What followed led us upstairs. Let's leave it at- we had little sleep that night. My wife is hot stuff. She can pick me up and dust me off after knocking me down. She doesn't see it exactly that way, but it works. I am a lucky man. She is a wonderful woman. Together, and with our boys, we are a fantastic team.

Chapter 61 – Formal Night

Katie spent the day at the Tanger Outlets in Deer Park, searching for a new dress. Since our move to New York and her new job in Manhattan, she has become a clothing diva. Besides, we have a black tie event in NYC tomorrow night. We both needed to look our best. John and Rebecca are flying up tonight. We offered our home but they already had reservations for the weekend at the Hilton on 6th Avenue. Rebecca loved shopping in the city. All the big guns will be there including the Vice President. Rumors had us believing the Chief would attend as well, but I was sure they were just rumors. As it turned out; correct as usual. It appeared that security details had been increased raising my curiosity. As long as I remained uninvolved, all is good. Besides, being a guest is nice. I needed to learn how to relax and schmooze, with no real objective putting pressure on the evening.

Friday came upon me like there was only a Monday to the week. I guess being busy has its merit. I left the office early. Fortunately, no demanding assignments held me there as is usually the case. Katie's car took up the wife's side of the driveway. You know, the side with the car that is always too far from the Belgium block edge and the trunk open. This irritates me, but then

I am greeted with a smile and a kiss that calms me and makes me forget about my little driveway OCD.

"Hi, Jack, you're home early." Now, in the movies that would have been preceded by *"Quick, get dressed my husband is home."* She smiled and I knew a request was to follow. "Please get the rest of the groceries from my car?" Ok, so there is a good reason the trunk is open. I brought in the four bags filled with food items. "Thank you, Jack, I picked up lasagna noodles. Rosa is going to cook for the boys tonight." Hmm, here's a thought; "Let's stay home, we can call in sick." I kissed my wife and subtly rubbed her lower backside in a place that made my intentions clear. "Don't worry, lover; Rosa will make enough for you to have tomorrow." Rosa's cooking is pretty good, her lasagna is out of this world delicious. "Not the lasagna, you know, me and you..." I winked and Katie disappointingly waved me off, then looked over her shoulder and smiled. We were on the same page; for the moment. She had me worried. "OK, it's the lasagna." My wife already left the room. I headed upstairs as well, to say hi to my boys and give them a big daddy hug.

The boys and I spent a good hour playing all sorts of silly games that made them laugh. The ping of the shower fell silent; my turn to get ready for our formal night out. The bedroom had puffs of steam clouds and I could see Katie wrapped in a towel, brushing out her hair.

I called to her as I began undressing. "What time is this thing called for?" She pulled one more stoke of the brush through her glistening hair and placed it on the counter in front of her. Then my wife, my incredibly sexy wife, leaned forward on the counter and looked over her shoulder towards me. If this was one of my dream fantasies, I never want to wake up. "You are one fantastic lady." I kissed her neck, still moist from the shower. She had rubbed moisturizer on herself and the scent stimulated the senses. She leaned back into me, making sure I knew what to do next. I tried to turn her around to face me but that is not what she had in mind. Not at this moment.

We heard the door chime; "Shower quick; Rosa just got here and we're going to be late." I did, and we were; late. My explanation to our hosts - my wife was in the mood and I had a husband's responsibility. They understood; I needed to seize the moment. Actually, we blamed the nanny.

Chapter 62 – Anastasia

As our town car drove up Fifth Avenue and approached our destination, the iconic landmark stood before us. The Plaza Hotel illuminated the whole area. We arrived only fifteen minutes later than the invitation called for. The driver pulled up to the main entrance where a ceremoniously dressed doorman opened the driver's side door for Katie. I waited, but he did not come around to my side, so I let myself out of the car. "Oh, look, Jack, Central Park. It's so beautiful." "Not as beautiful as you, my dear." Katie pushed my shoulder, "Cut it out. You never took me here, and I work a subway ride away. I have to come uptown one day for lunch." I took my wife's hand and lead her toward the grand entrance. "We can take the boys here on a Sunday and do the picnic lunch thing." Katie smiled, "I think they would love that." I told her, "Besides, it is a beautiful park, but I'm not so keen on you traversing its paths without me. Or at least with a few friends." Katie told me I was too paranoid and that the park is safe during the day. We left it at that.

I have to say the Plaza is a well-run establishment. It has been a true landmark since it's opening in 1907. The personnel are truly there to service you. I wanted to try something, call it research or profiling. I tensed up a bit and started looking in several directions. It took all of fifteen seconds and I was approached by a concierge who asked if he could be of service, "Perhaps sir, the lavatory?" *Now that was cool*.

Katie had my arm; she squeezed it tight, pulling me away from my new friend. "I told you to behave." "You are adorable when you scold me; it gets me, – you know..." Her stare told me what I should know. I made my serious face, and we both laughed. My wife, – she gets me. "Oh, hey, there is John and Rebecca." We walked over to them just as the concierge announced that we could enter the Grand Ballroom. I said, "Rebecca, you look absolutely stunning." She kissed me on my cheek and then attempted to rub her lipstick markings off. I whispered, "Leave it, a little jealousy perks up the marriage." She responded with, "OK, John Bobbitt." If you don't remember who John and Lorena Bobbitt were; he cheated on his wife, and she, cut his manhood right off while he slept. Only, it backfired on her. He had a new *one* attached. Bigger, and better, and became a famous porn star.

As you enter the Grand Ballroom, you have to be awestruck. You are immediately thrown back in time to the early nineteen hundreds. The room was brightly lit making the golden fixtures, and gold leaf trim of the walls and chairs glow. We could have been entering a fairytale palace. "Wow, there are a lot of tables in here. Let's sit at table number thirteen, it's my lucky number." John's turn to scold me, "I would guess, we are each assigned to a table. Rebecca and I are at table nine." I took the hint. With nothing further to do, I headed out of the fancy room into the fancy lobby to retrieve our fancy table card. All I kept thinking was that there would be no card with our name on it. *What if we weren't invited, or they forgot to add us to the list. After all, we are here as guests of John and Rebecca. I am, after all, part of the group that saved our great country from the perils of evil. My life put in jeopardy more than once. My family threatened.* Ah, there it is. All is good.

"Table seventeen; is that like in the upper mezzanine? Or in the lower deck, below sea level. I saw Titanic, and it didn't end well for those folks." John laughed, the women ignored me. "Your table is just two over from ours, Jack. Rebecca was always good with directions. "You guys can use hand signals." My jokes are funnier. The room filled quickly. We took our seats. The waiter came over to take our dinner order; meat for me, fish for Katie, and a double scotch. The live orchestra, very impressive, played some decent music. It was a formal night so no R&B or cool music. I asked Katie if she would like to dance. "What a nice idea, Jack. Do you think that cute guy over there is going to ask me?" She really is giving me a run for the money tonight. "I don't think so; I heard he can read minds and my mind just threatened his. Will *I* do for the first dance of the evening?" "I suppose." She smiled and said, "There is no one else I would want to dance with. Come on sexy."

We danced for a while and then took a beverage break. I kissed Katie, picked up my drink and headed over to table nine. The more *"elite"* group. "Jack, this is Ronald and Anastasia McDermott." Ok, so I guess this group does outclass me. "Mr. Speaker, Mrs. McDermott, it is a pleasure to meet you in person." The number three man partially stood and offered his hand. "Please, tonight it is Ronald and Anastasia and it is a pleasure to meet you, Mr. Owens; Jack. You are well known on the hill. Your past endeavors, and loyalty to our great nation have not gone unnoticed." Wow, I hope my head didn't get really big just now, it sure feels like it did. "It's what I signed up for Sir, and I worked with an incredible team guided by the best." I placed my hand on John's shoulder. Katie walked over and took my hand. I introduced my wife and told them she is the force that gives me the willpower to forge ahead in tough times. Everyone at the table raised their glasses, "To Jack, John, and the rest of your teams. God Bless America." The energy in the room just reached nuclear levels. We ate and danced and made small talk. Everyone tried hard to avoid real situation discussions.

The four other couples at our table were pleasant enough. We kept it polite and spent most of our time dancing and chatting with the members of table nine.

"You look so beautiful tonight, and your dress is a definite wow." Katie leaned her head on my shoulder, "You are pretty cool looking as well, my husband. I like you in formal wear." She knew I was out of sorts with my apparel but I have to admit, tonight it felt good. Katie spaced herself from me, still dancing in sync, staring into my eyes. "I am very proud of you, I love you." "I love you too."

"How about another round?" My wife smiled, and I took that as a "Yes." I left Katie at our table eating some foo-foo dessert. On my way back, I noticed Katie, still at our table, speaking with Anastasia McDermott who was seated beside her; they were chatting. I gave my wife some space and took a walk around, observing the variety of guests. Perhaps Katie might be headed for politics at some point. The number three lady is a good connection.

"So Katie, your husband is quite the guy; but I understand you are pretty impressive as well." Katie tried to hide her embarrassment. "Thank you Anastasia; I am new at my job and have a lot to learn, but I do love what I do." Anastasia smiled and touched Katie's hand, "You keep putting those bad guys away. We need more dedicated young blood, fighting the fight." Katie responded, "We have a great country and a justice system that works well. Our leadership is strong and finally things are turning around." "Katie, I am enjoying our conversation so much. I hope we get to talk some more soon. Oh, about your husband, the important work he and his team have done; don't you worry about him being on a hit list? I hope you are taking proper precautions. Our country needs him." Katie was taken back at Anastasia's last question, or statement. She couldn't be sure which she meant it as. "Excuse me, Anastasia, *but*-" Anastasia stood up, "I think my husband is about to make his presentation. We'll talk again, soon."

I took my seat next to Katie as the Speaker of the House approached the podium. His speech was typical, praised everyone, made no commitments and named no specific names. A true politician. Katie whispered in my ear, "What's your take on Anastasia McDermott?" I told her she was "Kind of hot, but not my type." "Jack, I mean her personality. She seemed nice, but said some creepy stuff. She asked me if I was afraid for you. That you are on a hit list, or something like that. Why would she even think it appropriate to ask me that question?" I didn't know how to answer her. "It's nothing Katie, just leave it alone. She probably had a few too many and did not mean anything by what she said." Katie shrugged her sexy shoulders; and mumbled to herself, "Creepy – like *Jane* creepy."

The trip home was quiet. Katie rested her head on my shoulder while gazing out the car window. I could tell her brain was in hyper-mode. The rest of the weekend remained quiet. We spent time as a family unit, mostly centered on what the boys wanted to do. We all had fun, and let the issues of adult life be forgotten for a day. Sunday, Katie worked from early morning until after ten in the evening, reviewing and preparing for court in the morning.

Monday would be a big day for Katie and the DA's office as the trial of the century began. Raul Espinosa's first court appearance started at nine sharp.

Chapter 63 -Escape

My Name is Jack Owens, I have travelled across great deserts to bring the defendant to this trial. I dined in stinky tents and made deals the devil would be ashamed of ... The courtroom was one of the larger ones I had been in. Sitting there, my mind began to wander. I could be called as a material witness to corroborate the information leading to Espinosa's arrest, and to validate the terms of his plea deal if needed. Looking across the courtroom at the DA's team I notice the beautiful ADA assisting in the preliminary trial. Katie looks so professional. She wore my favorite blue suit. Very attractive, and who cares if I am biased. I hope the Judge is able to concentrate.

It is unusual for a member of the *Agency* to appear in court, let alone acknowledge any connection to anything. Our close working relationship with the other agencies became a game changer. After the Yemen take-down a few years ago my cover had become non-existent. I took a seat far back, and would only be called if needed. I had to trust the DA on this.

Down below in the, what we in law enforcement called the dungeons, guards prepared Espinosa for his grand entrance. "I'll take that." Espinosa's sexy lawyer took the soft rubbery comb from the guard and ran it through her lover's hair. If things did not go well, this would be her last opportunity to touch him. Raul closed his eyes and took in the two minutes of simple pleasure as she did the chore so soothingly. The guard touched Adeen's shoulder, "It's time."

Solitary wasn't so bad, it was more for his protection than as a punishment. Worse than child molesters, traitors suffered physical hardships in prison. Early on in his first week in captivity, Raul spent one restricted hour in the yard for fresh air. He was fine until the third day. The bruises, mostly on his face were severe, and he had lost a tooth. He elected to exchange his daily reprieve for library time. Outside, an attack by inmates or guards? No way to tell. Inside, it had to be guards and their locations are tracked closely. Staying indoors seemed safer for him.

All that would change in a little while. He would be free to live and love with his Adeen or they would die together, only to be separated by their opposing Gods.

The room fell silent as the doors opened and Raul Espinosa, Drug Kingpin, enslaver of woman and children, financier to terrorists, entered the court room The judge introduced the players and the bailiff swore the prisoner in. The judge recited the charges and summarized the plea bargain deal. "Do you understand the charges and the terms of your plea arrangement?" The judge looked annoyed, more like disgusted, at the plea deal. He had difficulty reading it out loud. Even the judge was not privy to all the justifications for the deal. Only a handful of us had that information. Katie handed a group of documents to ADA Levine. "Your Honor, pursuant to the terms of our agreement here is documentation agreed to by us. Also in agreement, are the federal representatives mentioned in the secured documentation, you should have reviewed earlier today." I noticed DA Johnson sitting right behind Jason and Katie. Next to him must have been Michelle. I never met her, but thanks to Katie's vivid description, I was sure that was her; pointy teeth and all. Everyone looked so at ease, one would not expect that this trial had connections to a larger multinational conspiracy.

The judge sat back and scratched his head. What he said next shocked everyone on both sides of the legal lines. *"In all my years I have never had to deal with a more unjust trial situation as what is presented before me today. Mr. Espinosa, you are a criminal guilty of many things not listed here, this I am most certain of. What we do know as fact is that you are accused of conspiracy to promote terrorism by financing Al Qaeda operations. You have committed crimes against your own people in both the United States and in Mexico. Crimes of the lowest*

315

dehumanizing kind. What you have done to women and children is appalling and that is too kind of a word for you. Out of respect for these people, all of them, I cannot, in good conscience, allow this plea to be accepted by the court. With this in mind, I am remanding you to the state authorities where you shall spend your time in the general population until such notice of a new trial can be set or you are summoned to Federal court to be tried for your real crimes." He rapped his gavel and proceeded to stand. We all must have made a great picture, an entire courtroom, a rather large one with all its inhabitant's mouths wide open and in shock. There was not a sound to be heard.

"Gun!" The world exploded instantaneously as the words were shouted from an unknown mouth. People hit the floor as the shots rang out. Bullets flew from several directions. I clearly saw a firearm in the hand of Espinosa's attractive lawyer's hand as she grabbed the defendant and headed to the rear of the courtroom and the exit. Apparently several of the guards were involved as well. I had no gun, not allowed in the court. A deal was on the table, no one expected this chaos.

I stood up and jumped over three rows of seating to get down to the front where the DA and my wife had been. Katie was lying on the floor under the defense table. Our eyes met and I could see she was OK. I had to react and my tactical training kicked in. I ran to the exit behind the Judge's bench. I tripped on something, only to realize it was the Judge's dead body, which had caused my fall. I quickly made sure he was past any medical help and continued out the back entrance reserved for His Honor. He would not be using it today or any other day. I ran down the short stairway and out into the courtyard. There they were, getting into a black unmarked SUV vehicle. Why do the evil ones always have connections in high places? We were compromised. People were running all over the place, and sirens were screaming. Strangely, like they were invisible, no one attempted to stop the fleeing defendant or his evil entourage. I looked around and decided to commandeer the first car I could, which so happened to be right in front of me.

I pulled out my ID; *Jack Owens, analyst* and grabbed the young man by his shoulders, "Get out of the car! Official emergency business!" The guy had me pegged as a nut job, and tried to fight me off. One to the nose solved that problem. I took off in what I think was a late model Nissan Maxima; nice interior. I headed downtown about ten car lengths behind them. I prayed that they would not head for any bridges but traffic was light, and they had to get off the island to have any chance to escape. The Brooklyn Bridge was wide open, and we traversed it speeding in excess of ninety miles an hour.

317

The car's wheels held up despite the potholes. I could see a trail of flashing lights from police vehicles behind me. I am not sure who they were chasing. I had no official markings, no authorization and as far as I knew, no one was aware of my pursuit. So, I might have been the target. As we exited the bridge, two pedestrians were nearly hit by the getaway car. Another vehicle went out of control, almost causing me to swerve into a lamppost. Water Street was crowded and chaos ensued. I figured they would head for Interstate 278, otherwise known as the Brooklyn-Queens Expressway, and travel along the water. I considered they might run for Jersey via the Verrazano Bridge. It was a beautiful day for a drive along the water. Driving close to one hundred miles per hour made sight-seeing a tad difficult. What happened next was the beginning of the end. The first gunshot took out my windshield. Glass was everywhere, including in my eyes. I almost lost control of the Maxima, coming close to hitting several other vehicles. I figured the time had come to give up the chase. My vision, due to the flying glass, was not very good; and for some reason my body ached. The *rage* that spiked my adrenaline took a break; I eased my foot off the gas. Perhaps I decided a minute too late. Espinosa's car hit something, another car I suppose. Then it hit the guardrail and launched into the air. The getaway car somersaulted high above me, bordered by a beautiful cloudless blue sky, and went out of view for a split second;

318

time stood still. The car containing enemies of the United States landed in front of me making a tremendous noise. It folded like a pair of pants ready to be packed in a suitcase. I swerved, but could not avoid hitting part of what was left of them and then careened into the guardrail that stood between my car and the perky waters of Upper New York Bay. In slow motion, metal parts and glass, like shrapnel, flew all around me; at me. The water looked peaceful, not a bad way to go if this was my time. Traffic on Shore Parkway came to a standstill. I suppose that is not so unusual on this unusual day.

Epilogue

Dreams can be so intense. The sand reflected the bright sunshine as I dug a moat around my castle. I remember the first time William and I met. We fought over beach territory, "Mine!" "No mine!" A truce was made and we became best friends that lasted almost twenty years. Our friendship did not break up, William was taken from me, and from Katie. I miss those days. Things were simple and innocent. So much good has happened in my life; enough to outweigh the bad that had to be endured.

If this is the way it is supposed to work, reliving our past just before we pass on to the next world, then so be it. The last events I want to remember are of holding my wife, her warm and loving body pressed against mine. The world is ours. When we are together like this, or spending time with our boys as a normal family, that is what makes life perfect. All the evil that surrounds us is suppressed during those precious moments.

There was a noise; in an instant I was alone in my house. Instinctively, I reached for my Glock, and in the darkness, covertly made my way downstairs. As I turned the corner they stood still, I suppose listening for movement above. There were two of them with automatic weapons. Eerily I could see them but they seemed to have no sense of my presence, like I didn't exist. My heart pounded like a drum in a marching band.

....

Rage – the driving force behind many random acts that end badly. My mind seems to be in an endless loop of good and bad dreams. I have just re-lived my life from the outside looking down upon the earth. Telling my story like a rerun of the cable channel's favorite mini-series. I am not sure what is real, but now I know I am trapped in some strange state of mind. I am imprisoned in a third dimension, aware of everything and of nothing. Reality is only what I want it to be. Things I think of seem so real, then they seem completely surreal.

Sometimes I hear voices; I allow myself to imagine what they are saying. Katie is kissing me or lying next to me. We are naked and her body has warmth that I choose now and always to hold onto. It is so strange; I can smell her perfume now. It is more intense than I remember. I am lying on my side, Katie is wearing a pretty pink cottony dress. The dream is blurry but I can see what my mind lets me. She had the most awesome smile and tears. Why tears? She is touching my face, gently. I can feel it as if it is real. The sweetness of her perfume tingles my senses. Her touch is too much to bear. I want this to be real.

The beeping got louder and more annoying, everything went dark. My beautiful wife, the vision that keeps me sane; gone. The sensation of cold, my skin tingled and my head hurt. I am experiencing pain and it feels great!

"Jack Owens, time to wake up."

I opened my eyes and there she was, my beautiful wife, smiles and tears. Thank God I can dream again. "Hi." She spoke to me; Katie never spoke to me in my dreams. "You are in the hospital and you are going to be OK. My love, you are back with us."

The doctors evidently had placed me in a medically induced coma to allow my brain injuries from the crash to heal. For three weeks, I reviewed all that had happened to me. There is a lot that needs to be considered going forward. My family needs me and I need them.

Three months have passed. It seems like an eternity. As I lay here next to Katie, watching her sleep-in on this early Sunday morning, I remind myself as I do every day, how fortunate I am to be me, here with her and our two fantastic boys. I want to reach over and touch her, just to make sure she is really there. Oliver Jones,

322

who is laying at her feet licking his front paw and purring contently, looks at me and yawns while closing his eyes again, signifying "*Don't wake us up*." My insane escapades have left me assigned to a desk and a weekly visit with Dr. Zachariah Smith, Psychologist. I should be cleared for regular activity soon. My self-understanding of the out of control *rage* of that day, resolved to the agency's satisfaction. I have been assigned a partner. My boss's way of ensuring my actions remain level-headed. I will work more closely between agencies, but not much different than before. As far as my new partner, we have worked well together before. Trust, which is the most important link between partners in any form of law enforcement a key factor here, my partner has that under control. In fact, she requested the pairing. Marcia Gainsworth will own the keys to the car. Meaning, she is in charge. I can deal with that.

A few days ago, I received a letter from a guy named Pete from up north. Pete informed me that he is a close friend of Jane's and that she had pretty much told him everything about her life. I already knew about Pete from the files on Jane. At first, the Canadian authorities suspected him as an accomplice but later cleared him. He wanted to update me, saying she is doing well, and has turned her life into something better than before. Jane had told him that if there was ever trouble, I was the only person in the world he should trust. *"Jack, Jane has formed a relationship with her children, and is learning to respect others in a way she never understood how to do growing up. We have grown to care very much for each other. I have loved her for a very long time and I think, for Jane, she in her own way, loves me too. She defines friendship as trust and calls you a friend. She is not sure you feel the same towards her but does want you to know that you, alone, have earned her respect and her trust. She is indebted to you. I am asking that you avoid contacting her again. Please do not bring the old world she knew back into her life."* The letter ended leaving me in a sort of limbo state, glad that I did not need to worry about Jane being a threat to me or Katie. Somehow though, I could not shake the thought that Jane and I would meet again. Our story, is but another chapter, waiting for the next to be written.

Her eyes opened, Katie just looked at me with a smile that without words, said, *good morning my love*.

Book Three – True Deception

Speaker of the House Ronald McDermott lay in bed thinking about the crazy day he had ahead of him. His wife Anastasia, still asleep, looked so peaceful. In an awakened state she was usually hyper and somewhat intense. His wife as he often told his associates is a "Go getter." One of the things that most attracted him to her, was her ability to make the impossible happen. The charisma she emitted drew people to her. The *number three man*, third in line responsible for the most powerful country in the free world, looked at his wife. He had to get up, but did not want to awaken her. Their weekend followed a big night, Friday night. Ronald McDermott, Speaker of the House of Representatives for the United States of America, made his first public presentation since taking office earlier this year. His wife allowed herself to become involved in the chaos of setting up and planning the event. At least, she made time to socialize and enjoy the excellent fare and dancing.

When Ronald first met her through an introduction of a business associate he had just been offered a partnership at a prestigious law firm in Richmond, Virginia. For their first date, they met at Marcel's. The restaurant and its chef are one of the most highly regarded in the Washington DC area. As in most "first dates," the evening started off a bit awkward. Anastasia took control of the conversation, breaking the ice. She talked about herself and her ambitions. She expressed her fascination with politics, and politely remarked about how impressive his impending partnership was.

He only knew her for one hour and already Ronald McDermott found himself drawn to her like an addict to his drug. They discussed his college years and the hard work it took to get into Harvard Law. From her keen interest in his career and future potential for a political run, Ronald had her pegged as a possible *"gold digger."* None of that mattered to him, she had him at *"Hello."* And she could talk, but she kept the conversation interesting and allowed for him to participate.

As she questioned him about his family he interrupted her, "You are beautiful." Anastasia paused for a sip of wine, "What?" Her date's face flushed red with embarrassment. "I am so sorry, I didn't mean to – I was thinking out loud." Now his awkwardness returned but she again took control of the situation. "Why are you apologizing? Are you sorry for saying it out loud or for thinking it? Please, relax, you are very sweet." She took his hand, "I like you too."

Anastasia McDermott lay in bed, eyes closed but not asleep. Well aware her husband had his gaze upon her at that very moment. His love and admiration and most importantly, his trust in her, never wavering. So far her plan, her leader's plans, are moving forward. She is *their* last hope for success.

To be continued …

Note from the Author:

I hope you have enjoyed the second of three books in the Jack Owens series.

Any mention of named characters are completely fictional and are not based on any real people. Agent Oliver Jones is real and as of this printing continues his daily routine of surveillance. Like any fictional story, any depiction of religious beliefs are for entertainment and have no real bearing on the author's or publisher's political views.

Also, I just thought I would mention this, as my wife was sensitive to chapter 31. "*No Camels have been harmed during the writing of this book.*"

During the course of development, and actual writing of this volume, several world events have changed how people perceive safety at home and when traveling abroad. The third volume in the series will incorporate real life situations to give my readers a sense of reality through fictitious characters. New characters will be introduced. Old characters will prevail. Conflict between allies will threaten world peace.

We are supposed to put our faith and trust in our leaders. Who is real, and who is a Twin, may be resolved. Or, it may not.

Acknowledgement

Once again, I have to thank my friends Tom and Hillary for their dedication and encouragement to get this second volume completed.

I want to acknowledge Mark G. for his optimism and eagerness to read on in the life of Jack Owens. His professional background, and detailed editing, helped clarify and improve the reader experience.

A special thank you goes out to all our brave men and women who live every day to fight the fight against terrorism. You are our true heroes, keeping us, and our great country safe.

Thank you all, for your positive comments and support.